Ends of Being

ENDS DUET, BOOK 1

MERCYANN SUMMERS

Cover Designer: Jay Aheer, @ Simply Defined Art

Edited by: Kirsty McQuarrie, @ Let's Get Proofed

Formatted by: Kayla Loyed, @ The Bookish Girls Services

Dear Readers,

Thank you for downloading/buying this book and at least reading this page. I'm pleased my book caught your attention enough to peek inside, but I feel I'd be remiss if I didn't tell you what to expect if you decide to continue reading. If you consider yourself to be free of triggers and have zero issues reading any kind of questionable content, please feel free to skip ahead to the prologue to not risk any type of spoilers. If you find you are even occasionally triggered, please read this note in its entirety and make a conscious decision on whether you feel this book will be a good choice for you. Your mental health is important, always choose wisely for yourself.

While the Ends Duet is classified as a dark romance with stalker themes, it's a bit different than your standard dark romance. This book has jokes. Lots and lots of jokes. It's likely I'm not nearly as funny as I think I am, so I'll apologize now. Also, this being a duet, most answers to the story are found in book 2, which means there's a cliffhanger at the end of this book. Though I feel it's a medium cliffhanger as opposed to the level 10 cliffhanger that has you screaming into your pillow at 3am. Those kill me.

TW/CW: There is drugging/noncon/SA, though NOT between the MMC/FMC. There's a considerable amount of dubious consent between the MMC/FMC as well as kidnapping, suppressed memories, and some relatively mild bondage. There is blood play, breath play, and more naughty words and graphic depictions of sexual acts and violence than I would care to count.

This book is not suitable for persons under the age of 18.

Thank you for reading. I hope you love Darius and Antoinette, and their crew of miscreants, half as much as I do.

—Mercy

To the defeated. The wounded.
The wrecked. The misplaced.
I see you.
Take my hand.

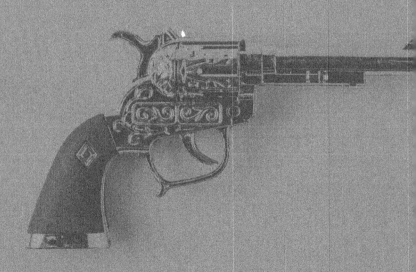

Prologue

TONI

"YOU'RE NOT BAD BOY enough to handle me..."

Though these words were said in jest, sometimes the joke misses the mark, and instead of laughter, you get...total mutiny.

And really, that must have been the beginning of the end.

The final nail in my coffin.

The last straw that broke the resolve of the man behind the curtain.

In complete fairness to myself, I had no idea he had it in him. I had no idea that sweet-man Clark Kent was a real-life beast under his starched white shirts and khaki pants. I guess I never even considered the possibility that he would have that much pent-up aggression built up inside him to pull off this kind of feat. Hindsight being what it is, maybe I should have known better.

Because that's what I do: I wind people up, drive them insane, make them become unhinged to the point they either step up and make me pay, or they high-tail it out of dodge. The vast majority run for the hills; however, occasionally, I'm pleasantly surprised.

Like, right now. I'm almost certain that this is how I ended up in my current predicament.

Tied up.

In a trunk.

I know, I know—who could possibly be happy about being tied up in a trunk, right? Well, I suppose it depends on how you ended up there, how you plan on getting out, and who put you in there.

You see, I'm a brat.

Now, I don't mean I'm a bratty toddler, a spoiled princess, or anything like that. No, my bratty attitude stems from something darker and a bit more sinister. I'm a smart-mouthed, snarky shit-talker who borders on blatantly disobedient. I yearn for a man who can handle me and has the power to control me, to make me want to submit to him and his will without a second thought, but I seem to lack the appropriate kink boundaries to make this a feasible reality.

Because I also have the added bonus of having an Alpha personality that overrides my brat side more often than it should. So instead of reaching the point where my brat will lay down and take her punishment as intended, my Alpha comes charging in, rearing her ugly bitch face and screaming variations of "bring it on."

And I fucking love it.

Obviously, this is an overly complicated situation that has no easy remedy. Because what man has the mental and physical fortitude to constantly be battling for domination in and out of the bedroom? So far, a big, fat giant nobody. Not one of the countless Dominant men I set my bratty sights on has had the mental and physical stamina needed to force my submission.

The process is almost agonizing enough that I'm starting to think that maybe I should just give up and release myself into the Dominatrix side of the kink world. If only having someone be subservient to me was my thing. Maybe there's something to be said about it that I'm unaware of? Was I wrong not to give them a chance? Was the quiet broody man the right man, after all?

I guess this is a question I get to ponder on my frigid, dark ride to the unknown. Is it the ones you least expect who will bring the biggest and most satisfying surprises? In all my years of searching for the perfect match to my insanity, I never once thought to look for the closet Alpha. Now, stuck here trussed up beautifully in the trunk of a car, the error of my ways is right in front of me.

Really, the clarity of hindsight is the most infuriating bedmate there is. All the obvious signs that were previously missed flash through my brain in slow motion. It's a kaleidoscope of missed opportunities, a decade worth of potential kink anarchy that I will never get back but could quite possibly make up for in future antics.

I'm replaying all those moments of quiet intensity where I thought he was praying I would leave him alone. The glaring looks that indicated he was picturing me being fired and removed from his presence for good. All the groans I thought were annoyance, the huffs I thought were exasperation, the growls I thought were his prelude to finally reporting me to human resources for my blatant outwardly unprofessional harassment of my coworker.

I had it all wrong this entire time. Sweet Little Dare wasn't glaring, groaning, huffing, and growling because he wanted me to leave him alone. He elicited these intense looks and primal sounds because he was actively controlling his baser nature to break me and bend me to his will. He was using phenomenal self-control to torture me. For fucking ages.

That sneaky motherfucker!

I giggle behind the gag in my mouth and squeeze my thighs together in anticipation. A small tear of giddy happiness soaks into the blindfold over my eyes as I picture my future with a man who will happily force me to my knees at any given moment without an ounce of hesitation on my part.

Seems wee Clark Kent has grown into a real-life superhero, after all.

I just hope he is ready for me.

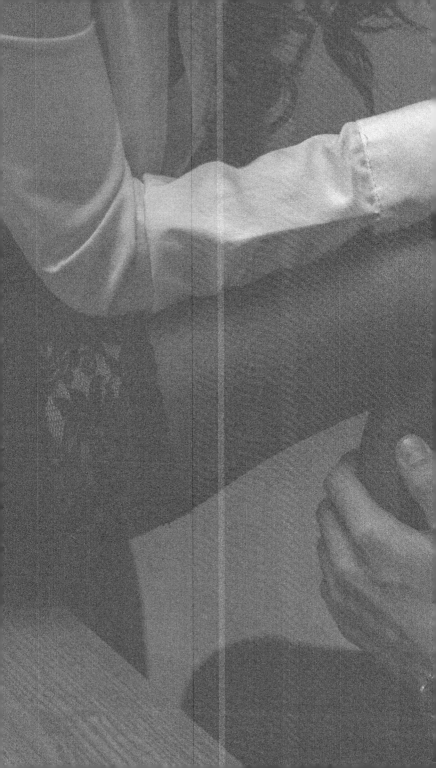

Chapter One

TONI

I'M UNBELIEVABLY BORED.

I've been sitting at my desk for hours, staring at a computer screen that has me seeing spots in my periphery. I'm at the stagnant point in the accounting process where the numbers on the screen swim in front of me, so I sigh in defeat and push away from my desk, stretching my shoulders and neck as I stand. I'm walking out my office door when I realize I have given myself a distraction mission.

Operation: Bug Dare.

I've been working at the same accounting firm as Darius Hughes for a while now and bothering that old stuffed shirt will likely never get old. He's not easily ruffled, but once you get him flustered, it's an exceedingly satisfying experience. His eyes get all squinty, and he starts to sweat. I can almost see the steam rising off his person as he undoubtedly daydreams about eviscerating me from his reality.

I know, I know—I'm a juvenile. But I'm a thirty-four-year-old single woman who chose a profession that doesn't allow for much in terms of daily excitement, and let's just say the average age of my coworkers is not exactly rave material. So that leaves Darius, or Clark as I like to call him to his face since it drives him absolutely batshit.

I can see his shadow hunched over his desk as I approach his office, and I'm surprised to find his door open, as he typically has it locked up tight. I sneak closer, easing myself into the doorway to spy on him for a few seconds before breezing in to make his day. His entire focus is on the screen before him, his index finger tapping on the mouse rhythmically as he takes in whatever fascinating information is before him.

I snort. He blinks and then sighs loudly, closing his eyes and muttering to himself.

I flounce in and sit down dramatically in the chair in front of his desk. "Hey, Clark. Whatcha up to?"

Dare squints at me. "Antoinette," he says blandly.

My smile widens; I can already sense his hackles rising at the mere sight of me. So, I sit back and adjust my pencil skirt just so as I cross my legs, showing him a little extra thigh for added effect. I unbutton the top button of my blouse and adjust my shoulders in a way that not-so-subtly pushes my breasts against the thin fabric.

The fucker doesn't even glance.

I cock one brow back at him, huffing a bit under my breath, "I was getting all cramped up staring at my computer screen and figured it was time for a break."

"And you thought taking a break in my office was a good plan?"

I nod enthusiastically. "Well, yes, of course. Where best to recharge my battery than with my good buddy, Clark!"

He squints at me again, inhaling deeply through his nose. His hands clench on his desk, his eye twitching minutely as he stares at me, silently.

I'm getting to him already. How unusual.

I jump up, moving swiftly around his desk to stand beside his chair. He doesn't change his position at all. He remains frozen in place, eyes still focused on the chair in front of him.

I lean down, my face hovering beside his. "You know what you need to do?" I ask in a serious tone.

He glances over at me wearily. "Oh, please, do tell."

I give him a closed-mouth smile, then roll my eyes slightly as I quip, "You need to turn that frown upside down!"

Now he groans outright, then pushes back from his desk, his hands coming down to slap the top of his thighs in frustration. "Why must you come in here and torment me incessantly? I've got work to do; I don't have time to be your entertainment."

I give him a stern look, "You know what they say? All work and no play makes Clark a very dull boy. You should consider breaking out of your shell and letting loose for a change. Maybe then, I wouldn't feel obligated to shake you up a bit."

His eyes meet mine sharply, his voice rough as he whispers, "Oh, Antoinette. You think you know everything about me, but I can assure you—"

"Come on, Clark," I interrupt, laughing. "You're not bad boy enough to handle me."

He doesn't say anything, so I glance over, surprised to find him staring at me intently. Then the corner of his mouth curves up ever so slightly, until he's almost smirking at me with the strangest glint in his eyes.

I shiver and laugh again, slowly moving away from the desk and edging toward the door as I say, "Always so serious, Clark."

He doesn't respond to my flippant remark, but his eyes are on me as I exit the room, and I can't control the shudder that runs up my body in response.

Dare

I will never forget the first time I saw her. She was a vision—all long, dark hair and big blue eyes. A sassy fucking mouth that will cut you up and spit you out without a care in the world. She was infuriating and mesmerizing, and I was gone for her in a blink of an eye.

Antoinette, or Toni as she prefers to be called. Oh, how she hates being called Antoinette, which means I only call her that. She goes out of her way to get a rise out of me regularly, so I have to do my part to subtly make her keep coming back to continue driving me crazy.

I never knew my deep masochistic tendencies until her. My intense need to keep her at arm's length, something I want with every fiber of my being, just to continue the delicious torture. It's like an illness, a disease of the senses, to keep me from taking her and locking her away in my basement.

I am, however, beginning to unravel.

If she knew the intense, ruinous thoughts going through my head, she would likely quit her job and move out of the area to escape me. Perhaps even out of the country. She would most certainly change her name and number as well as her postal code.

You see, I may be a bit of a psycho. Sure, I dress conservatively and speak softly, but beneath this boring demeanor is a beast just waiting to be unleashed onto the world. Or, in this case, be unleashed onto one smart-mouthed fucking menace so he can make her shut her fucking mouth for once in her goddamn life.

Sometimes, when she jacks the heat up on her harassment to upper inferno levels, I daydream about shutting her up by shoving my dick so far down her throat that she chokes on it. Denying myself the urge to make this daydream a reality often has me breaking out in sweats. The sheer force of will it takes for me to stop myself from cutting off her sharp-tongued barbs with my hand squeezing her throat and forcing her to her knees is excruciating, and I'm not entirely sure how much longer I can hold the beast at bay.

It doesn't help that she's never known when to stop. She has always missed my verbal and nonverbal cues on when enough is enough, and it's becoming increasingly apparent that she does it on purpose. For some reason, I'm her main form of entertainment in the office, as well as anywhere else I may have the unfortunate luck of running into her. Even if the majority of these random run-ins are engineered by me because I'm a glutton for punishment when it comes to her.

I can't breathe when she's in the room with me, busting my balls, but I also can't breathe when she is away from me for too long since, apparently, having my balls busted on the regular is akin to oxygen.

I'm a fucking madman.

Then, just when I'm close to my wit's end, she comes meandering into my office, not a care in the world, ready to push my buttons for her own entertainment. She then strategically adjusts her skirt to show as much thigh as possible, unbuttons her blouse a little, and squares her shoulders just right so her tits are pressing against the thin fabric. It's all I can do to stop myself from leaping over my desk, fisting that silky blouse in my hand, and ripping it to fucking shreds.

Instead, as she goes on about my office being the perfect place for her to take a much-needed break, I fist my hands on my desk and squint at a spot on the wall behind her. I grind my molars together almost violently and feel my eye twitching. I'm so focused on keeping myself together that I don't notice she's moved until suddenly, she's right beside me, her breath dusting my face as she speaks.

"You know what you need to do?"

No, but I'm sure as fuck you're going to tell me, and I'm also sure it's going to piss me off.

I glance over at her wearily. "Oh, please, do tell."

I force the words out through gritted teeth, not that she notices how tightly wound up I am. She's too busy working out how best to make me want to throw myself off a cliff to be worried that I might actually retaliate for once. And for the love of fuck, do I want to retaliate.

She gives me her condescending, closed-mouth smile, then rolls her eyes at me and says in her most jovial and mocking voice, "You need to turn that frown upside down!"

Now, I groan loudly as I push back from my desk, my hands coming down to slap the tops of my thighs in frustration. I'm nearing the end of my tether, I can feel it being yanked with every word that falls from her pretty little mouth, and I need to do something to get her the fuck out of my office. "Why must you come in here and torment me incessantly? I have work to do; I don't have time to be your entertainment."

She gives me a stern look, "You know what they say? All work and no play makes Clark a very dull boy. You should consider breaking out of your shell and letting loose for a change. Maybe then, I wouldn't feel obligated to shake you up a bit."

No, she fucking did not. Surely, I misheard her, and she did not just refer to me as a "dull boy." Dull. Boy.

My eyes meet hers sharply, my voice rough as I whisper, "Oh, Antoinette. You think you know everything about me, but I can assure you—"

"Come on, Clark," she interrupts, laughing. "You're not bad boy enough to handle me."

I blink at her, my brows furrowing as I let her words sink into my psyche, swirling around in the darkness.

I'm not bad boy enough? Me? The quintessential wolf in nice-guy clothing is not bad boy enough to handle little miss sassy pants? Who the fuck does she think she is making baseless assumptions about my bad-boy prowess?

I don't say anything else; I only stare at her intently. Then the corner of my mouth curves up ever so slightly until my beast smirks at her in anticipation.

Her body trembles ever so slightly, and she laughs again, slowly edging toward the door as she says breathlessly, "Always so serious, Clark."

Instead of responding to her flippant remark, I keep my eyes on her as she exits the room.

When she spins to strut away, I drop my head in my hands, gripping my hair and giving it a yank before jumping out of my chair and walking swiftly to the door. She's rounding the corner at the end of the hallway, and I step back out of view just as she turns to look behind her. What I want to do is go barreling down the hall after her, barge into her office, lock the door, then forcefully bend her over her desk and give her ass the blistering it deserves.

That's only for starters. A slow-mo movie of everything I've ever wanted to do to her runs through my mind until I'm a panting, ravenous beast when I sit back behind my desk.

"You're not bad boy enough to handle me..."

Those words keep repeating in my head, and the more I think about them, the more incensed I become.

I'm not bad boy enough to handle her, huh?

My blood boils in my veins. The beast rattles in my chest.

Challenge fucking accepted.

Chapter Two

TONI

EVER SINCE MY RUN-IN with Dare earlier in the day, I've had this deep sense of unease. It's like I'm missing some vital tidbit that is crucial to my health and well-being. Like I can feel eyes on me at every turn, and I keep glancing over my shoulder, expecting someone to jump out at me.

I know this is completely ridiculous; however, it doesn't stop me from checking all the stalls in the ladies' room when I enter. Nor does it prevent me from changing my stilettos for running shoes before leaving the office and heading to the parking garage. I have headphones in my ears, but no sound coming out of them, so I can be alert without anyone thinking I am.

I'm not normally this paranoid. Sure, I have a somewhat healthy sense of self-preservation—I always carry pepper spray in my purse and walk with my car key sticking out between my fingers. I always check under my car and in the backseat before getting behind the wheel. For fuck's sake, I even have a Louisville Slugger on my backseat, just in case I need to smash some shit on my commute.

I'm also pretty fit, thanks to consistent weight-lifting and my own unexplainable need to know how to throw down in a crisis. I may not win in a contest of brute strength, but I will definitely get a few pieces of them before they take me down and leave me in a ditch somewhere for being a mouthy bitch.

What I don't have is the ability to stop my intense level of excitement when the soft footfalls steadily gain on me as I make my way to my car. I even adjust my pace a couple of times to see if they do the same, and when they do, my little heart almost jumps right out of my chest in anticipation.

All that being what it is, I'm also not an intelligent person when it comes to fight or flight. As in, I have no flight at all. If I see an obvious red-flag situation a mile down the road, I'm definitely going to continue towards it rather than take any number of possible safer detours along the way. Basically, I totally deserve to be that dead bitch in a ditch, but even knowing this, I can't stop my forward trajectory into possible unnecessary danger.

So instead of hurrying directly to my car, jumping into the driver's seat, and locking my doors, I take the long way and meander a few extra laps just to see what my potential assailant will do. And also to confirm in my ridiculous mind that someone is indeed intentionally following me because, honestly, why would anyone peg me as an easy target?

Dare

Antoinette has been acting strange all day, almost as if she can sense chaos on the horizon. She's constantly looking over her shoulder, playing with the pepper spray she keeps in her purse, and adjusting her car key between her fingers. She even changed her goddamn shoes. I can almost see her envisioning her beloved Louisville Slugger that is a constant companion in the backseat of her car.

As if any of these precautions will protect her from the beast when he comes for her.

Now, we're in the parking garage, waiting patiently for her to approach her vehicle so we can pounce, but she's taking her sweet-ass time walking to her car. She's lapped the place a few times as though she couldn't remember where she parked, and a few more times, she even stopped in her tracks and glanced around in complete puzzlement.

Because the fucking bitch is playing with me.

I growl deep in my chest, settling back into the shadows to wait for her to stop being a pain in my ass and complete the journey to her car. I should've known she would do this, that something as simple as accosting her in a parking garage would go awry due to her incredible ability to fuck with me without even trying. She's naturally infuriating, and I can't wait to break her down and bend her to my will.

Oh, here she comes now, strutting towards her car as if aggravated that all her pissing about had zero results. I swear on all that is holy, if she detours one more fucking time, I'm going to change tactics and charge her like the raging bull I currently am.

She continues towards her car, her quick pace more determined than before, and I slowly ease myself out of the shadows and closer to my desired target.

That's right, come to me, baby girl...

Toni

Fucking hell, that was a complete waste of time and energy.

All of my excitement about my potential accosting has left me, and I'm now stomping toward my car, completely annoyed I let my overactive imagination get the better of me. As if anyone would ever attempt to steal me out of a dark parking garage in the first place. There's no way a criminal mastermind would ever stick around to watch their potential victim wander aimlessly in search of a car that is literally right under their nose.

I roll my eyes at my own idiocy, huffing more expletives as I go over all the reasons no one would attempt to kidnap me, even if they thought I looked like an easy prey.

I'm almost at my car when I notice movement in the shadows, and the subtle scrape of shoes on cement. My heart rate picks up again, my feet automatically picking up pace a bit as I draw closer to my intended location—the back driver's side door—and my trusty Louisville. I was excited in a morbidly fun way before, but now, I'm excited in a pissed-off and ready-to-smash-shit way.

I rush the final steps to my car, my hand reaching for the door handle when I'm suddenly shoved from behind. I attempt to push back, to force some leverage so I can maneuver into an offensive position, but I find myself unable to move with my face pressed against the cold glass of the car window.

My pulse is racing wildly, and I'm gasping for air. This is not a scenario I ever envisioned, being trapped and entirely incapable of fighting back. I attempt to struggle a bit and then freeze as a hard body presses fully against me, a strong hand flexing at my throat, and hot breath tickling my ear.

I hear it then, the deeply sinister chuckle that sends vibrations down my spine. The hand at my neck squeezes tighter, the hard body pushes in more forcefully, and then an eerily familiar voice washes over me.

"Mm...there's my baby girl," the voice whispers against my ear. "Let's see how much of a bad boy you can handle."

I freeze, my eyes widening in recognition. *What the actual fuck?*

I go to shout, to kick back and scream my bloody head off, but the hand at my throat tightens further, cutting off my voice and pulling my upper body back fully against his. His other hand comes up to my mouth, his thumb and index finger pinching my nose as his palm presses against my lips, cutting off my air completely. I try to rear back, to pull my face away from his pressing hand, to allow myself to breathe. But it's too little, too late, and the world goes black.

Dare

Well, that was exceedingly satisfying.

I stand back, my eyes skimming over Antoinette's beautifully trussed-up body lying prone in the trunk of my car and smile smugly at my handiwork. Even with her delay tactics, this could not have gone any better if I had spent months planning it.

I mean, technically, I've been planning this out in one capacity or another in my mind for ages, but that was only in theory. Execution of the plan is where it really counts, and I pulled off the snatching of Antoinette flawlessly. Oscar-worthy performance, for sure.

I double-check the ropes binding her and the gag in her mouth, making sure there's enough leeway that I won't accidentally suffocate her in transit. Now that would really piss me off. After denying myself her company for so long, to then have some accident tear her from me permanently.

I glance down at her again and consider removing the gag so she can at least communicate acute distress to me, but then, as I remember what a raging bitch she can be when riled, I tighten it a bit more so she can't get out of it. If nothing else, I know she'll be spitting nails by the time we reach our destination, and the less I hear from the trunk of my car, the better.

I slam the trunk lid down none-too-gently, a pep in my step as I walk around and climb into the driver's side. We have a bit of a drive before we get where we're going, and I want to be well on our way before she starts kicking and screaming. Well, wiggling and grunting in her current bound-and-gagged state.

I chuckle to myself, amused and relieved that there's no going back now. Even if I wanted to call the entire thing off and deposit her at home before she woke up, there's no way she didn't recognize me when I had her pressed against her car. I hadn't meant to say anything at all, my plan being to remain silent and get her incapacitated and into my trunk without much fanfare.

But I just couldn't keep my fucking mouth shut. As soon as I had her pressed up against her car, all previous planning went out the window, and I started running my yap like a goddamn amateur, and it would've served me right if things had gone south and I'd ended up with a knee to the balls. Calling her my baby girl and going on about bad boys, for fuck's sake.

A thump sounds in the back, so I turn the radio down and listen intently. The thumping sound comes again. She must have woken up already; that didn't take too long at all. The banging increases in volume, then in frequency, until it is a constant rhythmic noise in the back.

I laugh to myself, then turn up the hard rock song, "Highway to Hell", playing on the radio to drown her out. She'll be spitting mad by the time I open that trunk at our destination, so I may as well get in what little relaxation I can now.

I hope she's as ready for me as I am for her.

Chapter Three

TONI

I'VE BEEN MOSTLY AWAKE for a while. I did some thumping around initially, so he'd know I was awake, but then reverted to calmly resting my eyes as I plot my imminent revenge.

To say I'm shocked would be a serious understatement. How that boring son-of-a-bitch ever hid such an epic plot twist from me for all this time is beyond me. It does *not* seem possible, and part of me is concerned I may be incorrect in my recognition of the voice.

If that is the case, I'm definitely in a shit-ton of trouble right now.

Possible extreme danger aside, I'm mostly tickled with this quick turn of events. To think my sweet boy Clark is a devil in pastel clothing means the details I don't know about him must be epic.

Putting aside my delight in the potential dark side of Dare, I take stock of my current predicament—gagged and tied in the trunk of a car. The gag in my mouth is a bit uncomfortable, but nothing I can't manage for a great length of time. His rope skills, on the other hand, are a lackluster joke.

It only takes me a few minutes to squirm my hands free, then a few more to wriggle my feet loose in the cramped space. For once, I almost wish I was shorter or narrower or just smaller in general. The trunk of a vehicle is not a very forgiving place to be moonlighting as Houdini, that's for sure.

I loosen the gag in my mouth a bit, stretching out my jaw as I ponder my limited choices. I have no idea where we're going. I also can't be one hundred percent certain Darius is the man who has taken me. I can take my chances and tie myself back up, or I can prepare for a direct assault in the hope I can give myself a big enough moment to escape.

Tying myself back up definitely leaves me at the mercy of my kidnapper with a very slim chance of being able to escape. But if I attempt to escape as soon as the trunk opens, I might be able to use the small window of surprise to my advantage.

Given that both options have no guarantee, I put the gag back into my mouth then adjust my body in the trunk so my unbound hands are not immediately visible.

Then I wait.

Dare

I pull into the clearing in the woods, circling around and coming to a stop at the crossroads of the paths. Most people know New York for the vast city, but they don't realize there is wilderness within an hour drive.

And lots of questionable things go on in the wilderness.

I purchased this exclusive piece of property on the outskirts of the state park because I wanted seclusion and separation from the general outside world. I ended up having to buy several land parcels under a few aliases to get a sizable enough acreage to work with, but it was worth the hassle once my vision became a reality.

I glance around, then exit my car, strolling quietly to the rear while listening intently.

All is quiet.

Antoinette stopped the thumping a while ago, apparently growing bored with the uselessness behind it once I cranked the music.

Knowing her, she could quite possibly be asleep. She never has had a self-preserving bone in her body, and I highly doubt she's too worried, especially if she recognized me when I took her.

Or she's quietly plotting my imminent demise.

I open the trunk without any flourish, stepping back in case she's waiting to lunge for me or attempt to jump out and run, but there's no movement from her. She's partly on her side, facing me, and I can see the easy rise and fall of her chest.

I snort, shaking my head as I watch her sleeping form, tied and gagged. She truly is a piece of work, all fearless, brazen, and entirely infuriating. I want to protect her and spank her ass red at the same time.

I walk back to the driver's side, leaning in and grabbing the small duffel bag from the passenger seat. I pull out some zip ties and a bottle of water, close the bag and toss it back onto the far side.

A rustling of leaves sounds behind me, and I move to stand just in time to see the large metal object being swung at me with a surprising amount of speed.

Unfortunately, I don't see it in time to duck and take a glancing blow to the right side of my head as I attempt to dodge it too late.

I stumble back, the bag in my hand falling to the ground at the same time I'm falling against the car and a dark-haired she-devil draws back to clobber me again. I shake my head, my eyes quickly refocusing, and

I manage to right myself and get my hands up just in time to stop her from caving my head in on the next swing.

Antoinette looks like a fucking goddess, rage burning in her eyes as she cusses me out. I can't make out much through the ringing in my ears, but I gather she has nothing nice to say to me at all.

I ignore the buzzing in my head and smirk. "Come on, baby girl, don't be like that."

She pauses her attack, her face contorting in fury as she shouts at me, "You duplicitous motherfucker, making me believe you're a goody fucking two shoes for all this time instead of showing me how completely fucking unhinged you truly are."

I frown, my lips twisting in contemplation as I retort, "Unhinged seems a little dramatic. I prefer darkly eclectic."

What I find amusing is that even after me stealing her from the parking garage, she really has no idea how unhinged I am. She knows nothing about who I am besides the surface bullshit I allowed her to see. She truly believed I was nothing more than a boring stuffed shirt swimming aimlessly in my sea of mediocrity.

Antoinette glares at me, showing me her teeth as she lunges for me, her fist jabbing out and catching me in the side of my neck as I barely manage to shift away. I grab her by both wrists, quickly overpowering her and pulling her back against me, using her arms as restraints.

She's stiff at first, then slowly starts to melt, her torso sinking into me, her head coming back to rest on my shoulder, baring her neck to me. She's panting; I can see her pulse pounding beneath her creamy skin as I press my face against her, inhaling a line up right beneath her ear.

"That's a good girl," I whisper gruffly, pressing my lips against her soft skin.

She whimpers, her breath catching in her throat, and I loosen my hold on her arms, allowing her to bring her arms up, her hands tangling in my hair. I smile against her neck, a low growl building in my chest as she presses her body back against mine.

I'm so enamored with the feel, taste, and smell of her that I miss the obvious tell-tale signs that she is indeed preparing to make a solid move against me. Yes, I'm a fucking moron, and the next thing I know, the world has gone upside down, and I'm laid out in the dirt, my balls absorbing a direct heel kick from her trainers.

Well, I knew better than to let my guard down with her, but what can I really say other than I'm a blind fool for her. She has spent our entire relationship actively winding me up, and I can honestly say I would've been much less interested in her had she been even remotely sane.

So, that leaves me here, on the ground, holding my junk, groaning in agony, completely helpless to prevent her from getting into my car and slamming the door shut. The engine starts and then there's the whir of the power window being lowered.

Did she just spit on me?

"I will have you arrested and tossed in jail for kidnapping," she yells, and I'm certain I can feel her waving her middle finger at me.

Then she drives away, leaving me in the dirt, still holding my junk.

That fucking bitch.

Toni

That fucking bastard.

Who does he think he is? Thinking he can lie to me for our entire relationship, then kidnap me, toss me in a trunk trussed up like a prized hog, and not end up on his ass with my foot in his balls. As if I could even, in good conscience, just let him get away with it.

I'm so furious it takes me a good ten minutes to realize I'm driving aimlessly at a higher speed than is likely reasonable on a dark foreign road. I slow down, then pull over to the shoulder and stop, putting the car into park.

I rest my head back against the seat, close my eyes, and rub my hands over my face as I ponder what I should do next.

Maybe I should go back and get him? I snort, shaking my head as I toss that possible plan out the window. Fuck him if he thinks I'm going to take it easy on him after the shit he's pulled. Even if I could remember where I left him after my aimless drive in the wilderness, I'm not going back.

I could just go home. Have a bath and pretend none of this ever happened and see how it pans out in the office on Monday.

I frown, my eyes narrowing as I quickly toss that possible plan as well. *Fuck that. Fuck him. Fuck his stupid swanky car and his stupid paisley socks, and his stupid, lame-ass golf sweaters. Fuck him right in his tight, rock-solid ass. Ugh. That ass!*

I take a deep breath, my gaze scanning the interior of the car in fascination and horror. *What the fuck kind of fancy pants car does this fuckwit drive? And how the fuck did he manage to buy it on his accountant's salary?*

I start poking around, eventually settling on the touchscreen in the middle of the dash. *Or is it a television? Tablet? Whatever.*

After some more poking around, I finally manage to bring the GPS up. I frown at the screen, shaking my head at the idea that I'm in what appears to be a state forest an hour or so from the city. I'm in the goddamn woods with no real idea on how to get back home other than finding a road that goes south and aiming for the brightest lights.

I touch on the search icon, pausing as I start to input my home address and notice something very strange a few lines down on his recents list.

My address is...auto-populating from a recently searched address? A recently regularly searched address? What the actual fucking shit is going on here?

You know, I was mildly annoyed before, but now I'm livid. Not only is that asshole a deranged kidnapper, he's also some form of creepy stalker because, according to his GPS, he's been at my address repeatedly for what could quite possibly be months. I mean, the GPS location history doesn't go back that far, but statistically speaking, it's unlikely driving to my exact address was a new hobby this past week.

That dirty, no-good motherfucker. He's been hiding his deranged, creepy stalker ways from me for all these years, like the selfish prick he is. How dare he deny me the privilege of deciding if I want to allow him to creepily stalk me or not. And here I thought Dare knew me so well that he truly understood how incredibly fucked up I am since he never tried to do anything to make me stop messing with him. Turns out the candy ass doesn't know me at all, and that fact I find to be extremely disappointing.

With my mind made up, I go back to the search function, deleting my address and instead typing in "police department near me."

I promised him a police report and some jail time.

And no one has ever accused me of being a liar.

Chapter Four

TONI

SINCE I'M IN THE middle of nowhere, I have two options: head south and find the closest precinct or drive directly to the nearest police station and hope backwoods justice will suffice.

One thing that's funny about being in the wilderness outside Manhattan is that most of the time it doesn't take much to get out of it. Assuming you're headed in the right direction. In a car. And have a map.

I pinpoint the closest police station, which seems to be about eight miles from my current location. Which will take approximately three hours—on foot. *What the actual fuck?* I poke at all the buttons on the touchscreen, attempting to force it to give me driving directions, but the goddamn thing seems to think I'm stuck in the middle of the forest where there are no roads.

I peer out the window, out into the pitch-black night. I turn on the high beams, wincing at what appears to be a shit ton of trees all around me. I open the car door, stick my head out and check out the ground, hoping for pavement. I'm greatly disappointed.

How the heck I managed to drive as far as I did without driving into a ditch is a miracle. I'm literally in the middle of a forest on what appears to be a very rudimentary roadway, a road I drove blindly down, likely in the opposite direction in which I want to travel. A roadway that the super fancy GPS does not know about.

I groan, slamming the door shut and resting my head back against the seat. I'm a highly intelligent, well-educated badass woman, I won't be thwarted by this lack of a proper roadway. It really is unfortunate Dare didn't think to leave my phone in my pocket, though I suppose Uber may not come out this far.

I sit up, shake off the negative vibes, and start poking at the touch-screen again, panning the map out until I can see a road. It doesn't seem to be too far away, though I have no idea what kind of scale the map is using. And Dare obviously drove in here somehow, so there must be a hidden path back to the main road.

I ease the car back onto the poor excuse for a road, slowly inching my way along as I scour the tree line for a way out. At this rate, I may make it back to civilization before I have to be back at work in three days. I wonder how he'd explain my absence if I never returned and eventually, had to come out here to bury my carcass among the pricker bushes.

Ugh. Would he really not come looking for me if I was missing for a while? Would he leave me out here to rot? *I mean, I did toss him around and kick him in the balls, but he'll have to admit that it was a perfectly reasonable response to his deep treachery.*

Pushing the possibility of dying in the wilderness to the back of my mind, I focus on finding the hidden exit. I roll my eyes and scoff at the insanity of this entire situation. How very *Alice in Wonderland* of him, finding this little maze in the woods to bring his snatched women to.

Is that a shiny object in the trees?

I slam on the brakes, put the car into reverse and back up and around until I'm facing the tree that glimmered at me. I don't see anything now. I look at the GPS, the main road is literally right there.

Frustrated, I get out of the car, walking around the hood to take a closer look at the trees standing between me and freedom. The underbrush seems very thick here, but I can see where some of the plants have been flattened recently. I consider just crashing through it blindly, but knowing my shit luck, I would either crash into a giant oak tree hidden behind the bushes or there would be a deep ravine for me to plummet into.

I push through the bushes, slowly easing my way in by using the light from the car headlamps to guide me. Sure enough, a few yards in I can see where it clears out again, showing a better-defined roadway that must lead back towards town. I do a little shimmy then hustle back to the car, my spirits greatly improved knowing I won't perish in the middle of no where.

By the time I hit the main road, I feel like I've been out here for days. I press the gas pedal down, impressed by how quickly Dare's car accelerates as I speed towards the local police station. I wonder if he has managed to get himself up and out of the dirt, back to wherever he was trying to take me.

Before I know it, I'm pulling into the parking lot of the local police station. This is a large town considering I was lost in the woods not even fifteen minutes ago; however, I can only imagine what kind of operation I'm running into.

I walk towards the entrance, looking around for the way in, pulling on random doors. Everything is locked. I peer in the windows. No one is loitering about. *For the love of...reporting your own kidnapping should not be this difficult.*

I finally find an intercom system and press the button. And wait.

I press it a couple more times in case they missed it.

"May I help you?" a bored, crackly voice comes through the speaker.

"Yes, I need to report a kidnapping," I exclaim, nodding to myself.

"Excuse me?" the uninterested voice queries.

I frown, my hands fisting at my sides as I squint at the metal box in front of me and say slower, "I need to report a kidnapping."

"Hmm," the bland voice comes through again. "Someone will be with you momentarily. Please wait there."

Well, that response was certainly underwhelming. Should I have called emergency rather than drive down here? Maybe if I had been less calm and matter of fact and had been a sniveling, screaming basket case instead; maybe then they would be reacting with some sense of urgency.

It takes more than ten minutes for a uniformed officer to show up at the door to let me in. He pushes the door open, gesturing for me to enter and follow him. He glances at me blandly, obviously not overly concerned by my clearly disheveled appearance.

"What relation are you to the victim?" he asks as he leads me down the hallway.

"Me. It's me. I'm the kidnapping victim," I reply curtly, my hands gesturing towards myself emphatically.

"You were kidnapped?"

"Yes, I was kidnapped! Some asshole I work with snatched me from the parking garage!"

He stops walking, his skeptical gaze zeroing in on my face. "You're saying a coworker stole you from work and brought you here, to this town?"

"No, he brought me about ten miles north of here, but you're the nearest police station according to the fancy pants GPS in his car," I reply calmly, though I'm getting more annoyed with every question this guy asks me.

"You stole his car?"

I blink at him, truly startled this has shifted from me being kidnapped to me confessing to grand theft auto. I open my mouth to reply, then pause to contemplate if I need a lawyer.

"Of course, I took his car. The lunatic attacked me then tied me up and stuffed me in the trunk of his car. I had one chance to escape, and I took it."

"How did you manage to find an opportunity to escape?"

"Oh, I hit him with the little fire extinguisher he has in his trunk then I kicked him in the balls as hard as I could."

The man physically winces, his hands coming up to cover his crotch as he asks, "So you assaulted him and then stole his car?"

"What the ever-loving fu—"

"Oh, there she is now! Darling, I was so worried about you."

That fucking voice. That deep, dark, smooth-as-silk voice I would know anywhere is somehow behind me, calling me darling. *Calling me fucking darling!*

I'm truly speechless right now. I want to kick and scream and throw an epic hissy fit, but I have no words in my brain at all. I'm well and truly stunned into silence.

I slowly turn around, gritting my teeth as I see his annoyingly handsome face smiling back at me.

That fucking bastard.

Dare

I'm smug.

I fully admit it, I'm one smug fucking bastard right now.

And the look on her face. Priceless.

She looks so adorably confused and full of rage I honestly can't decide if I want to hug her or grab her by her hair and yank her head back to spit in her mouth. Maybe both.

I knew it would take her a fair amount of time to get herself out of my wooded maze, but it took her so long I was starting to get worried.

Since I was familiar with my surroundings, and had many options for transportation, I have been here for quite a while, regaling a small group of police officers with my tales of woe with my woman. How our role-playing rendezvous went awry, and she had gotten herself tangled up in the forest. They mostly thought it was a funny story and happily let me wait around for her to show up.

Because her reporting me to the police is always part of the show.

I think they appreciate that I came up with a feasible cover story rather than expecting them to cover up my potentially criminal shenanigans. I also brought coffee and an envelope of money that just happened to fall out of my pocket at some point in the hallway.

A growl snaps me out of my thoughts, and I glance at Antoinette's furious face as I ask, "Are you all right, darling? Are you injured?"

If looks could kill, I would drop dead in this very spot.

"I don't know, Clark,' she snarls. "How are your balls?"

I wince. All the men in the room wince.

I smile at her lovingly. "Oh, don't you worry about the boys. They've recovered just fine from your little slip-up."

She shows me her teeth. Time to go.

I turn to the closest officer, offering my hand. "Thank you for letting me wait here for her arrival. We'll take our lover's quarrel out of your hair for now."

He shakes my hand, grinning at me knowingly, "Anytime, Darius. We're always here to be your little safe space."

He laughs, so I laugh. Thank god for greedy bastards.

I put my arm around Antoinette, forcefully maneuvering her around toward the exit. "Just go with it, baby girl. You can murder me with your poetry soon enough."

She's vibrating with rage beneath my arm, and my cock hardens in my pants. I pull her closer to me, pressing my face into her neck as we walk down the hallway. She smells like musky earth and sweet cinnamon.

I narrow my eyes at her. "You ate my fucking Red Hots, didn't you?"

She smirks. "Every last fucking one of them."

"You are a very naughty girl, Antoinette. Whatever am I going to do with you?"

"Oh, I don't know. Maybe truss me up and stuff me in your trunk again?"

"Tempting as that sounds, I think our playtime opportunity has passed." I lean closer to her, smirking as I add, "For now."

She gives me a bland look and grunts at me.

I put my hand out. "My key FOB, please."

She stares at me for a beat. "It's in the car."

"You didn't lock my car?" I ask incredulously.

"Why would I be worried about locking your stupid car when I came here to report you for kidnapping me? You should be in jail right now."

I scoff, stepping closer to her. "It would take a considerable amount of effort to get me sent to jail."

She doesn't move away from me, her hands fisting at her sides as she asks, "Is that a challenge? Shall we see if I can come up with enough effort to make it happen?"

I chuckle softly, leaning down even closer until my breath practically paints her lips. "Oh, by all means, baby girl. Do. Your. Worst."

She glares at me, then huffs, jerking her body away from mine and taking a step back. I can see her hesitation; her typical response to me now stuttered and glitchy, and I'm filled with a sense of remorseful glee.

Will I miss our old dynamic now that she has glimpsed the real me?

"Can I have my phone and bag, please?" Her question breaks through my thoughts, and I glance up to see she's standing there with her hand out, waiting expectantly. *As if.*

"I will give them both to you when I deposit you inside your house," I say with a nod in case she didn't realize my decision was final.

"You don't need to bring me home. I'll call an Uber," she retorts, her arms crossing in front of her. Obviously, she gives no fucks about my feelings of overbearing finality. This I can work with.

"Over my dead fucking body." I grit the words out between my teeth, my hands clenching at my sides as I ignore my intense urge to force my will on her, preferably after forcing her onto her knees.

"That can be arranged," she shoots back, unflinching, her eyes shooting daggers at me.

I squint at her, contemplating how best to handle her in this new uncharted territory we've ventured into. What I really want to do—what my beast is beating up my insides to do—is to stuff her back into the trunk of my car, kicking and screaming and spitting, consequences and possible witnesses be damned. But no, I can't do that.

I scoff to myself, disgusted with how terribly wrong this entire evening has gone. *"Can't."* I'm not at all used to that puny, annoying little word, and it's already on my last nerve. Time to change tactics, time to put playtime and my attempt to overwhelm Antoinette into my way of thinking on the back-burner for now.

"Antoinette, there is no way I'm leaving you out here to find your own way home, so for once in your life, give it a rest and get in the fucking car." I open the passenger door for her, then wait for her to decide how we're going to do this. "The easy way or the hard way, baby girl, you decide?"

"Stop calling me that!" she shouts at me, her hands coming up to shove at my chest with all the rage she must have been harboring since waking up in my trunk.

I shrink back a bit, my hands coming up to deflect her attack. She is exceedingly strong, something I learned today when she tossed me over her shoulder and kicked me in the balls, and I won't make the mistake of letting my guard down with her again.

I grasp her wrists firmly but loosely enough that she won't feel I'm trying to trap her again. I pull her close to me, bending down slightly so I'm right in her face, my eyes seeking hers as she intentionally evades my gaze. I tighten my grip slightly, giving her a little rattle that snaps her focus to me, and I beam inside when I see the fire burning within her.

There you are, baby girl.

"Please, Toni," I say quietly, my words almost a whisper. "Allow me to bring you home, so I can be assured you got there safely."

She cocks her head at me, confusion shadowing her features as she contemplates my rapid shift in demeanor. She narrows her eyes at me suspiciously, then, thankfully, though with obvious annoyance and discontent, she does as I ask and plants herself inside the car.

I barely manage not to slam the door, instead closing it firmly, then walking around to the driver's side. She's sitting there like a stone, her arms wrapped around her middle, her left leg bouncing in aggravation.

I lean over the middle console towards her, chuckling to myself when she moves her body away from me. I look her right in the eyes while I grasp her seat belt and buckle her in.

She glares at me again, "Oh, so now you're concerned for my safety?"

"I'm always concerned with your safety," I mutter, turning away from her as I pull away from the curb.

She doesn't say anything, just remains quiet, tucked against the door. I sneak a glance at her; she looks tired. I almost feel bad for dragging her all the way out here and causing her so much grief. *Almost.*

"Don't you need my address?" Her question cuts through the quiet, her tone sharply innocent, making it incredibly obvious that she knows I know where she lives.

I don't respond. I'm also exhausted, and I don't see any point in wasting energy on rhetoric.

But she's staring at me, glaring a hole right into the side of my face.

"If you have something to say, Antoinette, by all means, spit it out," I bite out, my hands gripping the steering wheel so tightly my knuckles are white.

"How do you know where I live, Clark?"

Her voice is quiet, almost sad. I glance over at her, meeting her gaze as I reply, "I know where you live because I got your address off your license that time I saved you from that douchey women-drugging shitbag you dated a ways back."

"What are you talking about? Who are you talking about?" She seems genuinely confused, her brows drawing together as she contemplates what I'm telling her.

"I figured you didn't remember any of it, considering you never brought it up to me."

Her eyes widen, her brows punching together as she asks, "Then why didn't you bring it up?"

I shrug, "I didn't see any point in rehashing a situation best left forgotten."

"What the fuck, Darius!" Now she is shouting again. And bringing out the Darius instead of Clark. This isn't good. "Something traumatic happened to me that I don't even remember, and you didn't think that maybe I should know about it so I could prevent it from happening again?"

"Oh, the danger had passed, so your knowing was irrelevant," I say with another shrug.

She stares at me incredulously—for good reason. She knows damn well that I'm not a shrugger; I'm a matter-of-fact, shoot-from-the-hip, professional communicator, and now I have shrugged...twice.

I'm a dead man.

I remain quiet for the rest of the drive, knowing that her silence is just another trap. She's definitely sitting over there plotting her next move. Likely daydreaming about trussing me up and stuffing me in the trunk of my own car and dumping me somewhere unpleasant.

I continue to steal glances at her as I drive toward her residence, taking in her body language as she stares out into the darkness. I'm not accustomed to her being silent, and her stillness seems wrong compared to her typical bratty chatter. I'm not certain, but I feel like I'm not a fan of this Antoinette. Hopefully, it's a temporary response to the shock of the evening, and batshit crazy will be back forthwith.

Finally, we're pulling up outside her building. I park the car and then reach for the door, but her hand on my arm stops me. I turn to look at her, groaning inwardly as I see she's full-on stubborn bitch-face right now.

She crosses her arms, juts her chin out, blue eyes boring into mine as she says slowly and clearly, "I'm not getting out of this car until you tell me, in great detail, exactly what happened that led to you knowing where I live."

Fuck.

Chapter Five

DARE

Six months ago

I have been sitting at this table for almost an hour, listening to so-and-so drone on and on about so-and-so for most of it. Yes, both so-and-sos have a name; I just don't care enough to remember what they may be. Or if so-and-so is even talking about the same so-and-so.

I catch a glimpse of long dark hair in my peripheral vision. I glance over, allowing my gaze to drink her in before focusing my attention back on my date. I think she's still droning on about the same man, but it all blends together—is this an ex or a brother...a neighbor?

I do not fucking care.

Then that full raucous laughter drifts over and my gaze strays across the room again. I'd know that laugh anywhere; loud and annoying, and so damn sexy my cock twitches in my pants.

I turn my body toward the sound, squinting at the weird suit, leather-sport-coat jackoff sitting across from her. She's always had the absolute worst taste in men. And even though they are usually completely different, they always have the same underlying stench of douchery surrounding them.

It's also not lost on me that she tends to always bring her douchey dates to the same exact location I bring my boredom of the week to. Like we're using these other people as a buffer between what's been brewing between us since the day we met. As if the symbolism of dating other people detracted from the intense romantic relationship we're inevitably working towards, albeit in an untraditional manner.

I get out my wallet, pull out some bills, and toss them on the table. She pauses the yammering to gape at me in mock outrage. I put up a hand in a salute, then walk away from the table, heading to the far side of the restaurant where a small table is sitting vacant.

I know, I know—I'm an asshole. But am I really? She literally spent our entire date talking about other men while swilling top-shelf booze and hammering tapas plates. I don't see anyone crying over any supposed missed love connection this time.

I sit down, smiling at the waitress heading my way, likely to tell me I can't sit here. I hold out a couple of hundreds, "Sazerac, please, and as you know, I'm an excellent tipper."

She smirks at me, pulling the bills from my grasp as she asks, "Up to no good again, Darius?"

I smile at her cheekily, snapping my fingers as I reply, "You got me, Dee."

Dee rolls her eyes at me, then turns and makes her way to the bar to retrieve my drink, and I turn my attention back across the room. I have a much better view from here while also being a bit hidden from prying eyes. *My very own little creeper corner.* Yes, I chuckle at my own jokes.

Antoinette gets up and heads towards the restrooms, so I keep my eyes on the jackoff still sitting at the table. He glances at his phone, then reaches into the inside pocket of his stupid leather sport coat, pulling out a small bottle. He pours something out into his palm, capping the bottle and putting it back in his pocket before putting whatever he got out of the bottle between two spoons and pressing them together. He glances around, checking his surroundings before tapping the spoon into Antoinette's drink.

That motherfucker.

I clench my fists, forcing myself to stay in my seat, even though I want nothing more than to run over there and pound that jackoff into hell where he belongs. He looks pleased with himself, and my desire to destroy him rises even more.

Antoinette comes back from the restroom, sits down, and picks up her drink. She takes a couple of big swallows, and jackoff smirks at her slyly. My blood boils, and I don't even look up as Dee places my drink on the table.

He is a dead man.

They sit at the table for a few more minutes, and I can see her loosening up with every minute that passes. Finally, he leans closer to her, and she nods in agreement at whatever he says to her. He drops some bills on the table, then gets up, holding his hand out to her and helping her up, smiling down at her as he leads her away from the table and toward the back exit.

I stand up, walking down the same hallway, just far enough away not to draw attention to myself. I want to confront him away from witnesses, but I also don't want him to get so far out in front of me that I lose them.

I peek around the corner just in time to watch him lead her out the back door. I wait for a few beats and then I follow, stepping out into the darkness.

Antoinette is looking at me incredulously, her brows furrowed, eyes squinting as she processes what I've just told her. She gives me a suspicious look as she asks, "And that's it?"

I nod. "Yes, that's it. The douchebag attempted to roofie you, and I stepped in before he could do anything to you physically. I got your address off your license and deposited you there, safe and sound."

"And what happened to jackoff?"

"I knocked him around a bit and left him in the alley," I respond. "No idea what happened to him from there, but I would imagine getting caught attempting to drug you and then getting his face re-arranged may be a big reason why he ghosted you."

She snorts, rolling her eyes at me as she replies, "Yeah, I'm sure that must have been a real downer for him."

She looks sad, almost crestfallen, and she sighs. I don't like her feeling bad about anything, never mind her feeling bad about what some piece of horseshit did to her.

I reach out, resting my hand on her arm as I say, "Hey, that douchebag attempting to take advantage of you was not your fault. You didn't do anything to deserve it or ask for it. He was an asshole—a dirty, rotten, no-good shitbag who deserves to rot in hell for what he tried to do to you."

She glances at my hand on her arm before raising her eyes to mine. She nods. "Yes, I know, but knowing doesn't make it feel any better. And I really feel you should have told me. What if he hadn't ghosted me? What if he tried to go out with me again? I would've figured my spotty memory of our date was me overindulging and figured he was worth another shot."

"I would not have allowed that to happen."

She scoffs, "You couldn't have prevented it. You only ran into me by chance that one time, and the odds of you being able to intervene a second time are basically slim to none."

I mean, she isn't wrong, knowing as little as she does. But I was there, and I remember the entire story, so I know for a fact there isn't even a remote chance the jackoff will ever be calling her again.

But I can't really explain all of that to her.

I sigh, "You're right, and I'm sorry."

She frowns at me, her eyes narrowing as she snorts, "Seriously. You're sorry?"

Now it's my turn to roll my eyes, my hands coming up to flail around in defeat. "Yes, Antoinette. I'm sorry. Now get out of my car and get your ass into your building, so I can go home."

She squints at me some more, and I feel like she is staring right into my soul, siphoning out all of my secrets to use against me in whatever way she can. Finally, she nods, "Okay, Clark. Whatever you say."

Normally, I would get out and escort her to her door but not tonight. Tonight, I watch her gather her things and unbuckle her seatbelt, her hand reaching for the door handle before I lean across the middle console and say quietly, "But don't forget, Antoinette, we haven't finished our earlier business."

Her eyes widen as she pauses her movements, asking, "Business? What the fuck are you talking about?"

I smile at her wickedly, all teeth and glinting eyes, my hand shooting out, delving into her hair at the base of her scalp. I tighten my hold until the tension allows me to yank her head closer to me, and I lean further into her, my breath painting her neck as I whisper, "You'll see, baby girl."

She shivers, and I release her, chuckling darkly at the heat in her gaze. She doesn't say anything, though; she just exits my car and walks into her building without a backward glance.

That's my good girl.

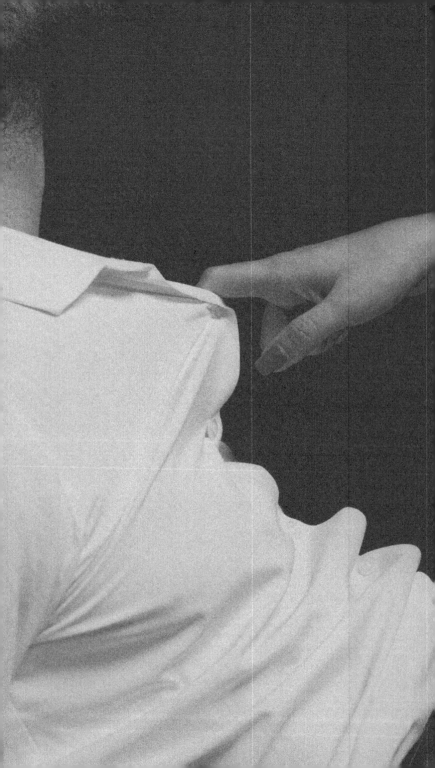

Chapter Six

Toni

I will admit, it's been a lot.

The last twenty-four hours, that is.

Once I got into my apartment last night, it took me a reasonable amount of time to grasp what Dare had told me in his car. I only vaguely recollect what had gone down with the jackoff, thus I figure he just decided he wasn't interested in me, and me not giving enough fucks to follow up on any of it, I left it alone. From what little I remember of him, I have a difficult time pegging him for a roofie-pusher; however, I don't believe Dare would make it up—he saw what he saw.

Of course, now that I know the douchebag drugged me, likely with the intent to do bad things to me, I kind of want to follow up for the sole purpose of beating the ever-loving piss out of him. And then ruin him financially and socially because that is more my style.

Now, as I'm lounging in bed, I smile at the thought of inflicting some vigilante justice on his douchey ass. I can only begin to speculate on how badly Dare must have beaten his ass to get him to never speak to me again. I mean, I assume, I likely blocked his ass and attempted to avoid him at every turn, but some men at least attempt to save face on a possible rejection.

And then there's Dare and his Jekyll-and-Hyde act.

Never in my wildest dreams would I have believed my dapper little Clark could be hiding such wickedness beneath his seasonal ties and floral-print shirts. Yes, I said floral prints, and not in the sense of a tropical vacation. This is more designer floral which should mean classy, but really, they just make him look like a painfully colorful accountant rather than the drab accountant he's supposed to be.

And now, I just want to see what those floral shirts look like on the floor. My floor, his floor, any old floor.

I narrow my eyes at my own thoughts, taken aback by how quickly my thoughts of Dare have shifted from affectionate mockery to complete bitch in heat. Don't get me wrong, I'm not blind; the man is attractive. You'd have to be dead not to notice his underlying sex appeal, and the idea of busting up his boring exterior only deepens this appeal.

The mere idea of pushing Clarkie-poo over the edge into beast mode has me rubbing my thighs together. I bet if I pushed him hard enough, he would come completely off his leash and take me to heel in a grand fashion. I shiver at the thought, my mind immediately going back to the last few seconds before I exited his car. *Business. Really.*

I huff to myself, rolling out of bed and making my way to the bathroom to wash my face and scrub the mothballs from my mouth. I didn't have an ounce of liquor last night, but the few hours of poor sleep have left me feeling less than refreshed.

Which means one thing—time for a run.

Dare

I had every intention of waiting.

After I dropped Antoinette off at her apartment, I went home, fully intending to have a nice relaxing sauna, a frigid shower, and a healthy shot of kombucha. I lasted about five minutes in the sauna, skipped the cold shower, and poured the shot of kombucha but never actually drank it. I attempted to find a new show to watch, then figured I'd watch something I'd already seen and enjoyed. No luck.

Instead, I sat there for hours mulling over her many possible reactions to the story I told her. Either it would deflect her anger from me, or it would fuel her anger towards me in a different way. And she may demand more answers as to what happened after I followed them out that back exit. I must be prepared for any and all possibilities because all it takes is one slip-up for her to jump on me.

And so, I told myself to give it some time, to give her some time, to give the entire sordid affair time to cool off and settle down before attempting to escalate the situation between us. Give her some time to process and digest the complete mind fuck I dropped on her not even sixteen hours ago. It's the right thing to do and the best option for the healthy development of a romantic relationship.

Fuck all that. Now, I'm standing in the shadows on her street, waiting for her to run by.

And yes, I know she'll run by this very spot likely within the next half hour because she is a creature of habit, and she pretty much never veers from her mood-driven schedule. At one point, I actually thought she took her own safety and well-being seriously, but after the jackoff incident, I realized she was a goddamn mess and required significant oversight in keeping her safe. I mean, she is a stalker's dream in that sense—same schedule day in and day out. Rinse and repeat.

Not that I'm calling myself a stalker or anything. I'm more of a distant admirer. A connoisseur of her comings and goings, who is intent on getting her going until she is coming. I only become intrusive in ways she is unaware of, though I suppose the closer I get to her, the more likely it is she'll catch me at my own games.

I hear her footfalls before I see her, her heels striking the pavement exactly how I have told her repeatedly not to run. I shake my head, sighing in exasperation. It's like she defies me at every turn.

I step back into the shadows, biding my time as she approaches, completely unaware of the danger she's running into. I'm sure she even has her headphones cranked up, drowning out the world around her. Perhaps these new experiences will make her more cautious in the future.

She's about to run right by me when I reach out and grab her by her arm, giving her a quick yank to throw her off balance, then placing a light canvas bag over her head. I have to use the element of surprise to my advantage and incapacitate her quickly and efficiently; otherwise, she'll either get in a lucky punch or kick, or she'll scream bloody murder and draw unnecessary attention to us.

I pull her against my front, wrapping my arms around her so she can't flail about as I lift her and walk toward my car, which is parked close by in the alley. She struggles half-heartedly, likely recognizing my scent or the feel of my body or some other romanticized reason she's not fighting me like the banshee she is. Or she's just tired and can't be bothered because she's also like that.

I press her face first down into the open trunk of my car, my knee in her back keeping her down when she briefly attempts to wiggle away. I truss her up in my best restraints, her arms and legs secure, and then swap the bag for a blindfold and ball gag. I won't be making any so-called amateur mistakes this time around.

I push her further into the trunk, arranging her just so before gently closing the lid. I walk around to the driver's side and get behind the wheel, feeling rather accomplished with how well that went. I learned my lesson last time, and there is no way she will get away this time.

Toni

Well, he certainly tried harder this time.

I'm genuinely surprised he decided to do this again so soon. I suppose I shouldn't be surprised, considering I likely know next to nothing about the man I have been teasing mercilessly for what feels like ages. For all I know, snatching unsuspecting women off the street is a weekly occurrence for him.

I snort as best I can behind the gag in my mouth. I could've done without that added bonus when he thought how best to restrain me. He must still be sore about the kick to the balls because he definitely wasn't taking any chances this go around. I can't move my hands at all, and I'm barely maintaining circulation in my hands and feet.

I kind of want to kick him in the balls again.

Whatever happened to just asking a girl out?

I mean, assuming he isn't taking me out to the middle of the woods to dispose of me once and for all, if he truly decided he had a thing for me, why couldn't he have just sent me a note or a text? Maybe knocked on my office door and asked me if I'd like to grab lunch or dinner or a drink with him. Anything short of kidnapping, maybe.

Okay, okay—yes, I would've laughed in his face and told him to stick with his merry-go-round of potential Stepford wives, and he would've been all butt-hurt and told me to suck a sock or something equally lame. But still, to hide his true persona for all this time and then just unleash his beastness on me without any warning whatsoever... that's just outright mean.

And now I'm mad all over again. *That duplicitous motherfucker.*

I have no idea how long we have been driving, but I can feel the terrain has changed from pavement to a rougher surface. Here we go again. Though I can tell this time will be a bit different since there is no way I'll be pulling off any kind of epic getaway.

The car stops, and I listen intently for movement from what I can only assume is the driver's side. I hate feeling disoriented, but I can't seem to get my bearings with the blindfold on, and I can't reach anything with how tightly my hands are bound.

The car door opens, then slams shut, followed by footfalls on gravel moving around towards the back of the car. Then the click of the trunk being opened, his hands pulling me out of the trunk, lifting me up, and swinging me over his shoulder.

I grunt, briefly wondering if I can throw him off balance by flailing about, but quickly accept that it would likely just earn me some bruises and not even a moment of freedom. So, I lay over that broad shoulder, blood rushing to my head with my tied arms becoming increasingly more uncomfortable with each jostling step.

I want to scream at him, but no real sound comes out around the ball gag. In normal circumstances, feeling this impotent would throw me for a loop, but it all seems pointless from my current vantage point. As much as I want to put up a fuss and kick and scream and murder, instead, I'm going to hang out here and see how this all pans out.

I'm a bit surprised that he isn't winded lugging me around like a giant sack of grain. I'm not a small person by any stretch of the imagination, and he's moving along at a decent gait, not even breaking a sweat. And now I'm even more annoyed that my hands are tied behind my back because, otherwise, I would at least be able to cop a feel.

Finally, he climbs up some steps, then I feel him reaching, hear the subtle squeak of a door sliding open, and then he steps forward, turns, and there's the squeak of the door again, closing. Next thing I know, he is moving downward, his steps quick as we walk down, down, down into what could quite possibly be a torture chamber.

I should be more concerned about that possibility than I am, but short of him having a horde of women locked away down there, I'm likely game. And I'm not even embarrassed about it, though there is no way I'm going to just roll over and take it. I'll make him work for it like he has never worked for anything before in his entire life.

Finally, he sets me down, pushing me back until the backs of my knees come in contact with something hard, and I automatically sit down. He unties my hands only to resecure them to the back of the chair, then does the same with my ankles, securing them to the legs of the chair. It's not the most comfortable position to be in, but mostly, I hate not being able to see. And my jaw is starting to hurt.

His voice, gruff yet quiet, cuts through the silence as he asks, "If I remove the blindfold and gag, are you going to behave?"

I immediately nod, and I feel his hands on the back of my head a moment before the gag loosens, then he pulls the blindfold off as well. I blink my eyes against the light, dim as it is, flexing my jaw in what must be the most unattractive pose possible.

I don't see Dare at first, so I glance around until I see him standing at a counter across the room. He turns and walks towards me, a bottle of water in his hand. He kneels down in front of me, helping me drink from the bottle before sitting back on his haunches and giving me a strange look. He looks like he's waiting for something, though I can't even imagine what, with me sitting here all tied up.

I glare at him, my words quietly menacing as I ask, "What the fuck, Clark?"

He smiles. The motherfucker smiles at me. Now, I don't mean he smirked or his lip twitched, no; he full-on showed me his teeth, all sparkly-eyed, and smiled at me. It would have almost taken my breath away if I wasn't so keen on giving him a hard time, but luckily my inner rage bitch dulls at the glorious sight a bit, and I'm able to continue being contrite.

"Let me go, fuckface," I seethe, shifting in the chair as I pull against my restraints. I try to stomp my feet, but the ropes prevent me from getting any leverage, and I mostly do a weird tap dance.

He tsks, raising his brows at me humorously as he shakes his head and says, "Now, why would I do that, Antoinette? Just so you can get a better shot at jamming your foot into my balls?"

I laugh at the memory, my glee likely coming off as borderline maniacal, but I genuinely don't have any fucks to give at this point. I have to cover up my other interest in his balls by making him believe I only want to stomp on them. "That's right," I taunt. "I bet I could really bust them up this time."

He winces, his eyes narrowing slightly as he watches me, but he doesn't say anything. I feel like he can see right through my ball-stomping bitch defense, and it makes me uncomfortable. I try not to squirm, but I fail, my wrists and ankles twisting in the restraints as I ponder how I'm going to get out of here in one piece.

Then, without warning, he strikes, his hand wrapping around my throat as he lunges forward. I would have toppled over backward if not for his firm grip on the back of my neck. He leans over me, his face so close to mine that I can only focus on one of his eyes as it burns with something unclear. Anger. Hunger. Ownership.

I try to gasp, but my air is cut off as he uses his grip on my neck to prevent me from falling further backward, and I can't help the thrill that goes through me at the increasingly feral look in his eyes. I try not to respond, but a shiver runs through me, and my eyes close of their own volition, my body relaxing into his hold.

He eases his grip just enough for me to get some air and then immediately cuts off my breath again, leaning forward until I can feel his lips against my temple, his breath fanning my hair as he says, "That's right, my little minx. Relax..."

Instantly, self-preservation is a beast raging inside of me. I want to fight back, to put up some kind of fuss, to kick and scream. I want to bite him, punch him, kick him, anything to get him to back up, to back off, to get the fuck as far away from me as humanly possible.

But I don't.

Instead, I practically melt into a puddle, my arms pulling against the ropes, my thighs squeezing together as a deep ache erupts inside me. I'd moan if I had enough air to do so, but all I manage is a whimper that gets caught in my throat, and my entire body is on fire.

Dare chuckles, the dark rumble vibrating over me as his grip on my neck relaxes, and I gulp air as I attempt to get control of myself. He doesn't remove his hand from my throat, but he doesn't cut off my air this time, just uses his light touch to force me to look at him. I don't want to look at him, once again fearing he'll see right through my tenuous façade into the real me.

He leans closer, the hand on the back of my neck moving to stroke my face as he eases the chair down. He glides his lips along my cheek, coasting up to ghost over my eyelids before doing the same on the other side. Then he bites me, sinking his teeth right into my cheek while holding me in place when I attempt to flinch away in surprise. His tongue comes out, wetting the bitten area soothingly, and I gasp, my breath catching in my throat as his fingertips gently caress my neck and face.

There's a faint ringing of a phone behind me, and he tenses over me, a low growl vibrating against my skin. He only pauses for a moment, then takes a shuddering breath, burying his face in my neck before he bites me again, his teeth digging in almost painfully, and I whimper in response. I'm like putty in his hands, incapable of pushing him away. Or maybe I just don't want to.

His phone rings again, this time with a different ringtone, and he curses under his breath. His hand on my throat tightens again, not enough to choke me but just enough to render me immobile. He skims his nose down my cheek to the corner of my mouth, and for a brief moment, I think he's going to kiss me.

But he doesn't.

Instead, I feel his tongue slide against my skin as he licks my face, leaving a wet trail from the corner of my mouth across my cheek to my ear. He inhales deeply, taking my scent into my lungs and holding it there for a few beats before exhaling slowly, a soft growl that sets off another tremor through me.

Then he backs away, moving to a spot in the room behind me where I can't see him. He rustles around, and I crane my neck around, catching a glimpse of him out of the corner of my eye. He seems to be checking his phone, and he doesn't seem too happy about it.

I return my focus in front of me, working on getting myself under control before he gets back to "torturing" me. I'm normally much more controlled than this, my frustration bubbling up as I think about things that may help ease the ache between my legs. I can't even begin to think about the ache in my chest, the heavy feeling that keeps me weighed down even when I want to fight back.

This entire scenario is so confusing, I don't even know where to begin to unpack any of it. Dare being a genuine bad boy is too shocking to even fathom; however, it already seems so normal that I question whether I had an inkling beforehand. There must've been signs; there's no way he managed to hide this part of himself for all these years without ever having a slip-up.

Suddenly, he's there in front of me again. He looks resigned yet determined and not even a little come-hither, so that's not a good sign. He presses his lips together, his hands on his hips as he looks me over.

After a few long moments of this, I finally snap, "So, are we done here?"

He smiles at me again, the glint in his eyes all fire as he stares at me intently. "Not even close, baby girl," he practically purrs. "We haven't even gotten started."

He moves around behind me, and then there's a clicking sound as he presumably resecures my restraints to the chair. He loosens the ropes around my wrists and ankles a tiny bit before coming back around to stand in front of me. He crosses his arms over his chest, eying me skeptically. "Unfortunately, I have been called away for an errand. Are you going to behave while I'm gone, or shall I put you in the box?"

My eyes widen in surprise. *The box?* I mean, I'm almost curious enough to make him show me what the box is, but there is that tiny warning bell inside me screaming for me to shut my fucking mouth, and for once, I listen to it.

I beam at him sweetly and reply, "Well, sure, Clark. You know I can play nice when I want to."

He snorts, then gives me an incredulous look, obviously not buying my story. I meet his gaze squarely, not flinching as he stares me down. He reaches a hand out, dragging one finger down my cheek as he whispers, "I guess we'll just have to see then, won't we?"

Then he turns on his heel, his long strides taking him toward the exit.

"What the fuck, Clark!" I shout at his retreating back. "You can't just leave me tied up down here while you fuck off to god knows where!"

He doesn't hesitate or acknowledge my words at all; he just walks up the stairs out of sight. The door creaks as it opens and shuts. Then silence.

That motherfucker.

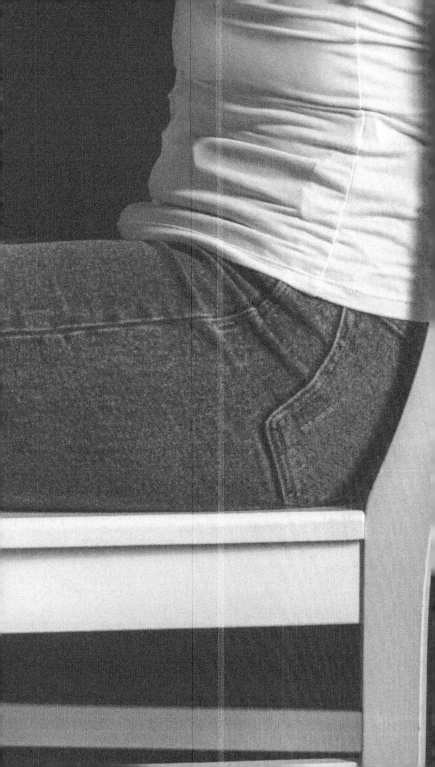

Chapter Seven

TONI

I'VE LOST TRACK OF the number of times in the past twenty-four hours I've thought to myself, *what the actual fuck?*

It has definitely been on repeat ever since Dare walked out of this fancy dungeon and left me tied to a chair.

Tied to a fucking chair. What the actual fuck?

I haven't tried very hard to get free, not wanting to waste energy on what may be entirely impossible. Mostly, I have been taking stock of my surroundings, making a mental note of the small windows that allow in some light but are an unlikely escape route. It appears I'm in a basement-type room, though obviously not fully underground, given the oddly placed windows. The way they're placed indicates they may have been used as emergency exits, but then someone came through and intentionally eliminated the option as an escape route.

Now, I'm seething at being left down here for some goddamn so-called important errand. How important could this errand possibly be to warrant abandoning me in an extremely awkward position?

I've been slowly twisting my wrists around behind me. The ropes have been secured to the chair by some kind of metal locking mechanism, so the odds of wrenching them free from the chair are slim. My only option is to free my wrists from the ropes, which will take a bit of time, considering I need to get the ropes stretched a tiny bit in order to pull my hands out. In this particular case, I'm lucky I'm not a small-boned woman because, with enough force, I can squeeze my hand through the loop and be free. Don't ask how I know this.

Once I painfully manage to get my hands free from the ropes, it's easy for me to reach down and untie my feet. I gradually stand, my extremities a tad numb from being stuck in such an uncomfortable position for so long. I take a few minutes to look around the room, a bit confused about how not dungeon-like it is. It's actually quite nice.

I could totally live here.

Not wanting to waste any more time, I make my way up the stairs to check the door. Shockingly, it's not locked. *Apparently, this guy is still running amateur hour at Stalkerville.* I slowly open the door and peer outside, not surprised to be completely surrounded by wilderness.

I stay in the doorway for a few moments, pondering my choices. *My phone!* He didn't bother patting me down, likely because the likelihood I'd get free was basically nil when he first snatched me. Which means I still have my phone in the side pocket of my super fancy running pants.

I pull my phone out, excited to find I have service. I figure I'm probably near where I previously escaped, so I bring up the map and check my location. Sure enough, I'm in the middle of the fucking woods, still relatively close to a road.

I have a couple of options here. I could call for rescue, which seems a bit extreme given I don't believe the dickhead is trying to kill me or anything, and obviously, him doing dirty things to me isn't exactly a horrible idea. He really could work on his approach, though.

Given no other immediate alternatives, I guess I'm going to have to hoof it out of here, and thankfully, I'm once again wearing comfortable shoes. I pinpoint a location I would like to exit the forest from and slowly start picking my way toward the road. Other than some dense underbrush and a few pricker bushes, it's pretty uneventful, though I'm not too keen on being lost in the woods ever again.

Of course, once I make it to the road, I have another decision to make on where to go from here. I'm not too far from town, so calling an Uber is probably fine; however, where to have an Uber bring me is the real question. My first inclination is to go right to Dare's house and stab him for leaving me tied up in a bunker in the woods, but since I don't actually know where he lives, that potential plan has to be put on hold.

This brings me to plan B; back to the local PD to get some fucking answers.

Dare

I didn't want to leave her alone in the bunker. The last fucking thing I wanted to do was to leave that delectable morsel tied to a chair without me there. I don't think I have to explain any further.

When the first call came through, I was hoping I could just ignore it, but that hope was quickly dashed when the second ringtone came through. We have this code when something is important enough to stop whatever we're doing and check-in. I was still hopeful that the check-in would just be a quick conversation for orders, but unfortunately, that was not the case. Having to deal with this bullshit when I have much more delicate priorities really pisses me off.

And I know leaving her down there is going to set me back a few paces or a dozen because she's not a forgiving type of woman. She will make a thing out of this for days, if not weeks, and since I can't tell her the details of why I had to leave her there, she will definitely drive it right into the ground. Even if I tell her my having to go was to benefit her, she still won't believe me without proof. I can't give her proof without divulging a lot of information that she's just not ready to hear. Honestly, she may never be in the right place to hear it, and if I have to keep taking the hits because of it, then I will.

I meet Tony—another reason I always use Antoinette—in the basement of a warehouse downtown. Most warehouses don't have a basement, but this happens to be a warehouse I own, so I may have added a basement. Blueprints can be deceiving, and that's the point.

Tony called to let me know there was some information I needed to attain from a person in his custody that could put somebody I care about in danger. I know Tony wouldn't have called me unless he believed this to be true, but I also know he wouldn't have told me it needed to be now if time was not truly of the essence.

So here I am, in the basement of a warehouse with Tony, one of his unnamed henchmen, and a crier chained to a wall, instead of in a bunker in the woods, teasing one furious hellcat.

Needless to say, I'm grumpy.

"To what do I owe the pleasure?" I ask with a good dose of sarcasm.

Tony laughs outright as he asks, "Did I interrupt a hot date or something?"

I scowl at him and say blandly, "Define hot date."

His eyes widen, a look of excitement in his eyes as he cackles, "You finally did it!"

I tilt my head at him, leveling him with my most serious gaze. "I haven't the faintest idea what you're on about."

He throws his head back and laughs even harder. "You dirty dog, you finally went ahead with the—"

I reach out and cuff him in the head, cutting off whatever he thought he was going to say about Antoinette. He takes a step back and stops trying to speak, instead continuing to laugh at me while shaking his head in amusement...at my expense.

I've known Tony Andersen for a very long time. He may as well be a brother to me since he's certainly as annoying as a blood relative, though maybe a bit more reliable. He knows everything about me, and I mean everything. That guy has so much dirt on me, I should probably marry him just to be protected by spousal privilege. I might even do so if I didn't also have all the dirt on him. We are equals in dirt. We are dirt brothers.

The best thing about Tony is he's ex-military, which means he is still military; he's just not on the official roster anymore. He has all the skills, connections, and no-fucks to basically get done any job you could ever think of. And I have done some thinking over the last few years in an attempt to find a hard no for him, and so far, nothing. He's all go, all the time. At least, for me.

But right now, he is still laughing at me.

"Seriously, Tony," I scoff, rolling my eyes at him. "You're being childish in front of our guest."

Tony slowly gets control of his laughter, wiping tears from his eyes. He gives me a sympathetic look, pats me on the shoulder, and says, "I'm proud of you, man. Finally taking that big first step toward your goal. It must have been scary to finally let go of the side of the pool like that and swim for the first time."

Yes, Tony knows about Antoinette. I rue the day I had to tell him the sordid tale, and I wouldn't have told him anything if not for needing his particular skill set to maneuver through some precarious situations that had come up since she flew into my life and blew it up entirely. Tony may josh me at every turn, but I've never doubted he has my back at any given moment, and in turn, would also have Antoinette's if her safety were ever to become his responsibility.

Don't get me wrong, I have every intention of staying alive so that job shouldn't ever be a real issue for him, but I take some comfort knowing I have a backup plan for her if things go extra shitty. She would be even more pissed since he would likely have to give her all the information I withheld from her, but hopefully, she would see the truth behind it and allow him to help keep her safe. I would tell her everything myself if I thought she would be receptive to the cold hard facts, but I'm relatively certain she would only see the truth behind it if I was dead. More's the pity, I guess.

Tony is grinning at me expectantly, likely waiting for me to take another shot at him. I shake my head at his antics, pointing at the crier as I ask, "What's the story with the pissant?"

Tony turns serious quickly, crossing his arms over his chest and glaring at the crier as he explains, "This here is one of dickwad's men. Got word he was overheard running his trap about a certain someone down at the local pub the other night. And from what I heard; it was not appropriate verbiage. About this particular someone, anyway."

I stare at him stonily as I ask, "You called me out here over some hearsay?"

He squints at me, then in the most condescending voice he can possibly muster, says, "No, Darius. I called you out here over some pissant telling his cronies he has orders to snatch an Antoinette from a parking garage over near 6th. I just figured the likelihood of his Antoinette and your Antoinette being a different person were basically nil, so here he is, you ungrateful fucklicker, ready to answer your questions."

"Fucklicker, really?"

"I call it like I see it," he taunts. "I already got him primed for you since I figured you were on a tight schedule given it is Saturday night and you have a hellcat..." he makes air quotes, "watch over."

I shake my head at him. "My god, you are such a prick sometimes, you know that."

He grins at me. "One more reason you love me."

I glare at him, shooting back, "If I didn't find you so useful, I would shoot you myself."

He laughs again, putting one arm around my shoulder and pulling me in close to whisper, "No way, man. You would totally gut me like the lunatic you are. Gotta keep it personal when it's personal, right?"

"Good point," I agree. "Dull knives, for sure."

A gruff voice interrupts us, "If you two are about done with your bromance, do you think we can get this show on the road?"

"Well, now, the pissant speaks," I mutter, leveling my stare at him. "I'm interested in what else you want to say to us."

The pissant is no longer crying and is now glaring at us in annoyance. He snorts, "I got nothing to say to you either."

"Oh, is that a fact?" I chuckle, almost good-naturedly.

"Yeah, I didn't have anything to say to your boyfriend over there, and I won't have anything to say to you either."

I look at Tony, who is smiling broadly at the pissant, his body almost vibrating with excitement because he knows precisely what's to come for mister I-got-nothing-to-say. Tony glances at me and shrugs. "I tried to warn him that he was better off just telling me what I want to know, but he was keen on meeting you. Seemed like it was a big challenge to possibly withstand your special kind of tactics. He wouldn't listen to me, not even when I explained how much you like dull knives in delicate places."

"Well, I don't go there first," I scoff. "See, Tony. This is how rumors get started."

"Rumors only get started if there is anyone left alive to start said rumor," he explains. "Hence why the only rumors there are about you are the rumors I have intentionally started." He beams at me again. "You're welcome."

I shake my head once more, not even sure what to say to that.

So instead, I turn to our honored guest, my smile all teeth and crazy eyes. "I guess it's time to get started, then."

Toni

By the time I get to the police department, I'm even more annoyed. I remember exactly how these assholes treated me last time I was here, and if they think I'm going to listen to their shit this go-around, they have another thing coming.

I poke at the intercom box a few times, then wait. Then press it again and again, over and over, until finally, it buzzes at me, then the bored voice is back, "Can I help you?"

"Yes, I need to come in, please," I say clearly.

There's a pause, then the voice returns, "State your business, please."

I roll my eyes, then shout, "How about I need to report a kidnapping!"

Static and then some rustling, a bit of muttering and what sounds a lot like squabbling. Then the uninterested voice is back, sounding a bit more frazzled than bored, "Someone will be right out to get you."

I step back, feeling proud of myself, then walk toward the door to wait. The door opens faster this time, and I'm surprised to see someone I assume is a plain-clothed officer staring at me expectantly,

"What are you doing here?"

I'm a bit taken aback by the question. "Excuse me?"

He motions for me to enter the building, then glances around once the door closes. "Darius isn't here," he explains. "So, what are you doing here? Is this a new part of your games?"

"Games?" I parrot, my confusion likely evident on my face as he stares at me. "I have no idea what you're talking about."

He studies my face for a few moments, then must believe what he sees because the next thing I know, he's throwing a few air punches. "That motherfucker," he spits out. He stops his air assault and looks at me, "He really did kidnap you, didn't he?"

I nod, not sure what to say.

"That fucking prick," he mutters, almost to himself. "Telling me fancy tales as if things had progressed naturally with his woman after all his pining."

His woman? Pining? What the actual fuck.

I make a face, my confusion growing with every word muttered by this guy. Surely, he's mistaken, and *his woman* is someone else entirely because the idea that Dare has been secretly pining over me for ages is completely ludicrous. He hates me. Loathes me even. Can't stand to be in the same room with me for more than a few minutes before wanting to bodily toss me out a window.

The officer is pacing around, still muttering to himself, "And I bet Tony knows all about it! I bet that fucking prick was in on this little turn of events the entire time, having a laugh at my expense."

I interrupt him, "Toni? But I'm Toni."

He spares me a glance, "No, you're Antoinette. Tony is Tony Andersen, Darius's bosom buddy and numero-uno bromancer."

"Huh," I respond. "Never heard of him. And who are you?"

He gives me a bland look, then finally holds his hand out as he replies, "I'm Chief Matt Shields. Nice to finally meet you."

"Finally meet me?" I ask incredulously. "Have you heard a lot about me?"

He snorts, "A lot would be an understatement, but that's really all I'm going to say about it."

I frown at him. "What? You can't be serious."

He just looks at me and doesn't say anything.

I raise my brows at him. "Then what are you going to do with me now that I'm here and Darius isn't?"

He mirrors my frown, "Excellent question."

"I guess you have no choice but to take me to him."

"Not a fucking chance."

Now he's pissing me off. It's obvious there is no way this asshat is going to be enforcing the law on Darius, especially since what I'm telling him would end up being my word against his. And he will definitely be team Darius unless I can come up with some kind of concrete evidence implicating Dare for something bigger than my current complaints.

I glare at him, crossing my arms over my chest as I ask, "What other choice do you have...Chief Shields?" I step closer to him, getting right up in his space as I continue. "Either you take me to Darius, or I bring a whole heap of problems to your house."

He eyes me suspiciously. "Either way, I'm fucked, so I'm not sure your way makes me any less fucked."

I shrug. "That sounds like a you problem. But let me assure you, if you attempt to double-cross me on this, I have people waiting for me to check in and my location is shared with them in case I suddenly go dark."

This isn't even remotely true, but I pull my phone out and send a message randomly anyway, giving the impression that I'm not full of shit. My gut tells me he won't try to pull anything, but I know my gut isn't always as fortuitous as I would like it to be. I have to plan for the worst and hope for the best. Whatever the fuck the best scenario would even be at this point.

He sighs deeply, running his hand through his hair in agitation as he mutters to himself some more. Apparently, this is a more difficult choice than I would have thought, and I can't imagine how or why. This could mean this guy knows a lot about all the Darius stuff that I really want to know.

Finally, he stops his muttering and walks around me, holding the door open as he looks at me expectantly, "Well, let's go," he says. "May as well get this over with."

I'm not sure what I should think at this point, so I walk out the door and wait for him to lead the way.

To where? I guess I'll find out.

Chapter Eight

TONI

OUR DRIVE BACK TO the city is rather tense.

Chief Shields, as I will be calling him, made it quite clear to me that he would not be listening to my questions at all, never mind answering them, and the blaring metal music he put on the radio pretty much cemented this fact. I'm not at all accustomed to being ignored, but I figure I may as well give him the win because, at this point, I don't even know where to start.

So, the silent ride gives me plenty of time to ponder every possible fucked-up scenario in the history of fucked-up scenarios. And plenty of time to slyly scope out Chief Shields while he's distracted by traffic.

At first glance, he appears to be another strait-laced white brief kind of guy. He has sandy blonde hair that's grown a bit too long and the palest green eyes I've ever seen. He's dressed in a drab, almost ill-fitting suit, and I can't help but reach a hand over and pull his suit jacket open a bit in the hopes of seeing what he might be hiding under his boring costume.

He slaps my hand away, giving me a dirty look before focusing back on the road. I roll my eyes, huffing a bit as I go back to looking out the window, allowing thoughts of Darius to flood in. The unknowns I have about Darius seem infinite, and my mind spins when I try to break it down. The amount of stuff I don't know about this man is mind-boggling, and I'm torn between being furious and a little sad.

Don't get me wrong, I know a healthy chunk of the blame for this is on me, and that's just the baseline without knowing any of the dirty details. I'm generally unapproachable and entirely irredeemable in how I intentionally keep myself distanced from people. The fact I lack the necessary social skills to be willing to learn anything important about other people is also on me. Instead, I allow myself to fall back on whatever assumptions I can come up with based on my own inner resentments because, frankly, people are shit.

Not that I think Dare is shit. I'm relatively certain he's a hell of a guy, given what little I know about him. And this fact just makes me push even harder to keep him at arm's length because deep down, I'm not a good person, and a hell of a guy really deserves a hell of a girl. I just don't believe I'm deserving of the attention and affection of this particular guy. Honestly, he would be better off slamming the door in my face and keeping it locked up tight because I would likely bring nothing but trouble down on his head anyway.

I know…this all sounds very dramatic, and I suppose some of it is. But in my weak defense, it can be difficult to unravel yourself from the diatribe that has been woven around you for your entire existence. Not even decades of therapy can fix that kind of mental trauma, and I know this firsthand. Once you've been smashed up into small enough pieces, it becomes almost impossible to find the entire you who once existed before all that bad shit tore you down.

But enough of that. Back to me being a bad bitch.

I think what bothers me the most about my current circumstances is how much time was wasted, seeing as it appears we're a pretty decent match. Somehow, he obviously understands me on a deeper level, even though, as far as I know, I've never given him any inclination as to what level I'm on other than being a bratty little shit. Or maybe that's what does it for him. If he sees that bratty side, and he's just like, *"Hey, now. I got you."*

I kind of wish he would've gone and said that rather than going to the extreme lengths he's gone to, but I accept I probably wouldn't have been receptive to the "normal" approach because I'm a raving asshole.

Between being lost in my inner thoughts and sending out messages to give the impression I'm checking in with someone, I miss most of the drive into the city. I'm not even sure exactly what neighborhood we're in when we pull into the drive of a rather nondescript two-story house. I can tell it's a nice house, so I'll assume it is in a nice neighborhood and likely cost a pretty good chunk of change. Mostly, I'm surprised Dare lives in the 'burbs. Because this is definitely the 'burbs. I pegged him more for a high-rise, penthouse kind of guy, with all of his drab suits and shiny loafers.

Chief Shields turns to me, his face serious as he says, "You should probably stay here while I check to see if he's home."

I snort, shaking my head emphatically as I reply, "Not a fucking chance. Since he thinks I'm currently tied up in a bunker, I highly doubt he's here hanging out for the night. And if he is, he's definitely a dead man, so I'm coming with you."

He gives me a skeptical look, raising his brows as he mutters, "You two are perfect for each other."

He gets out of the car, so I follow him, quickly catching up to him on the walkway toward the front door. He knocks and rings the bell, then waits a few minutes before checking his phone again. He makes a frustrated noise, obviously not too happy with the current situation, then turns to me and says, "We're going to step inside for a moment just to make sure he's not here, and then we can try somewhere else I think he may be, since he's not answering my texts."

He turns back to the door and some fancy keypad thing, and I don't even know what he does, but eventually, there's some beeping, and the door opens. I'd like to know what the fuck is with all this fancy tech shit since he couldn't even be bothered to lock the door of a bunker where he had somebody locked in against their will. Fucking unreal.

We step into a foyer, which is all white walls and dark beams, simply decorated and understated. The house seems quiet, and at first glance, there doesn't appear to be anyone here. Chief Shields glares at me, putting his hand up as an indication for me to stop where I am, and murmurs, "Fucking stay here, okay?"

I nod in agreement, but of course, I won't fucking stay there. As soon as he walks out of sight, I scurry off up the stairs because if he was on the ground floor, then it's likely we would be able to see or hear him from here. Apparently, police work is my thing, and Chief Shields needs to go back to the academy.

I peek into each room as I walk by, seeing as the doors are open, until I finally come to a closed door. I peer at it skeptically—every horror movie I've ever watched telling me not to open it—but we've established I'm not always the safety-first type. I'm definitely that bitch who gets slashed in the shower.

Not surprisingly, the door is not locked, so I push it open slowly and peek inside. I can't make out much in the darkness, so I reach over and feel for a light switch on the wall, then flip it on when I locate it. It's pretty obvious what I'm seeing as soon as the lights come on, but I think it takes my brain a full minute before I can actually fathom what the actual fuck is in here.

It's me.

Everywhere I look, all I see is my face.

There are literally thousands of pictures of me on the walls, on the ceiling, on the tabletop. There's an array of computer monitors that, thankfully, are black because I fear my face would be on those as well. I have to laugh a little at this completely insane sight before me, even if my laugh comes out more like a pained sob. I'm not sure if I should be angry or scared, but mostly, I'm just numb. Because seriously, what the actual fuck. How the fuck did I miss how clearly unhinged my boring little Clark is?

For a brief moment, I ponder if maybe Chief Shields is trying to put one over on me. Maybe this is his house, and he's going to come up here to find me at any moment to do the things that no one wants done to them. I quickly discard that theory because if Chief Shields wanted to do bad things to me, he could've easily done that without bringing me to this house.

I wander around the room slowly, my fingertips touching different images of myself, trying to pinpoint exactly how far back this clear obsession began. I step up to the desk and shuffle through the pictures there, and it appears there is a picture of me at every bar I've ever been to in at least the last few months.

There's a manila envelope sitting near the keyboard with what appears to be a pile of newspaper clippings in it. I open it up, squinting as I try to figure out what it's all about. The articles all seem to be about the same missing person. I don't recognize the name, so I leaf through the articles one by one until I come across an article that includes a picture.

It's jackoff.

Apparently, jackoff has been a missing person for some time. So again, what the actual fuck. Chills run down my spine, my guts cramp, and my breath catches in my throat as the clear implications of this information jump into my head. Also, slightly annoyed that jackoff had given me a false name, but this current issue seems to take precedence.

I feel the envelope fall from my hand and watch as all the clippings float to the floor and spread out before me like a fan. All I can do is blink down at them, stunned.

At that moment, through the buzzing in my head, I hear a commotion downstairs, several raised voices, then feet pounding up the stairs. I can't move—don't really see any point in moving—and the next thing I know, Dare appears in the doorway, obviously furious, his eyes wild as he locates me in the room.

"Antoinette," he says softly. "Are you okay?"

I don't say anything; I just stare at him. Has he looked around the room I'm standing in? Is he so fucking stupid he doesn't realize what I have seen? How incredibly fucked up it is?

He takes a few steps toward me, and I don't move until his hand reaches out for me. I flinch and take a step back. I raise both my hands in front of me and luckily, he takes my cue for what it is and stops moving toward me.

"*Do not* touch me," I say firmly, grateful there's no tremor in my voice. "You just stay the fuck away from me. Do you hear me?"

Dare nods at me and replies, "I hear you, Antoinette. Please, just let me explain."

My eyes widen at his words, my hands fisted at my sides as I practically screech at him, "Let you explain?" I stomp my foot and shout, "And what exactly is it you're going to explain here?"

I start walking around the room like a crazy person, pointing out things as I go and explaining as sarcastically as I can muster, "How about this picture of me, which appears to be taken in my own home while I'm sleeping?" I move on to the next one and go on, "How about this one that appears to be taken while I was on vacation—a vacation that wasn't even in this country?"

Finally, I stop in the middle of the room with my arms spread wide to showcase the newspaper clippings spread out before me. "Or how about this mess? Is this your fun little trophy to your murder scheme or what?"

He eyes me warily, starts to take a step toward me again, then stops when I immediately put my hands back up. He sighs, then replies, "I swear, I can explain everything if you just give me a chance."

I cackle. I don't giggle or laugh or chuckle; I outright cackle. I'm bent over at the waist, hands supported on my knees, outright cackling in what can only be described as a truly maniacal manner. It's all too much; I just can't deal.

He doesn't say anything else as I continue to laugh, and eventually, I run out of steam and manage to stand upright, wiping mirthless tears off my face.

Chief Shields is standing in the doorway, leaning nonchalantly against the doorjamb, eyeing both of us like we're ticking time bombs. I glare at him, then stomp my way across the room until I'm right in his personal space and seethe, "Well, *Chief* Shields, aren't you going to do anything about this?"

His eyes bulge almost comically, and he stands up straight, puts his hands on his hips, and asks, "And what exactly would you like me to do about it?"

"Oh, I don't know. Maybe you should do your job and arrest him," I retort.

He raises his brows at me and asks, "Arrest him for what exactly?"

"What do you mean for what?" I'm almost shouting again, my hands flying around to emphasize my words. "Isn't it obvious? Stalking? Murder? Being a fucking insane person? Pick something!"

Chief Shields tilts his head at me, obviously unsure how to proceed now that I've hit crazy town. And I'm definitely in crazy town right now. I feel completely unhinged and out of control, but I feel like I have to do something in an attempt to put things back to some sense of normalcy. As if there is anything I can do to backpedal this current situation.

"I'll make this easy on you," I say clearly and calmly. "Either you arrest him for any variation of the legitimate charges that are in this house, or I will make some calls and have someone else do it for you."

Chief Shields glances over my shoulder, most likely reading the forecast on Dare's face. Then I hear him behind me, his voice irate as he sputters, "Come on, Matt. You can't actually be considering doing this."

I spin around to face him, pointing a finger at him and spitting, "You shut your mouth. You have no right to be saying anything right now, and I don't advise it without your lawyer present."

Chief Shields sighs again, this time in obvious resignation, then walks over to Dare, speaking softly to him so I can't make out the words. Dare looks him in the eyes and nods, then says something else incoherent. Finally, Chief Shields turns to me and says, "I'll take him in and book him, but I need you to do me one favor in return."

I scoff, but the look on his face makes me relent, so I ask, "Fine, what is it?"

"I need you to allow my trusted colleague to escort you home."

I frown, sighing as I ask tiredly, "And who might this colleague be?"

A new voice pipes up behind me, "Well, that would be me."

I turn around, startled to see a dark-haired stranger now leaning against the same doorjamb Chief Shields had been previously leaning on. I shake my head in exasperation and ask, "And who are you?"

He steps forward, holding a hand out to me, "Well, now, I'm Tony

Andersen. Nice to finally meet you."

Finally? Again?

I eye his hand skeptically, and after a moment's pause, I reach out and grasp it firmly. He gives my hand a small squeeze, his twinkling gaze meeting mine almost reassuringly. I squint at him a bit, then let go of his hand, annoyed with myself that I don't automatically hate him. He seems the unlikeable type, especially given the information Matt shared with me about his ongoing bromance with Darius, but for some reason, I'm inclined to have a tentative trust in him, which annoys me even further because I shouldn't trust any of these assholes.

Everything is so incredibly fucked up. Two days ago, I lived in ignorant bliss, happy to continuously ruffle the feathers of my exceedingly dull coworker. And now, here I am, standing in the middle of this personal stalker drama. I sigh in defeat, then look over at Chief Shields and nod my head, stating, "Fine, this guy can escort me home. Now, lock that fucker up and never let him out."

Dare raises his brows at me and snorts, "Seriously, Antoinette? Never let me out?"

I glare at him and then retort, "Whatever gets you away from me the longest."

Tony and Chief Shields both chuckle, giving each other rather knowing looks as Tony and I head toward the door. Dare walks over toward us, and I scurry behind Tony so he can't get near me. It's not that I'm afraid of Dare or worried he'll hurt me, I just feel like if he touched me, I might either fall into him or explode at him, and neither scenario is ideal at this moment.

Dare leans into Tony, once again saying something that I can't quite make out, and Tony nods his head in agreement before motioning for me to exit the room ahead of him.

I can't say I fucking care about anything at this point. I'm exhausted, and my entire body hurts, and I just want to get out of there as quickly as possible.

So, I walk out of the house, not even flinching as the door slams shut behind me.

Chapter Nine

Dare

LET'S JUST SAY THINGS have not gone according to plan.

Hindsight being the little bitch that it is, I probably should've known things wouldn't have gone as smoothly as anticipated, given nothing that pertains to Antoinette has ever gone smoothly. She's the opposite of smooth. She's a rough-and-tumble, abrasive, intentionally aggravating firecracker. Right now, I want to murder her almost as much as I want to ravage her. Sometimes, it's a fine line.

Obviously, I knew I should've secured her better than I did, but frankly, my heart wasn't in it. I want her to bend to my will, but I also want her to do so comfortably. I couldn't have her sitting in that chair for hours with her hands and feet numb. Then I got concerned she wouldn't be able to get out of the building if there was an accidental fire or a flood, so I unlocked the doors so they would release from the inside.

So, it's official; that woman has made me go soft. Not just soft but also sloppy, amateurish, and outright inept. Tony will have a complete field day with this when he sees me next, and I should be glad for the reprieve of having him stay with Antoinette whilst Matt got to have the joy and privilege of fake arresting me.

Matt decided to cuff and stuff me, somewhat for effect, because he thought her witnessing the whole ruse might make her feel a little better, but also just because he thought it was funny as fuck. I could also see Tony attempting to cover his own smirk as he sat watching the show, but he couldn't give too much away in case Antoinette noticed. And Matt definitely secured those cuffs a little tighter than they needed to be, given the odds I was going to attempt to escape were nil. Even if I was, I would've waited to choke him out when we got to our destination.

Of course, now that he has me in the back of his car, he's refusing to pull over and uncuff me and allow me to sit up front with him. Because as he says, and I quote, "Bad kids get to ride in the backseat."

The fucking prick.

He's been mostly silent for the ride up, which is incredibly annoying because Matt is not a quiet person. He basically never stops running his trap, and even when he does, he's normally humming, singing, tapping, or just being annoying in general. Which means he's sulking over something.

Finally, growing tired of the quiet, I sputter, "For fuck's sake, man. Just spit it out already."

Matt glares at me in the rearview mirror, making a rather rude sound before saying, "I don't really think that there's anything to be said here, Darius."

Oooh, he brought out the *Darius*, which means he's big mad.

I still can't help but roll my eyes. Matt has always been the drama queen of our group, and man, can he hold a grudge. Unfortunately, we don't have time for grudges right now because we have some serious problems on the horizon, and they don't give a fuck about grudges.

So, I give him my most innocent look and say, "Sorry, Matt."

Apparently, that was the wrong thing to say because the next thing I know, the car is pulled over on the shoulder of the road, and I'm being yanked out of the back of the car and tossed about. I can't help but laugh, even though I'm sure there's nothing remotely funny about it. And, of course, my laughing only incenses him even further, which leads to a couple of extra kicks he otherwise would not have inflicted upon me.

"Fuck, okay. Matt—stop!" I shout, attempting to get my feet underneath me. "I think that's quite fucking enough! If you've got something to say, then by all means, say it; otherwise, we have bigger problems to deal with right now than your hurt little feelings. And frankly, if anyone should be pissed off right now, it should be me because you brought my girl to my house when you had explicit instructions never to do that!"

Matt reaches out in an attempt to give me another swat as he yells, "Your girl? Your fucking girl? Seems to me, you deluded fucking asshole, that all of this could've been avoided if you had just been truthful with me in the first place!"

Okay, so maybe he has a point. But in my defense, messing with Matt Shields has been one of my favorite sports for most of my life. Actually, Tony and I have even turned it into a betting game, a game that Matt is none too impressed with.

I nod my head in agreement. "You're right. In this particular case, I shouldn't have dicked you around about it, and if I had just told you the truth in the first place, none of this would've happened."

He gives me a shocked look, his hands coming up to fist on his hips as he retorts, "Seriously? You're just going to admit you're wrong that easily?"

I simply nod and say, "Yes. I was wrong, and I'm sorry."

Matt gives me a pained look and groans loudly as he mutters, "Fuck me. This must be bad if you're going to apologize without a fight. And I knew this was going to happen. I knew our little plan to keep you in check wouldn't last, and you'd go off half-cocked and do something completely unhinged and then I'd be the one stuck here holding the goddamn stick as if I was the asshole who fucked us again with his diabolical fucking urges to possess someone who doesn't even fucking remember anything!"

I stand there for a moment, my hands on my hips, watching Matt completely lose his shit on the side of the damn road. Now, I have no idea what the hell he's talking about, and he's so wrapped up in his ranting that it takes him a minute to realize I'm just staring at him in confusion. He pauses for a breath and then continues. "Of course, you have no fucking idea what I'm talking about. Why can't anything ever be easy with you? For fuck's sake, this is totally a Dare thing to do, I can't even look at you. You know what, I can't do this right now, so just spit it out and tell me what's going on, so I can decide what I'm going to do next."

"You gonna uncuff me?" I ask hopefully. Because even though he seems to accept my apology, that doesn't mean he won't take advantage of the situation and still attempt to pound the snot out of me at every turn.

He hesitates for a moment, obviously considering said pounding, then finally gives me a small nod and walks over behind me, removing the handcuffs.

As we walk over to the car, he rests his arm on my shoulder in silent reassurance. "Alright, lay it on me."

Toni

Here I am again, in a car, with a strange man.

At least this one is undoubtedly much more approachable than Chief Shields. On the flip side of that, I'm also relatively confident that taking anything he says seriously is a mistake. He seems like a real jokester, and sometimes this crazed look in his eye catches me off guard. I haven't decided what to do with that.

I shift my body in the seat, looking over at Tony as I say, "Can I ask you something?"

He glances at me and smirks. "Well, you can ask."

I can't help but laugh, shaking my head as I say, "But no guarantee you'll answer, eh?"

"No guarantees at all, I'm afraid." He shakes his head at me.

"Do you think Dare is unhinged?"

For some reason, this has him laughing out loud, which makes me a little suspicious that maybe he is also unhinged, but there's not much I can do about it now.

So, I throw my hands up in the air in defeat and mutter, "You're all fucking crazy."

"We're all crazy in our own special way, sugarplum." He glances at me, a teasing glint in his eyes.

I have nothing to say to that. I feel like I should be nervous in my current situation, and I'm not certain I can trust Tony. But for some reason, I feel comfortable with him. He's one of those unassuming guys with subtle handsome features that turn full-on electric once he focuses his gaze on you. The dark, skillfully styled tousled hair, the gold-green glint in his eyes, straight white teeth behind those full, smirking lips. I would even go so far as to call him panty-melting, if I was at all inclined.

It isn't until we're pulling up to my building that I realize this motherfucker has driven me home without asking for my address.

And once again, I'm questioning everything I think I've ever known about Darius.

I take my seatbelt off and then turn my body to face him, staring at him expectantly. He turns to me and raises his brows like he's waiting for me to say something.

"How did you know where I live?"

He grins and says slowly, "Dare told me?"

Now, maybe I would've believed this if he hadn't worded it as a goddamn question, but at this point, I also know that all these guys are completely full of shit. At least when it comes to me. I don't know why, and I don't know how, but somebody's going to have to give me some fucking answers.

Sensing my unease, Tony puts his hand on my arm, getting my attention. "Listen, Antoinette," he says quietly. "You're right to be suspicious and angry, perhaps even a little scared, but I promise everything will come to light, and everything will work out."

I peer at him quizzically, contemplating how to take such a strange declaration from someone I don't even know. Common sense would have me calling bullshit at this point, running from the car screaming, but this little tiny voice in my head keeps telling me to go with it. That it's not bullshit.

So, I simply nod and say, "If you say so."

I start to get out of the car when his voice gives me pause, so I turn back to look at him again as he says, "Do you have a parking spot available?"

I frown at him. "Yes, I have a parking spot. What does that have to do with anything?"

He gives me a very patient look and answers, "I need to park my car so I don't get towed."

I laugh, shaking my head as I reply, "You're not coming in."

All humor vanishes from his features. "Yes, I am."

"No, you absolutely are not. That is entirely unnecessary."

Tony just gives me a look and then starts the car. The locks click as he starts to look around, almost like he's going to pull back into traffic. "Where the fuck are we going?"

He shrugs. "You're not gonna let me come up, so you'll just have to come with me, then."

I growl, my head falling back against the headrest heavily as I groan, "Why are you being difficult? I just want to go home. I just want to be alone; I don't see what the problem is."

He doesn't say anything for a beat, and I can tell he's getting impatient with me, but he finally says, "Listen to me, Antoinette. I know you're frustrated I can't provide you with specific details on what's going on, but I need you to trust me on this. My orders are to stay with you, and I will stay with you until those orders are retracted, whether you allow it or not. So, this means you have two choices here: the easy way or the hard way. You choose."

I glower at him, the knowledge that this is the second time I've heard this line directed at me in a very short time span not being lost on me. "What do you mean, orders to stay with me? Orders from whom?"

He gives me a bland look but doesn't even bother replying because obviously, I know where the orders came from. It just never occurred to me that Dare was all about giving orders to people. He's a fucking accountant, for fuck's sake. Last I knew, the only person he gave orders to were the copier repairman and maybe Accounts Payable for some new pens.

This is all so fucking weird, and there doesn't appear to be anything I can do about it. I'm pretty sure giving him the slip either wouldn't work or would just put me in a hell of a lot of hot water. And what if it's true? There must be a reason he has these orders to stay with me.

I huff, glaring at him as I say, "Just tell me one thing. On a scale of one to ten, ten being life or death, what is the risk factor here that keeps you with me?"

He doesn't even glance over as he replies, "Solid ten."

My frown deepens, but I sit back in the seat and put my seatbelt back on. "Fine. Circle around the other side of the block. There's a parking garage entrance under the building. Number fifteen. My car is still at the office parking garage, so my spot here is empty right now."

Tony looks at me and smirks. He doesn't say anything. I groan, then give him a knowing look that basically says *my car isn't still there, is it?*

He just smiles some more.

That fucker.

Chapter Ten

Dare

I HAVE TO SAY, being in jail hasn't been terrible...so far. Of course, my "jail" consists of whichever room I feel like taking over within the police department. I did coordinate the "official" paperwork to have charges brought up on me and having me publicly denied bail was a pretty genius decision from Matt. Due to the events of the last forty-eight hours, it seemed best if I was on record as a guest of the local police department. That way, there is no question as to my whereabouts for the time being.

We've gone to great lengths to cover up the interconnected trail between me, Matt, and Tony. While most people know Tony is a colleague of mine, it would be almost impossible for anyone to locate the very beginning of our relationship. And the same goes for my relationship with Matt. There is a professional trail, and then there is a somewhat discreet, borderline-criminal trail of breadcrumbs that have been strategically placed wherever we want them to be found. There is a defined path for Darius the accountant, and another defined path for Dare, the less-than-upstanding citizen who may or may not exist.

Not that I consider myself a bad guy. I'm just more in that whole gray area of "I'll do what I have to do regardless of what society tells me is morally correct" kind of lane. Society has a very skewed compass on what is morally right and wrong. We like to think that the moral high ground is differentiated clearly in black and white; however, there will always be that gray overlap where good and bad kaleidoscope together for survival. It just happens that I tend to live there most days.

The good thing about using the police department as my headquarters is that it's very difficult for anyone to surprise me if they were to come look for me. Having to make an appointment to get a face-to-face with me makes it easier to be prepared when the name on the sign-in sheet doesn't match the face of the person who will be sitting before you. And since I'm not a moron, I have a good idea who will be coming to pay me a visit. Dickwad.

One thing the three of us have always done is work in codenames, and because of this, we never mention the real names of anyone directly. For example, "jackoff", "pissant", and "dickwad" are all codenames. It's not that I believe we've been bugged or that anyone is eavesdropping; it's just easier not to slip up if you always do it. You never know when there may be little ears tuned in to finding certain names being uttered at any given moment.

I'm not a crime lord or a crime boss, and I don't live in the criminal underbelly of the city. I'm more that guy in the shadows where you can fuck around and find out. When I was younger, I had established a fuck-off reputation out of necessity. I was always the smart guy, the nerdy guy, the kind of guy the bigger guys thought they could push around until one day, I made the decision that I wasn't going to allow them to do it anymore, and that's when things got ugly.

At first, all it did was cause more drama, more chaos, and more ridiculous violence that finally escalated to the point they realized they had two choices: leave me alone or die trying to destroy me. I wouldn't say the "bullies created me"; all I'm saying is the bullies were the catalyst that pushed the beast out of me, giving him flesh and bone and breath. And the beast ruled me for many years until, eventually, I had built up an impressive enough reputation and wealth that returning to a so-called civilized existence was possible.

It took me many years to learn to be Darius again. To be able to distance myself from the darkness that drove me to an almost mythical level of Dare, the Beast, within the underground organizations. A few people made half-assed attempts to eliminate me, and a few more attempted to force me back to my morally-questionable alter-ego; however, after a few tries, they mostly gave up and left me alone.

And I had just started to master the art of being Darius the accountant when suddenly Dare the Beast was ripped back out of my body by one very sassy woman named Antoinette.

A lot of people think I'm a monster, an entirely ridiculous assumption given a monster doesn't care about the black and white. A monster doesn't care about gray areas. A monster doesn't care about the well-being of society or family or a friend. If I was truly a monster, I wouldn't have followed Antoinette out into the alleyway, and the events from that moment forward would have had no bearing on my existence at all. But I did, and they did, and here we are, once again ready to see who all wants to fuck around and find out.

It was such an odd feeling for me to suddenly be responsible for someone else. I'd been responsible only for myself for so long that the idea of being worried about the health and happiness of another person was entirely foreign to me. Initially, it gave me pause, and it took me quite a bit of time to grasp the fact that this other person's life was important to me.

Okay, important isn't a strong enough word to describe my feelings for Antoinette's safety and welfare; possessed, obsessed, maniacal, and unhinged are some words that could be uttered with some level of accuracy throughout the last six months. The lengths my team and I have gone to keep Antoinette safe are extreme, and never once has anyone from my team made any comments on how completely out of character and potentially self-serving this mission has been.

Granted, I no longer employ very many people, and even of those few, Tony and Matt are the only two I trust without question. But having someone watched every minute of every day requires a certain amount of planning and strategizing that requires more than the three of us. Especially given the fact that Matt and I have to at least give the impression to outsiders that we're living our normal, everyday lives. This is far easier for me since I always have the guise of working from home, and for the most part, my job is a show of smoke and mirrors in making other people money. Namely me, and all of my aliases and shell companies and whatever else I decide to tinker in.

Matt has to make a bigger public show of it, though he does have far more spare time since he took over at a smaller police department than the one he used to work at in Manhattan. At first, he was angry he was having to uproot his life and redirect a career path he had devoted many years to, but after a while, he seemed to enjoy the change and the flexibility it allowed. Unfortunately, there likely will come a time when he'll have to choose between his life in law enforcement and his life as my morally grey counterpart, and that time seems to be drawing closer at an alarming rate.

Tony is more into freelance work, so he has the luxury of coming and going whenever he pleases, and I'm pretty sure he feels a special kind of kinship to Toni at this point. He'd never actually met her but had spent so much time in her company without her even knowing it that she started to grow on him like a little sister. He actually dubbed her "Sugarplum" as a codename.

At one point, he found himself checking in so often when he wasn't the person designated to be responsible for her that he asked me to punch him in the face repeatedly. I mean, I happily knocked him about just for sport, but I totally get what he means. I'm probably the worst of everyone as my entire existence revolves around her day in and day out into a level of obsessive compulsion that almost chokes me.

And every once in a while, it all feels completely pointless because nothing has come of the incident. There was no whispering, no movement, and no call to arms; it was all just eerily quiet. Which was especially alarming hence our decision to stay operational twenty-four-seven. And it's now, at this moment, as I'm standing in the corner of this room waiting for my visitor, that it's all going to come to a head. This is the pinnacle. This is the deciding factor. This one conversation will tell me if everything we've done over the last six months was for nothing or if we were correct in our need to be proactive.

With how resourceful the true bad guys are, I find it hard to believe that somebody out there hasn't managed to connect some dots between Chief Matt Shields and me. Which makes me wonder why anyone would even attempt to sign in with a false name, considering we all have eyes, and everyone and their mother would recognize that face. And since I know that all of these evil crime-lord people do everything for a purpose, I have to take a minute to try to contemplate what purpose that may be.

Some people use intimidation, but I highly doubt they believe intimidation tactics would work on me. I understand no one is infallible; however, when it's my time, it's my time, and I won't go out begging.

Dickwad appears smaller in person. And older. That doesn't detract from the deadness in his eyes as he stares at me. It takes all of my self-control not to smirk at the air of superiority surrounding him, and I know it's not even intentional after decades of being the head honcho of a lot of dangerous people.

Dickwad doesn't truly know me, though he may have heard of me. He may have seen me around here and there, maybe even found a calling card of mine a time or two. But he doesn't actually know me.

All I know is that when all of this comes to light, if the truth ever comes full circle, he'll have no choice but to drop a hammer on all of us for what we did. It doesn't matter if it was accidental, and it doesn't matter if it was deserved. In fact, the circumstances that led up to the end don't actually matter at all. He will have no choice.

He levels his gaze at me. He isn't smiling, but he also isn't posturing or acting aggressively. He looks tired. "Why did you have to let him go?"

I'll admit, I'm startled. Is this the first question he's going to ask me? I'm not even entirely certain who he is referring to, though it is a pretty short list of men I have ever let go. I'm almost certain he's referring to pissant. Someone who I did not intend to let go, but once he finished spilling all of his dirty secrets, I felt I had no choice but to use him to deliver my message. A little bait and switch, if you will.

I'm not normally thrown off. I'm very rarely surprised. However, right now, I'm at a loss for words because never in a million years would I have seen those words coming out of his mouth.

I cock my head, raising my eyebrows almost like a question. "I haven't the foggiest idea who you're referring to."

He stares at me, his arms coming up to cross over his chest as he snorts, "Like fuck you don't, Dare. You intentionally let that little asshole go so he could deliver me a message. If you'd just kept your fucking mouth shut, we wouldn't be having this conversation right now."

Okay, now I'm definitely flummoxed. In what fucking alternate universe would a head honcho, like dickwad, meet with me to tell me that I should've kept my mouth shut. It's a pretty well-known fact that when something is done to the family, restitution will be sought regardless of circumstances, and what dickwad seems to be saying to me right now is the opposite of that.

I glare at him, my hackles rising as I say, "And how would I know that? What you're insinuating right now goes against everything you all have ever said about loyalty, family, and the job."

He strolls over to the table and pulls out a chair, turning it around backward and sitting down with his arms crossed over the back. He levels a serious look at me, shaking his head. "All you did was show them your weakness. Now they have a weapon to use against you, just like they try to have a weapon against all of us."

This conversation keeps getting more and more insane, and I'm almost afraid to keep on with it for fear of what other insights might come to light. Having no other choice, I continue, "Who is it you're referring to? Because I was under the impression you were the person I had to worry about."

He looks me dead in the eye as he softly replies, "The Dead."

The hairs on the back of my neck prickle as a chill runs down my spine, but I remain outwardly unfazed, unblinking as dickwad stares at me knowingly.

Well, fuck.

Toni

I was right. Tony Andersen is kind of a fucker. But he's the kind of fucker that grows on you. You get so accustomed to having him around you almost don't even notice he's a fucker anymore—he's just Tony. It's all fucking weird, just like this fucked-up situation.

When Tony said he was going to stay with me, he was not at all exaggerating. Somehow, stuff just started magically appearing in my apartment until he had basically moved himself right in. It wasn't anything we discussed or anything I agreed to; it just happened.

I haven't heard a peep from Dare or that prick Chief Shields since I saw Dare carted off in cuffs. Tony did show me where Dare had been booked on kidnapping charges and that he was denied bail, so he's still in jail. Which makes me chuckle a little because Dare insinuated it would be impossible for me to get him thrown into jail, but there he sits.

I can't decide if I feel bad about it or not. Every now and then, I get a bit morose about him being in there, but then usually, I get right back to furious because he basically begged for it with all his kidnapping and stalker-like antics. Never mind the fact he's quite likely a murderer, but I try not to think about that part too much.

I've decided, though, I'd rather he not end up in jail for a long period of time because I kind of miss messing with him. My favorite pastime used to be giving the boring accountant down the hall a hard time. I'm entirely certain that winding up the bad-boy accountant down the hall would be even more fun, once he has adequately explained exactly what has happened and what will happen, of course.

But back to this fucker, Tony.

It's frightening how much information Tony can withhold while it feels like he's openly sharing information with you. It isn't until long after the conversation is over that you realize he didn't tell you anything.

Tony is also a master at getting you to do whatever he wants without you even realizing that you're not doing what you wanted to do. It's infuriating. Then he convinces you that it's in your best interest to do what he says, to such an extent that you truly feel like you can't argue with him about it. I don't understand it. It's like hypnosis. It's just fucked up.

The first thing Tony convinced me to do was to work from home for the week. He has literally been my shadow, which should've been extremely annoying if not for him being such a great roommate. He cleans up after himself, cooks, and even does the laundry. Like, who does that?

And even after being cooped up with this guy for three or four days, he still isn't super irritating. I mean, I often get on my own nerves after three or four days, so it doesn't make sense. That's why I live alone. I like things a certain way, and very few people have ever liked things the way I've liked them before.

Unfortunately, Tony is a closed book whenever I mention anything about Dare. His past, present, or future—nothing at all. I mean, I totally get it. It's obvious they've known each other for a long time, and "bro-code" aside, you don't talk about your friends behind their backs, even if said friend has kidnapped, restrained, locked up, and possibly murdered people.

I'll admit to being a little envious of that kind of loyalty. I've always been more of the lone wolf, mostly content to find my own way, but I suppose having a strong support system would be beneficial overall. On the other side of that, it sounds like a lot of work. So far, I haven't found a lot of people who were too keen on putting up with my shit unless it was going their way. People love a good-time girl, but surprise, surprise, they're not so keen on the shut-the-fuck-up girl.

It was actually getting quite late on Friday when I realized I had a work function that evening. And the only reason I remembered was because my dress was delivered. Luckily, it was delivered early enough that I wasn't surprised when the makeup and hair people showed up to take care of business. I'm not a hair and makeup kind of girl, that shit has to get hired out if I don't want to look like a complete clown.

Tony was a little taken aback when it all came around. I had to let him know that this time, he was not going to win because I had to go, and if he didn't like it, he could hire himself a tux and tagalong.

It was quite comical how insulted he was that I'd think he'd have to rent a tuxedo. Apparently, he has a closet full of fancy wear at his disposal. I guess I should've known better considering how incredibly debonair he is, but just to be a complete show-off, he had a brand-new tuxedo delivered to my door in record time.

And here we are, sitting in my bedroom, getting pretty for the fancy party. Tony is looking exceedingly dapper in his midnight-blue tux. At first, I thought it was black, but upon further inspection, it is the darkest blue I've ever seen. The material is so soft that I can't stop touching his arm.

"For fuck's sake, Nettie. Stop putting your greasy fingers on my sleeve." He yanks his arm away from my grasp and moves out of my reach.

"But it's so soft," I whine. "I want to wear it."

He gives me a disgusted look, shaking his head as he asks, "What the fuck is wrong with you?"

I laugh, and the woman painting on my fancy face tsks me to sit still. So, I face forward, keeping my face as still as I can as I whisper, "So many things, right?"

He smiles, "*So* many things."

Okay, so we've gotten to know each other pretty well in the time we've been living together. Or at least, well enough for him to have dubbed me with a new nickname and for us to have acquired an inside joke or two. I can't tell if Tony is mostly humoring me, but I find it hard to believe anyone would be able to put on this good of an act for this length of time if they weren't at least having a little genuine fun.

We're still joking around in the car on the way to the event, laughing as we get out of the car in front of the high-end midtown hotel where the event is being held. It's quite busy already, and there are fancy-pants people milling around everywhere.

I'm wearing a short strapless number, also in a midnight blue that's almost as dark as the suit Tony is wearing but for the shimmery lace overlay. It's a short A-line because I don't like to be boxed in. The corset-style top keeps everything where it's supposed to be while accentuating all of my important bits. I chose a flat sandal in silver that wraps up my calves just to make it a little classier. I may never wear heels again after all the drama because fuck me if I ever get lost in the woods wearing stilettos.

This work event I'm being forced to attend is some frilly gala being put on by the supposedly influential board members of the company Darius and I work for. Normally, I wouldn't attend, even if they tried to make it mandatory, but since this is a charity gala, I always attempt to at least make an appearance, even if I don't stay all night.

It was fun getting ready with Tony, and having someone drive us to the venue was a luxury I don't typically spring for, never mind the professional hair and makeup and extravagant, fancy dress. The fact that I'm having a good time should probably be a huge red flag for me, but I'm not known for listening to red flags anyway, so here we are.

Tony says we need to make a stop regarding security before heading into the main event and indicates I should follow him down a separate hallway away from the ballroom. We walk down the hallway until we reach a lone door. He reaches over and opens it, motioning for me to go in ahead of him into what appears to be a utility closet.

But then, instead of following behind me, he pushes me forward, hustling me up against the counter, facedown. I start to scream, but then I feel the familiar smoothness of a ball gag being shoved between my teeth, and he mutters near my ear, "Nothing personal, Nettie. You know I don't make the rules."

He makes quick work of securing my arms behind my back, then slips a blindfold over my eyes. I feel something pressing against my ears, then the soft whoosh of white noise floods my eardrums as I'm thrown headfirst into the void of pitch-black silence.

And, once again, *what the actual fuck?*

Chapter Eleven

Dare

Just as before, I had every intention of waiting.

I was going to give her some space to come to terms with the events of the past week, and I'd planned on giving her adequate time to work through what she thinks she might have found in my house.

Yet, here I am. Giving her neither space nor time like the raging asshole I am.

And I can't even bring myself to feel one iota of guilt or regret for it.

Tony did try to talk me out of it briefly, and I did listen to his weak argument and even considered what he was trying to tell me. But at the end of it, I decided I wanted to do what I wanted to do and to fucking hell with everyone else. I was tired of putting off the inevitable, and I'll be damned if I would let another day go by without being near her.

So, Tony agreed to lead her into my trap and was considerate enough to truss her up for me quite nicely. The white-noise head-phones are a nice touch, and I'm sure she's seething behind the blindfold and the gag, completely unable to do anything at all to vent her fury.

I can't help but chuckle to myself as I walk closer to her. She tilts her head a bit, almost as if she can sense me near her, and she makes a garbled growl from behind the gag. She pulls on the restraints around her wrists and ankles, and for a moment, I wonder if she'll be able to slip out of them. But they hold, and she relaxes against the wall.

Tony did an excellent job of putting her on display for me. I assumed he would just tie her up and secure her to a chair, but he went the full-on professional route and left her spread eagle against the far wall. The sparkly strapless dress adds to the delectable package. It's a short dark blue number, and even though it is on the cropped side, it still has a slit up one leg, almost like the skirt was supposed to wrap around, but they ran out of fabric. When she shifts around, I can make out the top of her thigh-high stockings, and I lick my lips in appreciation.

I stop directly in front of her, relishing the vision she makes with her shiny red lips stretched around the ball gag, her chest heaving from exertion. There's a slight sheen on her skin, and I have to force myself not to reach out and stroke her collarbone.

I finally move closer, grasping the headphones and gently removing them from her ears. I toss the headphones onto the counter, then step as close to her as I can without actually pressing my body against her. My breath fanning her ear as I say, "I know it doesn't feel like it right now, but I want to reassure you that you're still in charge here."

She tenses as I speak. Her head cranes closer to me, so I press my face into her neck, inhaling her scent deep into my lungs. Shockingly, she doesn't attempt to shake me off, so I press closer until my body is touching her from hip to chest, and I bring one hand up to gently grip her neck. I run my tongue up her neck to her ear, gently biting down on her earlobe. She shakingly inhales through her nose.

Well, this is encouraging.

But I know better than to get cocky with her. This is a positive turn of events, but it would be just like Antoinette to play the lamb to get me to drop my guard, only to shift into a full demon at the first opportunity. For all I know, she already has those restraints figured out, and she is waiting for the first opportunity to choke me out with them.

I step back from her, reaching into my suit jacket pocket and pulling out a ball. I press the ball into her hand and say, "Hold on tightly to this ball, Antoinette." I wait for her hand to tighten around it before continuing, "I have taken your sight and your voice from you, but you still have all the power here. If at any moment you want this to stop, all you have to do is drop the ball. Do you understand?"

She doesn't move or twitch or even breathe, so I raise my hand up and stroke a finger gently down her face. "I need you to acknowledge what I have said, Antoinette. Simply nod your head or drop the ball. Everything will be well, regardless of what you choose. Do you understand?"

She waits for a beat and then nods her head. I exhale heavily, relieved she didn't drop that ball like it was red hot in her hand because part of me recognized the outcome could go either way. She doesn't owe me anything and given the number of shocks I have given her recently, another heel kick to the balls seems imminent.

I bring both hands up to her neck, stroking my fingertips down across her clavicle to ghost over the soft swell of her breasts where she has them pushed up with the corset top of her dress. I skim my hands down her torso, feeling the shape of her beneath her fancy dress before sliding one hand up her leg to stroke along the top of her stocking, and I feel her thigh twitch against my hand.

She's breathing heavily through her nose, a small whimper letting loose from behind the gag, and I lean forward, brushing my nose along her cheek as I press my lips against the corner of her mouth. She turns her face toward me, and I flick my tongue out, licking at her lips stretched around the gag. I want to kiss her. I want to yank that gag off and plunder her mouth, lick and bite at her lips and suck her tongue into my mouth to feast on.

But I don't. I don't dare give her an easy out by returning her voice to her too quickly. She wouldn't last two minutes before her mouth dragged us out of this moment and right into another argument, once again thwarting my plan to worship her. So, I won't kiss her sexy mouth just yet. I'll save that for last, after I'm finished with her.

She tries to lean closer to me, but the restraints restrict her movements, keeping her shoulders pressed firmly against the beam Tony placed behind her. She makes a frustrated groan, her arms and legs yanking viciously to no avail, and her noise of frustration increases. I can't help but chuckle. My breath on her neck earns a small shiver from her, so I open my mouth and bite down a touch harder than might be pleasurable, and she shudders in response.

I attack her throat with my mouth, using my lips and tongue and teeth to lick, suck, and bite every inch of her neck from one side to the other. She whimpers, a low sob catching on the gag, and she trembles against me, an invitation for me to double my efforts, but this time with more finesse.

I blow softly on the damp skin where her neck and shoulder meet, then scrape my teeth lightly as I lick a new trail up to her ear and back down again, feasting where I can feel her pulse pounding beneath.

She's practically boneless by the time I move on, my lips and tongue hot and wet on the skin of her breasts as I reach behind her and release the ties of her corset top. I yank the fabric down, baring her to me, and waste no time diving in, using my hands to push her breasts up so I can easily lick and nip one hard nipple and then the other.

She moans, her upper body pushing closer as I scrape my teeth against her tight peak. My cock is painfully hard, pressing against the zipper of my slacks, and I reach down to adjust myself, squeezing my rigid flesh that's aching for relief.

I rub my face between her breasts, one hand moving behind her, squeezing her ass while my other hand strokes a line from the top of her leg to the back of her knee, pulling her leg up to hook around my hip, stretching the fabric of her dress until it tears.

I can't help but situate my hips against her hot pussy. I press firmly against her, hearing a muffled moan and feeling the heat in my blood rise even further. I'm not sure how much more I can take of this.

She still has the ball held firmly in her grasp; her knuckles white with how fiercely she's holding it. What little movement the restraints allow has her writhing and twitching in an attempt to get closer to me. I bring the bottom of her dress up further, wrenching the two sides until they come apart in my hands, and then I chuckle darkly at the fact she's not wearing any undergarments other than her thigh-high stockings.

I shake my head, leaning my upper body toward her so I can whisper in her ear, "You naughty little minx," and she gives me what sounds like a garbled laugh, which is cut off by another moan.

My hand grips her bare ass, my fingers dipping between her ass cheeks to touch the very edge of her pussy lips. I feel how wet she is, how hot, and her hips undulate against my hand in invitation. It's all I can do to stop myself from getting my cock out of my pants and impaling her in one go.

My beast rumbles in my chest, roaring to be unleashed onto her, to fuck her into oblivion until she can think of no one but me for the rest of her days. I stop my movements, squeezing my eyes shut and taking several deep breaths as I remind myself of the lines I can't cross tonight. There's a dark path of secrets still standing in the way of any kind of real future, and until those lines have been cleared away, I must keep to the clear boundaries I've put in place for myself.

This is another reason I have taken her voice because I know she would say and do anything within her means to break my control and make me take from her so that she wouldn't have to give it freely. I can't have that. I refuse to give her the ammunition she needs to shove me aside later or give her the words to throw back at me to force me to turn my back and walk away. I won't do that.

She whimpers and squirms against me, likely wondering what made me stop touching her. I wrap myself around her, my face once again pressed into her neck as I shush her. "Settle now, baby girl. Just give me a second." She's panting heavily through her nose still, and I can feel the tension radiating through her body, but she stops moving. Her body sags against me, allowing me to take her weight as I press into her fully, my pelvis pressed tightly against hers.

Antoinette takes a shuddering breath in, relaxing into me completely as she turns her head toward me, where I'm still breathing into her neck, and I feel her exhalations against my cheek. I slowly release my grip on her, and she pulls away a bit, attempting to stand on her own, and my hands come up, tugging the blindfold over her head.

Her eyes remain closed for a moment, and slowly, her lids flutter and then open, and I'm met with her fiery blue gaze darkened with arousal. I don't say anything. I don't feel a need to. Instead, I simply lean my forehead against hers, our eyes locked in silent communication as we simply breathe each other in.

Toni

I can't say I'm entirely unhappy to be in my current position.

I will admit, when Tony first shoved me in here and trussed me up like a prized hog, I was a little pissed off. Even a bit hurt, though I always knew deep down where his loyalties would fall if push ever came to shove, so I haven't a clue as to why I was completely shocked he so easily, quickly, and thoroughly threw me under the Darius bus.

I shouldn't have been at all surprised, given the fact that he's been very clear with me. Even though he likes me well enough, if it came down to me vs. Dare, he would never choose me. I mean, maybe he never said that specifically, but it was most definitely implied with his complete refusal to speak of Dare to me at all. So, I guess I may also be a bit envious of the situation, and I'd actually be upset for Dare if Tony was ever to abandon ship to my side.

I wouldn't trust that fucking traitor anyway.

So now, I'm basically spread eagle against the wall. That stupid fucker Tony even managed to place a wooden post behind me just so, meaning my arms are strategically stretched out and behind me. I can't even attempt to bring my shoulders up to remove the headphones or attempt to remove my blindfold. I'm getting the impression that he has definitely done this before, and I have questions.

It was not without some sense of relief that I felt Dare's presence when he drew close to me. If he wanted to keep it more of a secret, he should've taken my sense of smell along with my other senses. Taking my voice from me is more a relief than an upset. It gives me some freedom to willfully experiment with what I'm willing to accept from him. If I had my voice, I would feel required to verbally spar with him, to challenge him and force him to break free from the chains of his normal restraint and go full feral beast on me.

I wasn't even sure how I was going to react to having him near me until he pressed his face into my neck and inhaled, long and deep, drawing a shiver from my body.

Honestly, even though I've been attracted to him over the years, this was the first time I truly could accept how deep my attraction ran. All the guy had to do was smell me, and I was panting after him like a dog in heat. It's almost embarrassing, but I get to hide behind a blindfold and a ball gag.

When he first removed the headphones from my ears, the sudden hush disoriented me to where I felt like I was going to panic. It was his whispered voice in my ear that centered me back down to reality and allowed me to get my bearings. Even in a situation where he literally had me tied up and at his mercy, he still gave me reassurance that the situation was not out of my control.

At first, I was startled and unsure how to even take it. But then, when he provided me with a tool to use as a red light, I allowed myself to relax more into the scene. I'm not the type of woman who allows herself much leeway in taking a chance in a potentially emotionally lethal situation, but in this case, with neither sight nor voice, I gave myself a free pass to explore.

Of course, I gave myself this permission with no idea how far I would allow it to go or how far he would push it. As much as I've always wanted to relinquish control to another person, I've never had an opportunity where it felt safe for me. And as much as Dare has thrown me for a fucking loop in the last week, for some odd reason, I do hold a certain amount of trust in him. I have no idea why or how, and I should probably question it a little more deeply than I have, but for now, I'm going to let it go.

Consequences be damned.

Now, I'm barely managing to stay on my feet after he licked, sucked, and bit me, then squeezed, pinched, and fondled all over my body. My biggest concern is being torn between my need to be eaten alive by him and my fear of him eating me alive. Since, at the end of the day, which is more detrimental to our overall well-being? Need or fear?

I could feel him starting to lose control. He was holding it together famously until he realized I "forgot" to wear undergarments. The corset top doesn't require a bra, and underwear interferes with the shape of the skirt, so I left it at thigh-high stockings and called it good.

Then, when he dipped the tips of his fingers down around my ass cheek to brush against the very edge of my pussy, his entire body seized up, and I was happy that the gag in my mouth prevented me from outright begging.

Not that I'm above begging in the right situation, but it feels too early for me to be begging Dare to fuck me senseless, and I do have my reputation as a sassy, bad bitch to protect.

Dare remains motionless for a few moments, then wraps his arms tightly around me, once again pressing his face into my neck and inhaling deeply. I can feel a slight tremor in his body, and when he quietly asks me to settle, I do so. Though, I'm not entirely sure why, considering I normally go to great lengths to wind him up.

Instead, I allow myself to lean into him fully, turning my face toward him, breathing him in as he runs his nose along my neck. I feel his arms loosen, so I do my best to stand upright on my own two feet. Then he releases me, and I feel his hands pulling off the blindfold. When I feel the fabric release and the rush of cool air over my skin, I don't immediately open my eyes. Part of me wishes he would put it back, that we could just leave me silent in the darkness indefinitely, but I know that can't happen.

Slowly, I open my eyes, immediately drawn to his dark golden gaze that's seemingly staring right into the very heart of me. He doesn't say anything, just leans his forehead against mine and continues to stare into my eyes searchingly.

I'm so lost in his gaze that I miss the ruckus at the door behind him until suddenly, his eyes glint with anger, and he turns to glare over his shoulder and shout, "Get the fuck out!"

I glance over his shoulder, a sheepish-looking Chief Shields standing with his back mostly to us, his hands up in surrender as he says, "No can do, Darius. We're out of time; we need to go now."

Dare growls in his throat, his eyes swinging back to me as he says, "Sorry to cut it short, baby girl, but you heard the man."

He's already reaching for the restraints, carefully releasing my wrists, and placing my hands on his shoulders as he kneels down and releases my ankles. He stands up, pulling his suit jacket off and helping me put it on to cover my ruined dress. He helps me to move my limbs as I adjust to standing normally again.

The entire time, his eyes are locked with mine, and I can see the hunger and regret in his gaze as he asks, "Are you okay? Can you walk on your own?"

I nod my head. I'm shaky and thankful for my footwear choice, but certainly capable of walking on my own, even if I would prefer that he toss me over his shoulder and march me somewhere quiet, with fewer interruptions to get in our way.

He levels his gaze at me again, squinting as he says, "Are you going to give Tony a hard time for helping me set this up?"

I frown, then shrug. I'm not going to make any promises one way or another on that fucker Tony right now.

Dare curses under his breath, rubbing his hand over his face as he turns to Chief Shields. "You better go with her in case she decides to fuck around with Tony."

He turns back to me, pulling me in close and pressing his lips against my cheek right below the corner of my eye, then nuzzles my ear, whispering, "I don't want this to end here tonight, but I have some complications that require my immediate attention." He pauses, biting my earlobe before continuing, "Behave, and you'll be greatly rewarded."

Then he turns on his heel and disappears out the door without a backward glance.

I'm definitely getting a bit sick of him playing the cool, calm disappearing act, but there isn't much I can do about it right now, anyway. I roll my eyes, huffing to myself behind this stupid gag that he intentionally did not remove before he left.

I attempt to raise my hands to remove it, but my numb fingers won't cooperate, so I look at Chief Shields expectantly, pointing to the ball gag and miming a question. He chuckles, walks over and helps to unbuckle it. My jaw is tight, and it's almost painful when I first force my jaw closed, and I give it a few good chomps before it starts to loosen up.

Chief Shields is watching me suspiciously. As much as I want to give him a hard time, I realize I have no idea at all what's going on. Intentionally sabotaging his orders to secure me—whatever the fuck that even means—would be incredibly stupid. I'm a general pain in the ass, but I do have a healthy sense of self-preservation when the need arises. Well, sometimes...

I motion toward the door. "By all means, Chief Shields, lead the way."

He hesitates for a moment, his suspicious gaze never leaving mine. After a few beats, he walks over to the door, opening it and peering out into the hallway before motioning for me to follow him.

I sigh, once again rolling my eyes at him and my current situation before I quietly follow him, leaving our little playroom behind.

Chapter Twelve

TONI

I'M A CAGED ANIMAL.

When Dare gave the order to "secure me", I had no idea he meant the equivalent of being locked in an ivory tower with no access to anyone or anything for an indefinite period of time, without any type of clear explanation as to why this is necessary. I'm literally climbing the walls in frustration.

Of course, Tony and Matt are of little use because they refuse to tell me anything without explicit permission from Dare. And since, as far as I can tell, there has been no communication at all from him, said permission is denied. I haven't even had the satisfaction of pushing either of my jailers over the edge as they are basically uncrackable.

Not that I can utilize my full arsenal of tactics in my mission to defeat them since I seem to have some hard stops in the types of methods I consider appropriate. And I blame Dare for this, even if I can't explain it or understand it myself.

I'm rather disturbed that after our little playroom closet experience,

I've not heard from him at all. I know, I know—if he's too busy to report to his comrades, then he likely doesn't really have time to assuage my fragile, needy feelings. He probably doesn't even realize I have fragile, needy feelings, but knowing this doesn't make it any less annoying. I'm also on the brink of being sex mad, with no easy outlet for my sexual frustration.

So basically, I'm a horny, caged animal.

Don't get me wrong, I have read enough "why choose" romances to have dabbled with the idea of possibly seducing the two men that are with me twenty-four-seven. And I believe most people can get behind that whole "forced proximity made me do it" mentality. I've also considered hitting on them for the sheer purpose of making them uncomfortable, in the hope they will reach out to Dare to let him know that I need to be dealt with. I've not shelved this idea entirely because, at some point, I'll have to get the big-girl guns out and start calling everyone's bluff.

I'm almost certain I could make them snap without having to touch them. If I just start taking my clothes off randomly, what are they going to do? Blatant innuendo is my forte, and I'm not afraid to use it.

And then there's my arsenal of spicy audiobooks. Actually, that may be first on my list. "Whoops, was that not connected to my headphones? Oh, my! I'm so sorry that you had to hear Sebastian York speak of such wild indiscretions. Would you like to hear more?"

I'm pretty sure they would lose their minds rather quickly. That could also earn me a smashed device or two. So, maybe not.

It's also difficult coming up with a game plan when you're not certain how far the people in question would go in retaliation. I'm relatively certain Tony would have no problem trussing me up and leaving me in a closet for a few days. I actually think he would enjoy that. And Dare may not care about it as long as I was "secure" so it all seems pointless.

Having to make so many plans based on a huge steaming pile of speculation is a problem for me.

I'm in the middle of my revenge fantasies when Tony comes in, motioning for me to get a move on. I roll my eyes at him, muttering nonsense to myself as I slowly start walking toward the door, where Matt is standing, holding the pre-packed bag that they forced me to put together in case we needed to make a move swiftly.

I consider putting up a fuss, having a bit of a tantrum, and demanding answers. I stand in the doorway and look between them waiting for me in the hallway. They both put on a decent game face; however, I can see the subtle signs of stress on their features, the tension in their shoulders, and the worry in their eyes.

So, I sigh, taking my bag from Matt and moving between them as they once again lead me into the unknown.

Dare

Thwarting the potential evil deeds of a criminal organization is not going well.

My years of strategic evidence-planting, witness-tampering, and every other variation of carrot-waving appear to have been in vain, all because the information I received six months ago ended up being bullshit.

Turns out, the person I thought jackoff to be is not the person he actually was. If his true identity had led to where it was supposed to, all of this would be moot, and we would be in the clear. Unfortunately, that was not meant to be, and I'm outright perturbed that he wasn't linked to dickwad as I initially thought.

It was my understanding that he was an heir to the main criminal organization in the city; however, I'm finding out now that he may have been an heir to what may be the largest underground criminal organization in Russia. One of those organizations most people think is just a myth. And it seems this Russian entity has hired another so-called mythical organization to track down whomever took out jackoff.

Now, I know for a fact, "The Dead" is not a myth whatsoever. They have an extensive, deeply entrenched network of "death for hire" and are not known for asking questions or sorting out facts before they come for you. I've done everything in my power to try to throw them off the trail, and as of yet, all of this effort seems to have failed.

But if the real threat is coming from this Russian network—well, that's a whole new ballgame.

I've also queried if they would potentially consider a trade, but it doesn't seem like they're too inclined to consider this option at this point in the game.

Don't get me wrong, I'm not afraid to die. There's a very small number of people whom I would miss if they died, too. My main concern is what they would do to those few people before killing them. Especially under circumstances where they feel they have to make an example of a situation. The last thing anyone in these organizations wants is to give off even the tiniest showing of weakness. All it takes is one crack in the foundation for a rival organization to infiltrate and take it down from the inside.

And I should know, considering that's one of my specialties.

Now, here I am, sitting in a dive bar, waiting for god only knows who to show up to inform me where we stand in this whole shitshow. I honestly have no idea if my initial plan is at all salvageable, but the fact I was summoned to this meeting isn't a bad sign, assuming the contact who turns up is who I think it will be. This means they likely came across some of the strategic crimes I had committed and are following up on what the fuck it is I think I'm doing other than doing a shit job of getting their attention.

I do have my suspicions as to the intentions behind this meeting. The little I know about The Dead organization is that they rarely have any kind of conversation about their plans. They gather information on their own, decide on their method of execution, and it gets done. No checking or following up on it; they just drop the hammer—done.

For all I know, I'm sitting here watching the clock wind down on my entire existence. I showed up alone and unarmed in an attempt to make a show of good faith. This was either an excellent tactic or a deadly mistake. I'm relatively certain, though, if I vanish on this night, Matt and Tony will light fire to the underground in retribution. And they'd just say that's what you get for fucking around and finding out.

I also hate mid-morning meetings. The so-called acceptable alcoholic beverage choices for the morning are terrible. It's not that I'm opposed to drinking a bourbon at 10 a.m. in public, but I know I need to keep my wits about me.

Not that my wits will save me if this is a trap because if it is, I'm as good as dead, anyway. All I can do is hope they're keen on using the opportunity to drag some information out of me first, but that isn't typically their style. If they're coming to kill me, it's because I don't have any info they need, and they won't waste time on questions or give me the opportunity to escape. It's unlikely I'd even see them before I dropped dead. Another reason why I will consume no food or drink while in this establishment. I can't even trust sealed bottles.

And now, I sound crazy. I don't think I'm meant to lead a life of paranoia, so I'm hoping I'm just being overly dramatic.

I seat myself against the far wall, close to an exit. I don't want to take the chance of someone coming up behind me, but I also don't want to corner myself.

I'm genuinely surprised when a blonde woman enters the bar, walking directly to my table, where she stops and stares at me blankly.

I raise an eyebrow questioningly and ask, "May I help you?"

The smile she gives me is almost blinding. Her blank expression blooms into one of excitement, and I'm sure the look of bafflement on my face is fairly obvious.

She pulls the chair out, yanking it back abruptly, then flopping down onto it as she says, "Well, Darius Hughes, I have come all this way, so I certainly hope so."

I frown at her, leaning forward and squinting as I shake my head and ask, "And you are..."

To say this is not the person I was expecting is a gross understatement. I don't know a lot about The Dead's underground network, but I don't recall any chatter about a petite blonde woman being a contact. Though, if I think about it, it is a brilliant idea because no one in their right fucking mind is going to take a look at this woman and think "ghost-like assassin." Not that she necessarily kills people for a living or anything. I suppose she could just be The Dead's secretary, odd as that sounds, though also a little genius in theory.

I recline in my chair, sighing deeply as I look her over. She doesn't say anything, just smiles even wider as she says, "I'm so excited to finally meet you. I honestly wasn't sure if you would even show up for fear you could be walking into a trap."

This time, I raise both brows at her and respond, "I'm still not convinced this isn't a trap."

She throws her head back and laughs a full belly laugh, and I'm starting to wonder if this is a prank. I can't decide if this woman is certifiably insane or just playing the character so well that it's impossible to differentiate between fiction and reality.

As someone who's not typically thrown off in any situation, I'm beyond flummoxed. I guess that's what happens when you attempt to deal with a mythical entity. Without any concrete information to go on about The Dead, it will all be news to me, and it's an incredibly uncomfortable feeling floating out here in an ocean of possible misinformation.

Who's to say if this crazy woman is even a part of The Dead's organization. For all I know, she's just a decoy to throw me off in the hope I'll give something away. I also have to consider that they likely know the whole truth already, and this entire meeting it's just a ruse in order to get to their actual target.

I pull my phone out of my pocket, glancing at the blonde woman apologetically. "Excuse me one moment. I have a scheduled check-in I can't miss."

I quickly type out a message to Tony and Matt, letting them know it's time to make a move, and they acknowledge immediately, pinging me the code stating where they won't be going. When we first started using the code system, we all laughed, thinking it was overkill, but as the years have gone by, it has saved our asses more times than we can count, so we kept up with it.

I turn my attention back to the woman across from me, leaning back in my chair in what I can only hope is a relaxed position considering I'm feeling anything other than relaxed at this point.

I incline my head towards her and state, "Well, you obviously have me at a disadvantage here, Miss..." I leave the question hanging, hoping she'll give me the information rather than making me ask outright who the fuck she is.

She smiles at me again, reaching her small hand out to me in greeting as she replies, "Lilith, but you can call me Lils. It's a pleasure to finally make your acquaintance, Mister Dare."

I have to laugh. Regardless of her true intentions here, she's a character, and I do enjoy a character.

I take her hand, giving it a solid shake, "Likewise, Lils. Even if
I'm not exactly accustomed to being confused, I guess that's certainly
better than being bored."

Her eyes widen in excitement, and she nods. "Oh, yes. Boredom is
certainly like a long death."

"So, what is it you've come to tell me? I can't believe you've come all
this way just to shake my hand and give me compliments." I put my
hands up in surrender. I'm enjoying her enthusiasm, twisted as it may
be.

And just like that, all humor vanishes from her face.

It's as if an invisible switch has been flipped, and all inklings of her
sparkling eyes and magnetic smile melt from her features in an instant.

A slight shiver runs down my spine, the hair on the back of my neck
prickling, and I'm even more intrigued than I was before. I lean closer
to her, examining her features, as I whisper, "How intriguing. Are you
all right, Lilith?"

Her features don't change at all, her once animated face now that
of stone as she gives me a curt nod and says in a cool tone, "Quite all
right, Dare. Business is business, correct?"

I straighten in my chair, mirroring her serious expression as I nod.
"You're correct. Business will always be business."

She is sitting pin-straight in her chair, her hands folding in her lap
and her gaze boring into mine as she states, "My name is Lilith Ferro,
and I come with a message from The Dead."

I keep my features impassive as I tilt my head in acknowledgment
of her words. Any kind of message from The Dead is typically some
form of a death sentence, and there really isn't anything I can say or

do to unring that bell, as they say. At this point, all I can hope is that I'm able to steer the sentence in an acceptable direction, but this also means my option of leading them astray with any cover story is off the table.

Because they know.

I expected this, but it doesn't make it any easier to accept, given the repercussions that I'm certain will be coming down the pipeline. So, I don't waste any time.

"Let's hear it."

She tilts her head at me as she asks, "Would you like the long game or the cliff notes?"

I shrug, giving my head a barely there shake as I say, "Cliff notes will suffice unless you think there's a chance in hell I can change the outcome here."

"Cliff notes it is."

I give her a small nod. "Carry on, then."

Cliff notes: I'm fucked.

Chapter Thirteen

TONI

I WAKE IN STAGES, my eyes blinking into the darkness as I try to pinpoint what woke me.

I've been in this new location for a few days now and am still getting accustomed to the new space. I figure just as soon as I get comfortable, they'll just move me again anyway, so I'm trying not to settle in too much, too soon.

They confiscated all of the electronic devices, giving me a burner phone, which only had three contacts programmed into it, and a new Kindle that does not have cellular access. And then I was informed I was on extended leave from my job for a family emergency, which totally pissed me off, but it's not like I can do anything to change it.

I stopped asking questions as soon as we left the last apartment and other than the daily niceties, I haven't gone out of my way to bug Tony or Matt. It's actually a bit amusing to see how suspiciously they watch me, but frankly, I'm just sick and tired of the whole thing.

As for Dare, well, he has mostly been out in the world, attempting to right a wrong or whatever the fuck they want to call it. I still have no idea what I have to do with any of this other than maybe someone wants to use me to hurt him. But even that seems a stretch, considering we haven't so much as gone on a date.

The room is quiet, still under the cover of darkness, but I can feel a presence near the side of the bed.

I can't see him, but I know he's there, so I speak out into the darkness, "Come here."

He moves, and my eyes shift to the chair in the corner of the room where he must have been sitting, watching me sleep.

I sit up, resting on an elbow and pulling the blankets aside in invitation. "Are you going to just sit there and be a creeper all night, or are you going to join me?"

He chuckles, getting closer before I actually see him, and then I'm startled as the bedside light clicks on, and he's standing next to the bed, not even a foot from me.

I roll my eyes at his magician skills, then pat the mattress beside me as I shift over to make room for his large frame.

He slides in beside me, his eyes taking in the silk shorts and cami set I sleep in. I blush, forcing myself not to cross my arms over my chest or to try to hide my body from him. I don't believe he would let me anyway.

We're lying on our sides, facing each other, not touching. It's shocking how comfortable the silence is, especially given how crazy the last few weeks have been and the fact we haven't had time to clear the air regarding his moonlighting as a stalker and potential unaliver.

He raises a hand, brushing his fingertips lightly down my cheek, over my jaw, and down along my collarbone. I sigh in pleasure, my body instinctively shifting closer to him until he's wrapped around me like my very own man cocoon.

He strokes his hands everywhere he can reach, my back, my side, my hip. He reaches a hand down, squeezing my ass, and then with his other hand, he palms my breast, and it's like an inferno has erupted inside me. I'm shocked at how consumed with need I am for a man I used to intentionally terrorize.

"Do you want to fuck me?" The question falls out of my mouth before I even realize I was thinking it, and I stare at him in horror, wishing I could take it back.

He raises a brow at me, giving me a baffled look as he replies, "I'm certain you know the answer to that question, Antoinette."

I give him a pointed look. "That's not an answer."

He sighs, "Yes, Antoinette. I want to fuck you within an inch of your life, and then I want to nurse you back to health just so I can fuck you to death again."

I laugh. "Oh, how romantic. You want to fuck me to death."

He chuckles, shrugging as he replies, "I never pretended to be romantic, but I suppose it depends on what your personal idea of romance is."

"I wouldn't really know. I don't think I have ever been romanced."

He squeezes me, jostling me around a bit as he says, "Maybe you were romanced, but you missed it because their romance and your romance were just too different."

I ponder this theory, unable to tell if it's accurate or not since I'm uncertain what would feel romantic to me. I don't give a shit about flowers and chocolates and jewelry, and since I've been taking care of myself for quite a long time now, I can't imagine what kind of romantic gesture would even get my attention.

I pull back to look at his face, then ask, "Would you let me tie you up?"

I have no idea why I ask or where it came from, but there it is, out in the universe.

"Is that what you want?" he murmurs, his face giving nothing away as he waits for me to respond.

I don't know what's holding me back, but for some reason, the idea of freely giving and taking with anyone sends me into a panic. So, if he isn't going to tie me up and use me, and I don't feel like I can handle the pressure of being free with him, that leaves two options—either he gets tied up, or we cool it.

And there's no fucking way we're cooling it since it has been weeks of build-up now, and fuck if I know when his next appearance will be, so it really is now or never.

I nod. "Yes, I think I would if you're okay with it."

He doesn't say anything for a few moments, just stares into my eyes as if he's searching for something. Finally, he says, "The trunk at the end of the bed. Take your pick." He releases me, then lays back, stretching his long body out to get comfortable as I move off the bed and locate the trunk, taking a peek inside.

Take my pick, indeed.

The trunk is filled with all sorts of ropes and leather straps, gags, and toys. I give him an incredulous look. "What the fuck, Clark?"

He glares at me. "Don't start that Clark shit, Antoinette, or I'll beat your ass black and blue and then edge you for a fucking month."

My eyes widen, and I gasp in horror. "You can't edge me for a month!"

He simply smirks at me. "Try me."

Well, this is going pear-shaped real quick.

I frown at him, squinting as I relent and try again, "Looks like you have a regular party in this trunk. Have orgies often?"

He clicks his tongue impatiently, prowling off the bed and crowding me against the trunk. He bends over me, bringing his lips close to my ear and whispering, "Jealous?"

I mean, yes, a little, but I scoff, "Of course not, Dare. I just hope you properly sanitize all this shit in between skin soirees."

I groan inwardly as soon as the words are out of my mouth. I have no idea why I can't control myself with him. Why can't I just be nice and flexible and attempt to act like a sane, rational woman? Because deep down, I truly am a sane, rational woman, but with Dare, I'm a complete fucking lunatic, and I can't make myself shut the fuck up.

He reaches behind me, grabbing an object from the pile in the trunk before slamming the lid shut with a loud crack. I flinch, closing my eyes as I feel him press against me, and the next thing I know, I'm momentarily airborne as he tosses me back onto the bed.

I barely have a moment to catch my breath before his body is covering mine, his weight pushing me into the mattress, and I'm torn between wrapping myself around him and fighting him off. I push at his shoulders halfheartedly, giving him a shove, but then his hands are gripping my wrists almost painfully, and my hands are pulled up over my head.

"Let me be very clear with you, Antoinette," he says gruffly, his breath hot on the side of my face. "This bedroom you're staying in...this is my bedroom. And that trunk of goodies at the end of my bed is for you and only you. I've never had a woman in this house, never mind in my bedroom, and the only skin soirees I'll be having in this room or anywhere will be with you." He licks a line down my cheek to my neck and then up to my ear, where he says softly, "Got it, baby girl?"

I can't stop the shiver that runs through me, and I gasp, "Yes."

He laughs, the dark vibrations on my skin sending another shiver through me as he asks, "Who is it you're saying yes to, minx?"

I swallow, knowing this is a huge test, and any satisfaction I might get tonight is dependent on how I respond at this very moment. I want to fuck with him in the worst way, but I know it would be a mistake, and I'm trying to not make any more of those with Dare.

So, I drag in a deep breath, squeezing my eyes shut as I turn my head until my face is pressed into his neck and choke out, "I got it...Darius."

He growls deep in his chest, his hands releasing my wrists and moving to my head where one hand cups the side of my face and the other clutches my neck. He glides his lips over my face, hovering at the corner of my mouth as he pants, his hips and torso pushing me deeper into the mattress, and it's all I can do to not scream in frustration.

I whimper, struggling against his hold as I try to force his lips where I want them, but he shifts back, his grip tightening as he shushes me. "Look at me." His words are a pained whisper, and at first, I shake my head in refusal, but then he says, "Please, Toni. Open your eyes and look at me."

I freeze, panic bubbling up inside me at his words. I don't want to look at him. I know it's fucked up, and I know it doesn't make any sense. I want his hands on me, his lips and teeth. I want his entire body pressing me into the mattress until I can't breathe, his cock driving into me until it hurts.

But I don't want to look at him. I can't. It hurts.

Dare won't relent. He stills his movements, his grip on my face and my neck tightening until I can barely take in air. His whisper becomes darker with roughened edges, sharper, cutting into my reservations, my anxiety, and my fear. He gives me a little shake, his voice now directly in front of me, his breath painting heat against my lips as I try to swallow down the sob building up in my chest. "I won't touch you until you look at me." His hand on my throat tightens until I can't take it at all, and heat floods through me with a wave of relief as he takes my voice.

I don't know if it's the lack of air, the pressure in my chest, or the throbbing between my legs, but suddenly, my eyes are open, and I'm staring into his golden eyes burning for me. He looks resplendent, triumphant as he stares into my eyes as if he has won the ultimate prize. He relaxes his hands, and I try to take a breath, but I can't stop the sob that comes out just as he bends his head closer, the guttural sound becoming his meal as he crushes his mouth against mine.

This is no timid first meeting of mouths. There is no hesitancy or waiting. No gentle brush or apprehensive question. He presses his open mouth against mine and sucks out all the air, feelings, paranoia, and deep, gut-wrenching anxiety from me and feeds off of me with his lips, tongue, and teeth.

For a few moments, I feel paralyzed, completely overwhelmed by the intensity with which he touches me. Not only where his lips are moving against mine, but also his hand on my cheek, on my neck, his chest pushing against my breasts, his hips pressing the hard ridge of his cock between my legs.

It all feels like too much, but at the same time, like it will never be enough, and every instinct in my body screams at me to push him away and run. To run and run and run and never look back for fear I'll be completely changed by this unexpected beast before me.

He slows his assault on my mouth, his lips and tongue not quite gentle but persuasively demanding as he tries to coax a response from me. He growls against my lips, and it's his tongue stroking the roof of my mouth that breaks me. I come alive like electricity has been jacked directly into my soul.

I force my hands up between us, up around his neck, until my fingers delve into his hair, and I respond with every ounce of passion, longing, and need I've ever had, pulling his head down to meet my ravenous mouth. His growl turns into a dark chuckle, and I swallow it as I devour his lips and then suck his tongue into my mouth.

My legs come up, wrapping around his hips, my ankles locking against his ass, yanking his cock harder against me. I'm panting and moaning, emitting these guttural, animalistic sounds that barely sound human, but I don't even care. He pulls back from me, his chest heaving, and I practically snarl as his quiet voice breaks out, broken and breathless. "Oh, there you are, baby girl."

I glare up at him, muttering, "No words, Dare. No words."

His eyes darken, the look on his face primal and all-consuming as he leans in close to me and swipes his tongue across my lips. He drags his tongue from the corner of my mouth along my cheek, where he bites me just hard enough that I know there will be a mark there tomorrow. Then his voice is in my ear, "I'll do whatever I want, and there's not a damn thing you can do about it."

I practically scream in frustration as he pulls away from me, and I try to wrap myself around him to keep him as close as possible. He pulls at my arms, extricating himself from my grip, then pulls me up to a sitting position, his golden eyes boring into me as he says, "I think you're forgetting our deal."

He reaches behind him, grabs something, and holds it out to me. I'm panting, my heart pounding, and I feel like my brain is short-circuiting, so I just frown at his hand rather than taking what he's offering. My confusion must be evident on my face because he adds, "Tie me up, baby girl. I'm yours."

I blink at him, then give my head a little shake to clear the cloud of lust that one fucking kiss detonated inside me. I open my mouth to tell him it's not necessary, reaching out to push his hand away, but he forces it back on me, placing the leather objects in my hands as he leans in close to me.

"No take-backs, Antoinette. This time, we do it your way."

My breath catches in my throat, and it isn't until I feel his hot wet tongue licking a line up my cheek to the corner of my eye that I realize a tear has escaped. I remain sitting there as he maneuvers around me until he's lying on the bed again, stretched out, spread eagle.

He gives me a nod, his voice gruff as he says, "Go ahead, baby girl. This is your show. As fast or as slow as you want. The only rule is that you take everything."

I glance at the leather in my hands and then back up at Dare laid out before me. His body appears to be relaxed, but I can see the lines of tension around his eyes and how his hands keep clenching rhythmically. I can't believe he's prone to handing over control like this, and I'm somewhat shocked that he's decided to do so now with me.

Part of me wants to refuse, to put the restraints on myself and offer myself up to him. To beg him to punish me, beg him to lay me out with my hands stretched over my head and my feet stretched apart until it's almost painful. For him to slap me and choke me and pummel me with his body until I can't form a coherent thought.

But I see the look of determination on his face, his golden eyes focused on my face as he gives me another small nod.

I take a deep breath, then scramble up to the head of the bed, where I quickly wrap each leather band around his wrists. I glance around, unsure of what to do next until some hardware glints on the headboard. At first, it may be confused for decoration, but it's obviously strategically placed to secure various types of restraints.

I snort, giggling to myself as I contemplate which set of O-rings I want to attach the cuffs to, and with each click of metal against metal, some of the unease releases from my body. I sit back and view my handiwork, pulling the leather straps tighter until each muscular arm is pulled up and back.

I giggle again, trying to hide my smile behind my hand as I feel a blush rush up my neck and into my face. My heart races in my chest as I step off the bed, turning to look at him lying there, completely at my mercy.

All humor leaves me as I go back to the trunk, pulling out another set of leather restraints and setting them on the bed. He's still fully clothed in a white button-down shirt and black trousers, and for some strange reason, it's the sight of his bare feet that has me blushing all over again.

The dull ache between my legs increases at the sight of him, and I lick my lips, then crawl up his body until I'm straddling the tops of his thighs. I watch his face as I play with the buttons on his shirt, unbuttoning the top one and then the next before I grab each side and yank on it fiercely, popping all the buttons off in one go.

His eyes never leave my face. His mouth opens with a gasp, tongue poking out to wet his lips. His chest is heaving, and I feel him shift under me as he gives me a bump that slides me up until I'm once again pressing my throbbing pussy against his hard cock.

I make an appreciative noise, then tsk at him, shaking my head and saying, "Control yourself, big boy, or I may drag this out a little longer."

His eyes widen, and he gives me a dirty smirk but doesn't say anything. He just grips the leather straps tightly in his hands and pulls.

I move off him, kneeling beside him and then moving toward his feet, where I wrap the other restraints around each ankle. I get off the bed, examining the footboard for the O-rings I'm sure must be hidden somewhere, and sure enough, there are several sets in different locations. Another rush of excitement runs through me as they're secured, and I tighten the straps before returning to take in the sight of my handiwork. I'm sure the look on my face must be one of pure evil decadence—all gleeful, naughty.

I had considered removing his clothes before restraining him, knowing I won't be able to get them off without completely destroying them, but the idea of unwrapping him like a gift when he's completely incapacitated turns me on. And the picture he makes trussed up in his business wear is pure magic.

His shirt is open, exposing the golden skin of his muscular chest. I can clearly make out the line of his cock pressing against the fabric of his trousers, and I can't help but crawl up onto the bed beside him, brushing my hand against his erection teasingly before giving his rigid flesh a firm squeeze. He grunts, his hips pressing up into my hand as he pulls on the restraints.

I glance up at his face and ask, "Should you have a safeword?"

He makes a humorless noise, giving me a slight shake of his head in response, but I persist, crawling up his body until I'm inches from his face, staring into his eyes. And I say, "I'm going to need your words...Darius."

Now, he glares at me and spits out gruffly, "I do not need a safeword, Antoinette."

I glare back at him, then lean closer so I can trace his lips with my tongue, but I pull back when he attempts to capture my lips with his own. "And who is it you're speaking to, Darius?"

He glares at me again, and I feel the tension vibrating off him as he shows me his teeth, his tongue gliding over them as he practically snarls, "Don't play with me, minx."

I laugh delightedly, now fully committed to having this dominant, virile man at my mercy.

I crawl further up his body until I'm sitting on his chest with my knees straddling his head. I rock my hips, my silk sleep shorts doing nothing to hide my obvious arousal that's now on display directly in his face. His nostrils flare, and I feel his chest rise as he inhales, his head coming up off the mattress as he tries to get closer.

I lean over a bit, giving him a bit of slack in the straps securing him to the headboard, and then I shift my aching cunt closer to his reaching mouth. I feel his hot breath blowing against the fabric of my sleep shorts, so I slide the last inch closer until I'm basically straddling his face.

He growls beneath me, "Get that cunt on my face, baby girl. Let me have a taste."

White, hot heat rushes over me at his words, and I sink down until I feel his mouth pressed against my silk-covered flesh, his lips firm, his tongue seeking, and his teeth nipping. My eyes practically roll up into the back of my head as he works me through my clothing, and I can only imagine how amazing his mouth will feel on my naked flesh.

Abruptly, I wiggle around until I'm standing, shucking my sleep shorts and cami before I turn around, straddling his head while facing away from him. He mutters from underneath me, "Oh, for the love of fuck," and I hear and feel him yanking violently on his restraints.

I don't waste time with teasing niceties and go straight for the fastening and zipper on his trousers, opening his pants up and pushing at them until he raises his hips enough for me to force the clothing down far enough to release his cock.

I'm relieved to be positioned away from him so he can't see the look of fear on my face at my first glimpse of his massive dick. I reach out a hand tentatively, brushing my fingers over the swollen head, smearing the pre-cum around. He's unmoving beneath me and seems to be holding his breath as I lean forward, licking a line from the wet tip all the way down to his balls. He groans then, bucking his hips up in invitation, so I grip his length firmly in one hand and bend down to take the head of his cock between my lips, sucking and licking.

I begin to work him over, my mouth taking more and more of his length as I find my rhythm, my hand working in tandem with my lips and tongue as his hips flex.

I feel his mouth on my leg, his tongue licking, and his teeth sink into my inner thigh, and I moan around his cock in my mouth as he commands, "Sit on my face, baby girl. Let me have that sweet pussy," and so I do. I lower my hips down slowly, concentrating on his thrusting cock in my mouth and then his hot breath and spearing tongue on my pulsing, wet flesh.

He also skips teasing niceties; burying his face between my legs and feasting like a man starved. He licks, sucks, and bites my pussy lips, up one side and down the other, then spears my hole with his tongue as far as he can go at this angle, and I find myself paralyzed with pleasure, my saliva sliding down his dick and pooling around my hand before dripping onto his balls.

I sit back fully onto his face, bringing my other hand to wrap around his cock, and I do my best to focus on blowing him instead of what his mouth is doing to my throbbing pussy. I shift my body back some, grinding my clit against his lips, and he obliges my silent demand without hesitation, sucking my swollen nub into his mouth, flicking it with his tongue.

I pull my head back, releasing his dick, and he groans in protest as I remove my pussy from his face in order to shift down his body. I straddle his hips, reverse cowgirl, rubbing my slick heat along his length, then grinding against him to get the exact pressure I need on my clit. I gasp, a low moan spilling from my lips, my head falling back in pleasure.

"Holy fuck, Toni. What're you doing to me?" His words sound desperate, and I feel the tension in his body beneath me as I continue to writhe against him, so he continues, "There are condoms in the bedside drawer…"

I twist my upper body a bit so I can glance at him over my shoulder, my hips still undulating slowly, one hand squeezing my breast and tweaking my nipple as I gasp, "Are you saying I need one?"

He chokes out a laugh. "Fuck, no."

I whimper, the ache inside me building in intensity as I continue to rub my clit against his dick. "Then why offer?"

He shakes his head, his jaw tight as he grinds out on a muttered groan, "Just want you to be safe. Always want you to feel safe."

I shift my body without warning, raising my hips and moving my free hand to grip the base of his cock so I can rub the tip on my drenched opening. His breath catches, and he seems to be holding it, waiting to see what I'm going to do next.

I sink down an inch, then two, allowing my body to ease into the almost painful stretch of his girth. Dare curses behind me, yanking the restraints even harder as he grunts, "Toni, let me loose. Let me loose so I can touch you."

I ignore his plea, sinking down even further, then sliding back up until just the head of his cock is inside me. I bring a hand up to my mouth, getting a handful of saliva, then reach down to smear my wet hand onto his rigid flesh.

I glance back at him again, the utterly feral look on his face setting off another ripple of arousal through me, and I can't control the whimpering moan that falls from my lips as I sink down fully, taking all of him inside me.

I turn my body back so I'm facing away from him, bracing both my hands on his thighs as I start to move slowly up and down, then roll my hips to press him as deep inside me as possible.

He's panting behind me, his hips bucking up in search of more friction, so I pick up my pace, moving my hips faster until he's cursing and grunting behind me, "Slow down, baby girl. I'm going to lose it. You need to come first."

I stop moving, shifting my body so my feet are under me and I'm leaning back, one arm braced against his chest. My movement in this position is more restricted, but I feel him so deep inside me it almost hurts. I lick my fingers on my free hand, then rub them against my clit with purpose, knowing it won't take long at all with how turned on I am.

I grind myself down onto him, rubbing my clit in tight, fast circles, my eyes squeezed shut, my head thrown back, and my mouth falling open in pleasure as I whimper, sob, and moan. I spread my legs more, bracing my feet to increase my range of motion as I slide up and down, rolling my hips on the down stroke so he presses on that sensitive spot deep inside my pussy.

"Fuck. Fuck. Fuck. Fuck." Dare is muttering and groaning behind me. "Come, Toni. Oh, fuck. I'm going to come. I'm going to come so hard inside you, you'll be feeling me for days."

His words push me over the edge, and I sob with pleasure, grinding my pussy down hard on his cock, he curses as his hips buck beneath me violently. His cock pulses inside my twitching cunt, the feel of his hot release pushing me into another orgasm as I continue to rub my clit, drawing out my pleasure as much as I can before I finally slow my movements.

I'm panting and sweating as I push my sweaty hair out of my face and look over my shoulder at Dare, shaking my head at the look of utter satisfaction on his face. I gradually raise myself off him, releasing his still-hard cock from my body, and I can't help but snort as I feel our mixed releases drip out of me.

I crawl up to the head of the bed, releasing Dare's wrists from the restraints before I fall onto the bed in exhaustion. I know I should get cleaned up, and I will eventually, but right now, I can't move.

I feel Dare shifting around, likely releasing his ankles and adjusting his clothing, and I'm suddenly tickled by the fact I'm buck-naked and just fucked Darius Hughes while he was basically still fully clothed.

I must have dozed off because the next thing I know, I'm being roused by something tickling my thigh. I peel my eyelids open, blinking in confusion as I realize the tickling on my thigh is Dare's head maneuvering between my legs.

I go to reach down and push him away, but my arm won't move; it's been tied to the side of the bed. I lift my head, asking sleepily, "What the fuck are you doing, Dare?"

He raises his head to meet my questioning gaze, and I can't help but gasp at the feral look in his eyes as he replies, "Taking my turn."

Well, fuck me.

Chapter Fourteen

DARE

I PULLED A CHAIR up, sat beside the bed, and watched her sleep for an hour before I decided to proceed with my plan.

It took me that long to swallow the giant bitter lump of unease lodged in my throat at the thought of where this was headed.

I'm not one to give in to my emotions. I rarely show them, never mind flaunt them, and this strange warmth that bubbles up inside me when I look at her is almost enough to choke me.

Frankly, it pisses me off. It's as if this feeling festering in me for the last few months can no longer be contained, and I have no choice but to throw myself into it.

There's so much I want to say to her; however, I know she isn't ready to hear any of it. So, I'll continue to swallow it down and hold it where it won't hurt her.

On the outside, Antoinette comes off as a highly confident and emotionally healthy person. The truth of the matter is, she's a fucking mess.

I believe internally, she knows she's a mess, but she's unable or unwilling to confront the deep-seated issues that drive her on a daily basis. She's so accustomed to falling back on false bravado and overt sexual confidence that she loses sight of the possibility of legitimate deep connections with other human beings.

Not that I find myself having deep connections with human beings in general, but I at least have a handful of people I'd call on in the event of emotional turmoil. Not that I have a lot of emotional turmoil, but everyone has that one thing that's capable of ripping them to shreds.

Antoinette has managed to alienate herself into a corner where most people would never venture. Deep down, she's the type of person who would quite literally give someone the shirt off her back, but at first glance, she has a reputation for showing her teeth and flexing concrete boundaries that many people may deem inappropriate.

In many ways, I have her exactly where I want her at this moment. And I don't mean just naked in my bed.

I've finally managed to sneak my way past a few of her walls, and all I can do is hope that they're down for the duration and that I won't have to keep chipping away at them at every turn. She's exhausting and exasperating, and if I wasn't such a stubborn cunt, I probably would've told her to fuck off already myself.

I snort, the beast in me vibrating at the thought of letting her go. As fucking if that would ever happen, given my level of obsession is borderline manic and my need to possess her infinite.

It's quite likely she still feels she has choices. It's laughable, really. Because when it comes to me, she's going to find out all of her choices went down the drain the first time I stuffed her in the trunk of my car. I waited this long to make a move, and nothing will stand in my way now.

She shifts on the bed, drawing my gaze to her face, and I can't help but mirror the small smile on her lips. She sighs, and I sigh, and then my sigh turns into a groan as she turns her body just so, and I get a glimpse of my cum leaking out of her pussy.

My beast likes that, the sign of ownership, the primal sign of possession over her body.

She shivers slightly, so I stand, then crawl up onto the bed at her feet. I stroke my hand over her ass, my fingers ghosting between her ass cheeks, and then dipping into the wetness of my release, pushing it back into her body. She gasps and then moans softly, her hips squirming as I push two fingers up inside her as far as I can.

I pull my fingers from inside her cunt, moving up her body to smear the wetness across her lips, my beast practically purring as her tongue peeks out, licking around her mouth.

I go back to the trunk, picking out a different set of restraints, softer and more delicate. They also have a quick release on the off-chance that I get her exactly where I want her and I need to let her go quickly. I want to push her physically and emotionally until she's begging, pleading to be closer to me.

I pick up one of her arms, wrap the band around her wrist, and then ease her onto her back as I do the same with her other wrist. Moving both of her arms over her head, I connect her wrists together, then move to the head of the bed and secure her bound hands to the headboard. I tighten the straps until her arms are pulled up over her head just enough so her torso is bowed, her head back, and her neck presented to me.

I'm still wearing my clothes, mainly as a small barrier to keep me from going entirely animalistic on her. It's been quite some time since I gave in to my urges, and it's difficult for me to rein in my pent-up desire to consume her.

I know she'd enjoy it; that's what she wants, but this isn't about giving her what she wants. This is about getting what I want. I know I can have her body, that physically, she would be mine whenever and however I choose, but I want more than the physical, more than just her body. I want her mind, her emotions. I want her entire fucking soul.

I decide not to restrain her ankles, allowing her free movement of her lower body. I shift back down between her legs, spreading them wide, then bending forward and inhaling the scent of our mixed arousal. I know some men are scared of their own cum, but I'm no such man.

I softly flick her clit with my tongue, slowly licking along her pussy lips down to her entrance, where I fuck her a few times with my tongue. Her little noises increase in volume, and I know the exact moment she comes awake enough to comprehend what's happening. Then her voice breaks through the silence, "What the fuck are you doing, Dare?"

The question is breathless, and she pulls on her restraints as I give her a pointed look and reply, "Taking my turn."

I don't give her time to respond. I dive into her pussy, my hands sliding under her ass to raise her up, giving me better access. I suck, lick, and nibble every inch of her swollen, glistening flesh, allowing her legs to come up over my shoulders, her feet digging into my back. She's doing everything she can to grind against my face, so I bring one hand around, swiping two fingers along her wet entrance before pushing them inside her.

"Oh, god," she sobs, her gasping breath catching in her throat as her body winds tighter. I feel her climbing toward release, her body vibrating with need, her pants and gasps increasing in intensity the faster I work her over with my mouth and fingers. I twist my hand, pushing my fingertips up against her pelvic wall, and she freezes, her body strung tight as she reaches for her peak, her broken sobs quickly escalating in what I can only imagine being a well of pleasure.

And then I stop.

She screams in frustration, and I revel in the intense satisfaction that rushes through me. She thrashes on the bed, and it's only my quick reflexes that save me from the kick she directs up at my chest.

I grab onto her foot, squeezing her ankle tightly as I say, "Now, now, baby girl. Don't make me strap you down."

She glares at me, snarling, "Fuck around and find out. Right, baby?"

My eyes widen, and I'm sure I'm giving her an intensely smug look when I retort, "That's fucking right, and you've been fucking around for ages, so it's about time you find out."

She thrashes about once more, her arms pulling on the restraints with such force that, for a moment, I fear she may actually bust out of them. I question my decision not to restrain her entirely, but I want her to be able to fight; I want her to be able to lash out.

I turn my head, biting her ankle sharply until she flinches, then I move down her leg, biting into the meat of her calf until she cries out. I release her, looking at my bite mark with a growl of approval. I want to mark her everywhere. I want to leave my teeth marks on her neck, her face. I want to smear my cum all over her body so that all anyone will ever smell on her again is me.

My beast rattles in my chest again, and I grit my teeth, pushing back against my primal need to force her to my will because I know it would be a detrimental mistake. She's not the kind of woman you can force into anything; she has to be handled with care, tricked, and coerced into believing the end results are a result of her own making.

I release her ankle, lying flat between her legs and pressing my face into her pussy. I don't bother easing back in, instead driving three fingers into her and twisting them while working my lips and tongue against her clit. I'll have her bucking beneath me in no time. I carry on licking and sucking until I feel her feet pushing into my back, her thighs squeezing my head to keep me in place as she moans and curses, and I find myself smiling against her slick flesh as she attempts to force me to let her orgasm.

But it won't work.

Just as soon as her moans shift to keening cries, I tear myself away from her, this time moving off the bed to avoid her attempts to kick me again.

My cock throbs in my pants, so I unfasten them, reaching my hand in and squeezing my erection until it's almost painful.

She's beyond pissed, her eyes flashing at me and her teeth bared as she snarls like a feral cat.

And I fucking love it.

I shift up to the head of the bed, kneeling beside her, reaching a hand out to stroke her cheek. I barely manage to yank my hand back as her teeth snap at me in an attempt to bite me.

I chuckle again, taking her head between my hands and jerking her up so she can look nowhere but at me. I lean over her, my tongue lapping her upper cheek for a second before my teeth sink into her flesh, and she flinches. I lick my way down to her lips, swiping over her mouth before taking her bottom lip between my teeth and biting down until she sobs and the bitter taste of copper hits my tongue.

I pull back slightly, just enough, so my lips still touch hers as I whisper, "I can do this all night, baby girl."

Her eyes widen, the heat flaring behind the darkness: The turmoil, distress, anxiety, and fear. I lick her lips again, this time sucking her top lip into my mouth gently before shifting over to press my cheek against hers, whispering against her ear, "Don't be afraid, baby girl. I've got you."

She shudders against me but doesn't say anything, and I honestly have no idea if this is good or bad.

I move down to her neck, licking and sucking her pulse point, then biting down on the spot where her neck connects with her shoulder. My teeth sink in, my lips sucking her flesh into my mouth, reveling in how her breath picks up as she whimpers and moans.

I lick my way to the other side of her neck, where I leave the same mark, then slowly trail down her body, marking her breasts, her stomach, over her hips, and thighs, all the way back down to her ankles.

I sit up, giving her a feral smile, all teeth and wild eyes, as I take in my handiwork. She's a beautiful mosaic of teeth marks and beard burn that will likely bloom by morning. I can't hold back the growl that erupts from my chest, and I mentally count down from ten before proceeding, feeling myself on the cusp of losing control.

After a few moments, I kneel between her legs, bending down and working her over with vigor, my lips, tongue, and teeth working in tandem with my fingers. I edge her once, twice, three more times until she's a twitching, whimpering, writhing mess before me. Tears stream down into her hairline, her chest heaving, each exhalation a moan of incoherent words.

I get off the bed, maneuvering up to the headboard to put some slack in the straps to shift her exactly where I want her. I lean over her, gripping the back of her neck with one hand as I lift her upper body up, piling pillows beneath her head and shoulders so she's propped up at an angle that works for me. I tighten the straps until her arms are once again pulled over her head.

I walk to the end of the bed, closing the top of the trunk and shoving it out of my way so I can stand there, staring at her and the glorious picture she makes. She's propped up now, her upper body reclining, but she still has her legs bent, spread open for me, showing me her swollen, glistening pussy practically pulsating with need.

I want to give her a show as well, so, slowly, I remove my shirt, letting it drop to the floor at my feet, my eyes never leaving her face. I reach down, pushing my pants and boxer briefs down my legs, kicking out of them so I'm standing before her completely nude.

I stand there, watching her as she looks me over, her eyes trailing up my legs to my torso, over my arms, and up my neck until she's looking me in the face. I see the turmoil in her eyes, her lips pressing together in an attempt to control her breathy exhalations of arousal. But still, she lays there on display for me with her legs spread in invitation.

I crawl up the bed to kneel before her, my hand stroking up and down my cock before I lean over her. Now that I've got that image of her laid out before me engrained in my head, I release the tension on the straps so I can pull the pillows from beneath her shoulders. I pull up on her hips, and she braces her legs to assist as I place the pillows under her ass, her arms and upper body now flat against the bed and her hips raised up to allow for maximum penetration.

Then I'm pushing my cock inside her, the hard length of me sliding in where she's hot and wet, and I can't stop the groan that erupts from inside me at the feel of her clinging walls. I don't waste any time with gentleness, sitting back on my haunches, my hands on her hips bruising as I rut into her like a man possessed. It takes every ounce of self-control I have not to empty myself inside her almost immediately, and I know I won't last long at this pace. I move one hand from her hip, reaching around to pinch her clit, and I immediately feel her body coiling toward release.

I stop, abruptly withdrawing from her body and leaving the bed so I can retrieve a rubber cock-ring from the trunk. Returning to the bed, I resume my initial position between her legs. She's writhing and cursing, her eyes a fiery glare on me as I secure the rubber ring tightly to the base of my throbbing cock. I watch her face as I move back down her body, positioning myself between her legs.

She licks her lips, gasping, "Please. I can't take it anymore."

I grin in satisfaction, settling between her legs, my hands pushing her legs back as I shove my cock into her dripping cunt. I flex my body over her, my cock impaled deep inside her as my lips and teeth devour her nipples, switching from one to the other until she wraps her legs around my hips. She grinds herself against me, her hips bucking, her loud moans of frustration pleading and begging for me to move. But I don't.

Even with a cock ring physically preventing me from coming inside her, I can feel myself on the edge, my balls and dick throbbing for release. I squeeze my eyes shut, using what little control I have left to keep pushing her. I thrust until her pleas are no longer silent, and my mouth is moving from her breasts up to her collarbone and onto her neck.

I'm panting and grunting against her ear as I continue to pump into her. I feel her head lift, turning into me, her lips seeking purchase anywhere she can reach. She sobs, her arms yanking on the restraints, her legs tightening as she rotates her hips, and her voice broken and breathless as she moans, "Please, let me come. Please."

This is what I've been waiting for. The moment her fear and anxiety are overridden by her desire for me, and she's reaching toward me instead of fighting against me. It's as if I feel her inner animal calling to my own, overwhelming any thoughts of reason or self-preservation that would normally keep her from being in the present with me.

And then I hear it...my name uttered so quietly I almost miss it. It's not Clark or Dare or motherfucker or any of the other terms she has thrown at me, so I know it's almost time. I pull my hips back slightly, moving a hand down and releasing the offensive ring preventing me from release, then shove back into her fully once more.

With my body over hers, my hands gripping her ass and raising her hips to deepen penetration, I grind my pelvis onto her clit. Keeping my movements measured and firm, the beast inside me rattles as our mixed moans and curses echo throughout the room.

I sense the moment I have her. The moment when my name is no longer a whisper but a keening prayer on her lips as she begs me to push her over the edge into bliss. I move my hand from her ass, reaching for the cord to release her arms, and as soon as she feels the tension give on her wrists, she lifts them over her head and then over mine until she's gripping me around my neck.

She lifts her face, pressing her lips against my ear, her entire body now clinging to me, and I'm grunting with effort, sweat beading along my hairline. I continue to control my thrusts inside her, then she comes apart, and I feel the tremors running through her body as she sobs the beginning of her orgasm. I adjust my legs under me, moving my hands beneath her shoulders and lifting her torso up as I rear back, taking her with me so she's straddling me.

I pump my hips, slamming up into her, the sounds of her sobbing moans and the rhythmic slapping of our bodies quickly have my balls drawing up, and my cock pulses as I try to hold off.

She turns her head into my neck, her teeth sinking into my pulse point as she sobs, and then she's wild in my arms, writhing and moaning, her tits rubbing against my chest, her teeth devouring my neck as she leaves a mark of her own. I'm moving rapidly inside her when she releases my neck, her mouth seeking mine in frenzied need, and then she devours me with her lips, tongue, and teeth.

I suck in her breath and moans, taste the salt of her tears as she loses control of her senses, and it's my name on her tongue as she breaks apart. Her orgasm rolls over her in waves, and she sobs into my mouth,

"Fuck, fuck, fuck," pushing me over the edge with her. I pulse inside her with a guttural groan.

I ease her back down to the bed, bracing myself on my forearms as I continue to kiss her, our lips and tongues clinging, caressing. Soon, she's relaxing under me, her legs releasing my hips and falling into the mattress, and then her arms loosen their grip on my shoulders, her hand stroking down my arms to rest on the bed.

I'm watching her as we kiss, and she's staring at me with such intensity I fear she can see every dark secret I have hidden in my soul. But she doesn't flinch, she doesn't cower, and after a while, we stop kissing and just stare at each other, our breath slowly evening out.

She gives me a small smile, her eyes closing as a quiet laugh escapes. I lean closer to her, kissing each of her eyelids, her nose, mouth, neck, and shoulder before I get off the bed and make my way into the bathroom. I flip the taps on the tub to draw a bath, add in some bath salts, and then grab a mineral water from the small refrigerator under the vanity, which I pour into a glass and leave by the tub.

I return to the bedroom to find she hasn't moved an inch. She's still lying there on her back, completely relaxed, with the same small smile on her lips. So, I walk to the bed, remove the restraints still around her wrists, and then bend over and gently gather her against me, lifting her into my arms. She doesn't move, just sinks into me, resting her head on my shoulder, her hands in her lap.

I carry her into the bathroom, set her in the chair beside the tub, and I can't help but chuckle as she sits there with her eyes closed, still with the smile on her face. I'm surprised she doesn't just melt into a puddle on the floor, but somehow, she manages to keep herself upright, so I say, "I'm going to step out for a moment to give you a bit of privacy. Just yell when you're ready, and I'll help you into the tub."

She peeks one eye open and gives me a small nod, so I go back out into the bedroom, where I pick up the various restraints strewn around the bed. I check them to see if they need to be cleaned before putting them back in the trunk, closing the lid and placing it back at the end of the bed. I quickly remake the bed, then return to the bathroom door, just in time to hear her call out that she's ready.

I walk into the bathroom, stopping to check the water temperature before I scoop her up into my arms, and she shrieks, grabbing onto my shoulder as if she's afraid I'll drop her. I stoop over, depositing her into the tub, and then hand her the glass of mineral water. "Drink this. I'll be right back."

Taking a robe from the back of the bathroom door, I make my way down the hall to the other bathroom because I wasn't smart enough to use the facilities before sticking her in the tub. Once I'm finished, I make my way down into the kitchen and get the plate of fruit, hard cheese, and crusty bread that I asked Matt to put together for me. He had given me a bit of grief about it, but he did an excellent job.

I grab a bottle of white wine from the wine fridge and one glass because that's all we need, then make my way back up to my bedroom, stopping in the doorway of the bathroom to watch her. She's laid out fully in the tub, submerged to just below her collarbone. At first, I think she's asleep, but when I walk further into the bathroom, her head tilts toward me, and she asks, "Are you coming in?"

I'm relieved to see the soft look in her eyes, the corners of her lips still turned up in satisfaction. I know I still need to tread carefully with her; I may always have to tread carefully with her. It may take endless time, effort, and work to mold her into a woman who accepts that having soft edges with people you're close to is not a weakness, that if two people take those soft edges and fuse them together, they create an unbreakable bond.

I may only ever get glimmers of it, a revolving kaleidoscope of intimacy and affection blended with bits of resentment and a troubled soul. But after months of sitting back and watching her, keeping my distance and biding my time, I'll take it.

I walk over to the bathtub and place the plate of food, bottle of wine, and glass on the shelf by the wall, then grab another mineral water from the fridge, topping off her glass and handing it to her with a knowing look. She takes it from me without comment, gulping down half of it before giving it back to me, and I set it aside.

I sit on the side of the tub, picking up the bottle of wine and raising a brow at her questioningly. She gives me a small nod and a, "Yes, please."

I pour a modest portion into the glass and hand it to her. "You should eat something as well."

She glances at the food and then back at me, but I can see the confusion on her face. Then she asks, "Aren't you going to join me?"

"Would you like me to?"

She gives me another slight nod, and the beast inside me practically crows in victory. I'm surprised as I figured she may want to have a few moments to herself, but I'm not going to argue. I make sure I have everything we need close by, then strip my robe off, motioning for her to lean forward so I can sit behind her. She settles back against my chest, her head lying on my shoulder, and I pull her close.

She turns her head toward me and says, "You should also drink some water."

I chuckle, want filling my chest, so I reach for the remainder of her glass without comment and drink it down. She's not wrong.

I pick up a strawberry, holding it up to her mouth, and she eyes me suspiciously but takes the offering anyway. She looks at me thoughtfully as she chews and swallows, then asks, "What are you doing here?"

I meet her gaze, craning my neck around a bit so I know she sees the seriousness on my face. "Taking care of you."

She snorts. "Taking care of me? I thought that's what you just did in the bedroom."

I laugh again. "Well, that's a different kind of taking care of you. But if I only tend to your needs in one area, then that's not really taking care of you, is it?"

She's staring off into space as she quietly replies, "I don't think anyone's ever taken care of me."

I know this to be true. While she may not have had the difficult upbringing many people had, in some ways, she still grew up atten-tion-starved and goal-driven, always one step shy of perfection, as she and her siblings took the competition of childhood way too seriously.

As far as I can tell, she does get on pretty well with her family at this point in her life, but that's because she learned to put up solid boundaries and works hard to maintain them. She also lives thousands of miles away, so there's that.

Of course, this is all information I've gathered second and third hand from watching her from a distance. I just pieced together bits of information that somehow managed to establish a causation for her pattern of detachment and aloofness.

I pull her closer to me, whispering against her skin, "I will always take care of you."

She turns her head away a bit, her eyes still staring out into the distance as she says softly, "Until you leave me anyway."

I squeeze my arms tighter around her, my face pressing into her neck, my teeth nipping her as I say, "I will always take care of you, baby girl. And I would never willingly leave you."

She doesn't say anything else, just turns her body and leans into me fully, her face pressed into my neck. I feel her breathing me in, one of her hands clutching at my arm, so I squeeze her tighter as if I can force her broken pieces back together again just by the force of my arms wrapped around her.

All while trying not to focus on the tricky wording I used in my last profession.

Willingly.

Chapter Fifteen

TONI

WHEN I WAKE IN the morning, I'm not surprised to find I'm alone. Disappointed but not surprised.

Once Dare felt he'd taken care of me properly, he helped me out of the tub, dried me off, and even went so far as to slather me with moisturizer. Which just happened to be the same brand and scent I typically use. I probably should be annoyed or at least slightly creeped out, but I'm not. I actually think it's kind of funny. Which means I'm likely losing it.

I was annoyed, however, that he refused to fuck me in the tub, no matter how much I taunted and teased him. I recognize that he was probably right, that my body had been put through enough for one session, but that didn't stop me from pouting for a few moments. But then he kissed the pout off me and slapped my ass, which perked me right up. Again, I must be losing it.

Eventually, he helped me into bed and then went about tidying up a few things before joining me. I figured my brain would start to overthink and second-guess and question anything and everything I could possibly nitpick, but to my great surprise, nothing happened. It was all quiet—peaceful, even.

So, I let him gather me against him and hold onto me tightly from behind. I allowed myself to sink back into him and enjoy the feel of his face pressed into my hair, his exhalations hot along my ear and neck. He murmured quiet words of affirmation and reassurance, and I fell asleep, seemingly at peace with the situation.

I'm not exactly at peace now, in the light of day, but there are still remnants of a fire burning inside me at the thought of him, like actual butterflies in my chest.

I grimace. *Butterflies. Ugh.*

I have no idea how we jumped from bickering coworkers to this fire-injected inferno of near obsession, but here we are.

Or at least, here I am.

I suppose if we're having a contest on who could possibly be more obsessed, he would win, given how long he's been keeping tabs on me and the lengths he has gone to pursue me up to this point.

But I may not be too far behind him, and I worry this inferno will burn out, and I'll be destroyed. Or I'll destroy him because that's what I do—destroy people.

I let people get close to me, and then I shut off and close down; push them away until they finally get sick of my shit and stop trying to make it work. And that's not just with men; that's with everyone.

It's one of those situations where you're fully aware of your many toxic personality traits, but you can't be bothered to even attempt to fix them. Because that's just who you are at this point in your life, and fuck everyone who can't accept the bad with the good.

That's what's funny about this situation with Dare. All he has known of me is my complete toxicity, and he doesn't give a fuck. He's gone the complete opposite way, for that matter; he fucking loves it. How or why is beyond me, but I can't say I'm going to overthink that too much at this point.

I'm definitely still a bit freaked out about what I found in the upstairs bedroom of his house. Mostly, I'm shocked he put in so much effort to keep tabs on me for so long. Not that it detracts from the fact he has been stalking me for quite some time, but it is surprising he didn't grow bored with the situation and either make a move on me or move on from me.

See, here we have a toxic personality rationalizing the chronic stalking of a possible madman and turning it into a positive thing. Because surely that means he must think a great deal of me.

I wasn't surprised to find Tony and Matt back in the kitchen when I finally ventured downstairs. They both glance at me and then smirk at each other. I roll my eyes at them. "Don't start."

"I haven't the foggiest idea what you're talking about," Matt says with an incredulous look.

I snort, shaking my head at him. "I can see it in your eyes, Chief."

He laughs, then shrugs at me. "Oh, well, maybe you should've worn a turtleneck and a face mask."

I glare at him, well aware of the many marks on my body that are entirely obvious to anyone with eyes. I contemplated attempting to cover them up with clothing and makeup, but I hate turtlenecks, and really, I didn't see any point considering both of these men know Dare and that he was here last night. If they didn't know he was coming, they certainly would've caught on pretty quickly, considering what I can only imagine were incredibly loud noises coming from my bedroom.

I can't help but blush a bit, feeling the heat in my cheeks as Tony smirks at me knowingly. So, I glare at him, too. "Shut the fuck up,

Tony."

He grins at me, walking over with one hand in the air as he says, "Shut it, Nettie. High five."

I pretend to return his high five, then punch him in the gut instead.

Matt laughs loudly, so I shoot him a glare and say, "Do you want some too, buddy?"

"No, I'm good."

I bypass him and go over to the counter where there's food still out from the late breakfast one of them must've cooked. I add some of this and that onto a plate and then take a seat at the bar to feed my face.

We sit in companionable silence for long moments as I consume the food in front of me and internally ponder my life up to this point. Not that there's a whole lot of deep pondering going on, considering my mind keeps drifting off to the events of last night.

I can't help but shiver at the memory, and I'm not sure how many times Tony says my name before I snap to attention and glance over.

"What do you want, Tony?"

He gives me a hard look and walks up beside me to knock on the counter a few times as he says, "You're gonna need to put your dirty thoughts aside for now, Nettie. I'm not one for sharing much information with you, but there are a few points we need to go over because Matt and I have an errand we need to run later today, so someone else will be staying with you. We're going to move you again, temporarily, because we never have anyone outside of us three on this property."

I stand and pick up my plate, then walk over to the sink to rinse it off before I put it in the dishwasher. Then I turn to him, my arms coming up to cross over my chest as I say, "Okay, so do I need to pack a bag, or is this more like a day trip?"

"It should just be a day trip, but you may want to bring a few things to entertain yourself with. I don't like doing this, but we all agree that the errand that needs tending to can't go to anyone else but us. We could split up, but that's just not feasible. It's our only option to trust someone else with you."

I shrug my shoulders, puffing a bit. "I have read enough thrillers to know not to do anything stupid to open myself up to an outside threat. You could just leave me here if you think no one knows about the property."

"We did consider that, and we don't feel you're going to do anything intentionally that would draw attention to yourself. But this place is too far out, so on the off-chance someone did find you here, even with the cameras and alarms, it would take way too long to get somebody here to help you. And the camera trail is also lacking, unlike in the city, where there are so many more angles from where you can look."

I squint at him, my mouth twisting as I say, "Cameras?" I see Matt wince from the corner of my eye, so I turn to him as I ask again, "What do you mean cameras?"

Matt's the one to respond this time. "Dare definitely takes security seriously."

I look between the two of them, anger boiling up inside me, and I wish I was still holding a knife so I could stab one of them with it. I suppose I shouldn't be surprised, given the hard evidence I found in what must be his other house. If he didn't take all those pictures himself, he had plenty of eyes on me, and he must've known my every move.

At the very least, it seems he probably had cameras in my apartment and basically any place that I stayed in for more than a day. I guess that's something I'll have to take up with him next time I see him.

That fucker.

I open my mouth to say something, then close it, unable to get coherent words out through the anger burning inside me. I step toward Matt, and he immediately steps back, obviously not wanting to tangle with me today.

My gaze snaps over to Tony, who's watching me blankly, and I get the feeling he'd like me to make a move so he can shackle me up again. So, I don't give him the satisfaction and simply leave the room without another word.

Chapter Sixteen

TONI

THE TWO MEN THEY have assigned to me at the midtown apartment seem nice enough. Still, they're not exactly excellent conversationalists, so I soon give up attempting to have any form of camaraderie with them.

I poke around a bit on social media, then giggle over a few spicy TikToks before I finally settle on a book to read. I'm about a third of the way through when a thud comes from the living room. I put my e-reader down, quickly moving off the bed I've been sprawled on, and step out of the doorway to peek down the hallway.

I'm stunned to see the sprawled legs of a body on the floor at the end of the hallway and press myself against the wall of my bedroom, taking deep breaths in the hopes my heartbeat will stop galloping in my chest. My mind is racing, coming up with and discarding scenario after scenario of what these people might want and what lengths they may go to in order to get it.

For a moment, I consider trying to find a place in my room to hide, but that seems impossible, given I'm not exactly the right size to be hidden. I could possibly make it to the fire escape at the end of the hall, but it seems unlikely I would get very far, considering whoever is out there is obviously here on a mission to do harm.

I take a deep breath, accepting there's no use in me standing around here wondering what's going on. So, I stuff my feet into some shoes and grab my jacket off the end of my bed before exiting my bedroom and walk quietly down the hallway. I hesitate for a moment when I reach the sprawled legs that belong to one of the men hired to stay with me. I give him a glance, noting the rise and fall of his chest, indicating he's alive, then I school my features and continue into the room with a blank look on my face, my head held high.

They can fuck off.

Surprisingly, there are four of them, and they stand there, stonily staring at me. I wait a bit, thinking that maybe someone will say something, and when they don't, I bite out, "May I help you?"

The taller one motions to the one on his left, and I can only assume it's an indication that he should come and get me. Again, I contemplate fighting back, but I understand the likelihood of me escaping four people is pretty slim, so I put my hands up in surrender and say, "I'll go with you willingly. There's no need to use force."

The man who was coming toward me glances back at the taller man questioningly, and he must've given some kind of agreement because he continues walking over to me, reaching out as if to grab me by my neck. I jerk away from him and snap, "Don't touch me."

Again, he doesn't say anything, just glances over at the tall guy who finally says, "We're gonna need your phone."

I nod briefly in acknowledgment, handing my phone over and then motioning toward the door, saying, "By all means, proceed."

The two other men immediately head toward the door, and the

man still beside me indicates that I should go ahead of him while he and the tall guy follow behind. As we head down the hallway, I try not to think how ominous the click of the door feels as it closes behind me.

They lead me outside and around the corner into a wide alleyway where a limo is waiting. I hesitate, shocked to find a black stretch and not the van of the white windowless variety. The taller man grunts at me, giving me a little shove in the direction of the open door, so I get in. *And* I'm alone.

I sit there for a few minutes, then attempt to open the doors and windows, but they don't budge. The partition is up, and the windows are blacked out, so I just sit there in silence, twiddling my thumbs, and thanking my lucky stars that I'm not in the trunk...again.

We drive around for a while, then I feel the limo come to a stop. To say I'm astounded when the car door pops open and a blonde woman gets in beside me is an understatement. The door closes, and she turns to face me, her cool gaze scanning me all the way from the top of my head to the tips of my toes before looking me in the face.

Then it's like watching a flower bloom as her previously cool features suddenly transform into a beaming smile. It almost takes my breath away as she exclaims, "Antoinette, what a pleasure to finally meet you!"

I cock my head at her in confusion, frowning as I ask, "What?"

I know this isn't the most eloquent response, but it's all I can come up with, given how strange it is that I finally get kidnapped by someone other than Dare and it turns out to be this sunny blonde woman who's happy to meet me.

It doesn't feel right.

Then again, this is just as fucked up as every other fucked up thing that has happened over the last few weeks, so I guess it's par for the course.

She laughs, and it is this little musical number that almost has me smiling in response. I squash it down and slide myself as far away from her as I possibly can because, for all I know, she's going to stab me in the eyeball.

She raises both of her hands as if in surrender and says, "Relax, Antoinette. I mean you no harm."

I glare at her. "And who are you?"

She smiles again, putting a hand out to me. "My name is Lilith. I've waited quite a long time to meet you."

Tentatively, I reach out and take her hand in mine. It's soft and warm, her grip firm but not punishing. "Well, Lilith. It's nice that you know who I am, but obviously, I have no fucking idea who you are."

She tsks, her lips twisting a little, seemingly in annoyance. "I should've known he wouldn't mention me to you yet. He's such a shithead."

I raise my brows at her and ask, "Shithead?"

"Yes, Darius, the shithead. Apparently, he's incapable of following instructions. I'm going to have to teach him a lesson."

I huff and cross my arms over my chest in annoyance. "Oh, that's a fucking understatement. That guy doesn't tell me shit."

Lilith's frown deepens as she replies, "I'm sure he has his reasons, none of which any of us will find out until it's over. I just wish he'd told you about a few of the people you might come across so you would know when to be scared."

"Should I be scared now?"

She shrugs. "Perhaps." Then she beams at me again as she continues, "But no need to be scared today. This is just a brief conversation to force Darius in the direction we want him to go."

I shake my head and snort in response. "I don't see how any conversation with me would get him to do anything that he doesn't want to do."

"Oh, well, I guess this will be a good test, then."

She's still smiling at me like she's waiting for something. I look her over, getting even more annoyed with her tendency to speak in riddles. "What do you want, Lilith?"

"Call me Lils."

I roll my eyes, then say through gritted teeth, "What do you want, *Lils*?"

She turns serious, her eyes narrowing. "I want you to know that I'm not part of the endgame."

My glare deepens, my hands flailing about in frustration as I practically shriek, "Endgame? I don't even know what fucking game you are talking about!"

She nods, reaching a hand out and squeezing my leg as she replies, "I know." She looks at me thoughtfully, then continues, "Think of it as the ends of being—eventually, you have to let go of who you were and accept who you are."

I start to reply, but she's already exiting the car, the door slamming behind her with an air of finality. Then the car is moving, and I can only assume I'm being returned to where I was taken.

This "it's really fucked up" theme of my life lately is getting old. All this talk about endgames and identity riddles, coming from this blonde woman I've never met before is enough to make my head spin. For all I know, she wants to warm me up just so she can tie me up and lock me in a basement somewhere.

If Dare shows up in the middle of the night thinking we're going to have another sexy rendezvous, he's going to have a rude awakening. No parts of me will be opening up to him until he opens up with all the words he has been withholding. I can't keep wallowing around here blindly, never having a fucking clue what's going on. The next time somebody takes me, for all I know, they're going to slice and dice me and then have sex with my dead body.

I need explanations, I need answers, and I need to know the plan.

Abruptly, the car jerks to a stop, and some commotion erupts outside. I don't move, just listen intently as I try to figure out what's happening. I push buttons to see if everything is still locked down, but nothing happens. Loud popping sounds ring throughout the air, then silence, and my mind races as I attempt to make my body and brain work together.

My heart pounds in my chest, and I'm actively working on inhaling through my nose and exhaling out of my mouth. Suddenly, the door is yanked open, but this time, it's not Lilith, nor is it one of the men who took me previously.

This man smiles at me coldly and motions with his hand for me to come toward him. I repeatedly shake my head and press myself back against the door, my hand shaking the door handle again to no avail.

The sinister smile grows as he says, "Either you come willingly, or I drag you out."

I can tell he means what he says. The emptiness in his eyes, the glimmer of excitement that ignites with his words makes it evident. I give him a small nod, putting my hands up as I slide across the seat, hoping he'll let me get out of my own accord. A hope that's quickly extinguished as he grabs me by the back of the neck, yanking my hair as he drags me from the car. I trip over my own feet and almost fall over on the pavement, but his grip on my neck and hair tightens, keeping me upright.

My first instinct is to fight, so I thrash and kick, punching out blindly as I open my mouth to scream my head off. I'm quickly yanked around, and a sharp slap across my cheek snaps me out of my frenzy.

I stand there, frozen, my chest heaving and my scalp burning from where the man yanked viciously on my hair. My cheek is on fire, and I swallow down the panic that's blooming in my chest. I have to grit my teeth against the renewed urge to scream, so I stand up straight and try to shrug off the man's grip.

He loosens his fingers in my hair and stares me straight in the face as he asks, "Are you gonna give me any more trouble?"

I shake my head, but I don't say anything as I attempt to relax my stance. He lets go of me then motions for me to follow him, the rest of his crew falling in around us as he leads me into a narrow alleyway and then into a small parking lot between buildings. There's a van here, a windowless white one, and I can't stop the shivers that run down my spine at the thought of having to get in it.

Sure enough, he leads me directly to the van, where he opens the back doors, motioning for me to get in as he bites out, "Get in."

Everything inside me is screaming not to do it, and my heart is pounding with the panic churning inside me.

Every instinct inside tells me to take my chances with flight.

But I know it won't work. There's nowhere to run. Nowhere to hide.

So, I take a deep breath.

And get in the van.

Chapter Seventeen

Dare

I suppose I shouldn't have been surprised that someone would make a move, knowing we had our pants down.

I rarely use men I don't have a long history with, and this is just another example of why having to take Tony and Matt off Antoinette's detail was not my first choice. That's why the first time the subs missed check-in, I immediately went to COMs, and when there was no response there, I brought up the video feed.

Sure enough, I see the two incompetent fuckers lying on the floor, and I can't help but hope they're dead. Knowing time is of the essence, I immediately message Tony and Matt the appropriate code and call my associate to bring up the local video feeds and forward them to me.

My stomach is in knots, and I'm sweating as I make my way to our warehouse rendezvous point. I'm unfocused, and in my rush, I manage to miss my turn twice. I curse in frustration, my trembling hands slick on the steering wheel as I whip the car around and speed off in the correct direction of my destination. My mind races, and I have to force myself to stop thinking about worst-case scenarios, of Toni beaten and broken, of her gone forever.

I pull into the parking lot of the warehouse, my car screeching to a halt by the back doors, and I practically fall out of the vehicle in my haste to get inside and begin our search for her. Or what remains of her.

My stomach turns at the thought, and I vomit all over the pavement, the retching and coughing painfully purging these ends-of-being scenarios from my psyche. I stand there, hunched over and breathing hard, snot running from my nose, spittle dripping from my mouth, and I can't stop the maniacal bark of laughter that breaks free from my chest. Then the sickness eases, and I'm left with a deep, burning rage. My blood boils in my veins, and the beast reverberates in my chest.

They're all fucking dead.

Tony and Matt are already there when I finally manage to make it inside, and I see how furious they are. We knew this was likely to happen at some point; however, we were counting on it not happening just yet. Luckily, we have a plan in place for basically every possible scenario, so this just means we must move them up and adjust accordingly.

Recognizing my obvious conflict of interest, Tony is already prepared for me to defer to him on how to proceed. That's one thing about having people close to you who you trust implicitly. At any moment, complete control can be given to any one of us with the understanding that it's business as usual. With us, we have no ego, no arrogance attempting to lead us away from the mission at hand. It's just pure trust.

I try not to think about the fact there's the possibility that Antoinette is dead. My gut twists further, the reality leaving a bitter taste in my mouth.

I twist my neck sharply, giving it a crack as I try to shake off that darkness, and I level my gaze on Tony as I ask, "What do we know?"

Tony links his tablet to the screen on the wall as he explains, "They must've been sitting on her all day and somehow managed to figure out the timing of the check-ins because they made a move right at the top of the rotation. It wasn't difficult for them to get in, and it looks like they caught both guys completely off guard, considering they didn't just kill them."

I give him a dark look and mutter, "Doesn't mean they're going to stay alive."

Tony gives me a look, rolling his eyes as he ignores my comment and continues, "Surprisingly, Antoinette took it all in stride. She appears to be pretty calm and collected, given a crew of complete strangers popped in and knocked around her security without so much as a blink."

"She didn't put up a fight?" I can't help but snort, shaking my head in exasperation.

Tony shakes his head, "Not at all. It looks to me like she just gave him a bit of sass but then went along with whatever they were saying to her. She balks at one point, and I can't even imagine what that was all about."

Now, Matt laughs. "That sounds like Toni. She's just as crazy as the rest of us."

"I just hope she keeps her crazy in check long enough to not get herself killed. Have you been able to pinpoint her location?"

Tony winces then replies, "Sort of. I'm not sure where she is, but I know who took her."

I frown, huffing in annoyance, "Tell me."

He winces again as he mutters, "Lilith."

My eyes widen, my fists clenching at my sides as red-hot fury envelops me, and I grit out, "Are you sure?"

"Of course, I'm sure," he says, giving me an insulted glare. He pauses and looks away for a moment before continuing, "But that's where the trail ends."

I wave my hands at him impatiently. "For fuck's sake, Tony. Just fucking tell me."

He glances at Matt, then turns back to me. "I managed to contact Lilith, who confirmed she did take her, but also that she was returned to the apartment not long after."

I move to grab the tablet nearest to me to check the recent video feed, but Tony stops me. "She never made it back to the apartment, Dare. Someone else got to her along the way."

My blood runs cold. "What are you saying, Tony?" The look on his face tells me everything I need to know, and the rage and fear explode inside me. I bellow in fury, grabbing the closest object and throwing it across the room. "Fuck!"

Tony and Matt sit back silently and allow me my moment of destruction, then stand there while I attempt to catch my breath. Finally, Tony speaks, "You good?"

I nod. "Do you think Lilith is playing us?"

Tony shakes his head. "No way. The tantrum she had when she realized what happened was way worse than yours. She went ballistic—like, I had to hold on the line for ten minutes while she lit up the place. It was pretty epic."

I frown. "And then what did she say?"

"She said to give her an hour." He glances at his watch. "That was fifty-four minutes ago."

"Give her an hour to do what?" I practically shout.

Tony shrugs. "She did not elaborate, but from the way I heard her bellowing orders as she went to end our call, I have a feeling it is somewhere along the lines scorched earth."

My eyes widen. "Really?"

He nods, and I relax a bit at the idea that Lilith may also have the capacity to become completely unhinged when pushed into a corner. Given her connections to the deep underworld, it's likely she'll be able to locate Toni relatively quickly, or at least quicker than we can.

Tony's personal phone vibrates, and I give him a questioning look. "You gave her your number?"

He shakes his head. "No, I did not."

I grab the phone, accepting the unknown incoming call, and Lilith's voice barks out, "Come to the location I sent you." Then she hangs up without further explanation.

I check the messages and locations on Tony's phone but come up empty. "What the fuck is she talking about?"

Matt speaks up, "Check your phone, Dare."

I do as he says, then glare at my phone, as a message from an unknown number appears on my screen. *Now, she's just fucking showing off.*

I look between Matt and Tony, the unasked question floating in the air until Matt speaks up. "Well, let's go fuck around and find out."

When we arrive at the warehouse, the two men outside immediately lead us through a maze.

I'm on edge as I walk into the unknown. I still have no fucking clue who this woman is, but I'm starting to think that she's more important than I originally thought. Worst-case scenario, this is all a set-up, they have Antoinette, and I'm walking into my own death trap. I don't fucking care, but Matt and Tony are antsy, practically gnashing to get to the bottom of it all. I'm glad to have them with me, but at the same time, I wish we had a bit more to fall back on than our typical fuck-around-and-find-out mantra.

I have no idea what the main purpose of this warehouse is, but from what I've seen so far, none of it's good. And shockingly, it smells like bleach. I can't say that I've been in many cold, dark warehouses that smelled like bleach. It's disturbing.

We enter an expansive room which seems to be in the far recesses of the building, and I see someone standing in the very center of the room.

The screaming hits my ears before my eyes land on the body, and it's enough to make the hair on the back of my neck stand up.

After a few hasty strides into the room, I see Lilith standing in front of a man who is strung up from the ceiling by his bound hands. Her back is to me, but I recognize her blonde hair and slight build, and a coldness trickles down my spine as I take in the scene.

She's wearing all white—or I assume it used to be white—and she's barefoot.

I turn and look behind me at Matt and Tony, who are staring wide-eyed at the scene before them. I step further into the room and clear my throat, so she'll know I'm there.

She turns to me, the frigid look on her face immediately blooming into one of excitement, and she smiles at me, her eyes alight as she gushes, "Oh, Darius! So happy you could join us!"

This fucking woman.

I almost don't have words to properly describe Lilith in all her glory, but I'm not entirely convinced that she's crazy. Or, at least, I can't think of any one mental condition to use as a label for how wonderfully deranged she comes off. And then, there's the other side of her which is so lovely that you basically feel like you have to be on guard all the time because you can see how she may stop in the middle of a congenial conversation and slit your throat.

She wouldn't hesitate, and she would smile the entire time.

I glance behind me again, and I see Tony checking her out. I roll my eyes at the glint of admiration on his face, and I wouldn't be surprised if he was getting a hard-on standing in the middle of a bloodbath. I snake a hand out and smack him. His gaze shifts to me, and I give him a look that says to cut his shit. He just shrugs at me and smirks.

I turn back to Lilith and ask, "Did you find out anything?"

She claps her bloody hands together, blood spattering a bit on what's left of the white on her shirt. "Oh, I have, indeed!"

She turns back to the man strung up from the ceiling, one of her hands gripping him by the jaw so hard her knuckles are white. She looks at me as she says, "This here is Jimmy. Jimmy didn't have as much to say as the one before him, but he did have more to say than the two before that."

I can't help but raise my eyebrows at her. "Math isn't really my strong suit, Lilith, but that makes it sound like you've had at least four people in here."

She narrows her eyes a bit, then flits her gaze to the corner of the room and then back to me as she shrugs. I turn to look, and I'm surprised to see a whole pile of bodies there. I'm not sure how many at a glance, but definitely more than four.

I turn back to her, my hands settling on my hips as I say, "What the fuck, Lilith? You're going to need a backhoe to dig a hole big enough to dispose of this mess."

She gives me a small frown. "I don't think we own a backhoe, but not a bad idea."

She turns to the man sitting off in the corner, looking bored.

"Mickey, do we have a backhoe?"

He shakes his head, unfazed by her question. "That's a negative, Lils. Want me to get you one?"

She ponders the question for a moment before nodding. "Yes." She pauses, her brow furrowing in concentration as she continues, "And a farm. We can't have a backhoe purchase without anything to run it on, right?"

Mickey doesn't say anything, just reaches into his pocket and pulls out a flip phone. He pushes one button, then he puts it up to his ear, and after a moment, says, "Buy a farm. And a backhoe."

He doesn't wait for any kind of response, just flips the phone shut and puts it back into his pocket with a nod.

Lilith beams at him, then turns back to me. "So, would you like the good news, the bad news, or the super bad news?"

I grit my teeth, then spit out, "Just give me all the fucking news, Lilith."

"The bad news is I know who has her." She pauses for a moment in contemplation and then continues, "Well, that wasn't very clear. Let me start over."

She walks over to the pile of bodies and sticks out one of her bare feet and prods the leg of one with her bare toe. "This here is Abe. At first, Abe didn't have anything to say, but after a few twists and turns, he thought maybe he could come up with some stuff."

She stares down at the pile of bodies, appearing to zone out as she continues to speak. "One thing I thought to be odd during my inter-rogations is that I didn't recognize many of them. It's pretty difficult to get around this city without being recognizable in one way or another to me or any of my associates. So, I thought to myself, Lils, who in this giant fucking city would have balls big enough to bring in a ghost crew, right under your nose?"

She wheels around, her eyes meeting mine, and I see they're a little maniacal at this point. There's nothing cheerful about the smile on her face now, then her tongue comes out, swiping over her top teeth slowly before she continues, "But now, I'm ahead of myself. Before we get into what Abe told me, I have to explain one thing about The Dead. You see, we're going through a sort of organizational change right now."

I open my mouth to reply, but she holds her hand up and stops me. "Save your breath, Darius. Just let me get it out, and then you'll have your moment."

I give her a curt nod, and she turns back to the man hanging from the ceiling, walking over to him slowly. "We've had some trouble with upper management over the last few years, for many reasons, the first being someone's inability to see me standing at the top of the food chain."

Without warning, she hauls off and punches Jimmy in the kidney with enough force that he shouts in pain. I'm impressed by her aim and viciousness but refrain from commenting.

So, she continues, "The second reason is about some random jack-off who got himself killed a few months back. Some people took offense to it, and at first, I figured it must be due to a familial connection, but that turned out to not be the case which meant The Dead, as an organization, needed to be completely gutted."

She glances over at me, and her eyes twinkle as she says, "And that's when the heads started to roll. You know The Dead has a reputation of cold efficiency, and the same can be said for how we deal with our own."

She turns her attention back to Jimmy, a far-away look in her eyes. "But then, like all vermin, once they got wind that the fire was coming, they scattered into the sewers. I thought we managed to get most of them under control, either by elimination or intimidation, but it appears there are a few who were not tended to as previously thought."

She nods her head toward the pile of dead bodies. "Some of those are responsible for the spread of false information. Some are responsible for those being dead not staying dead, and some are responsible for Antoinette being taken." She turns her gaze back to Jimmy, still hanging from the ceiling. "And then, there's Jimmy."

She steps closer to him, her eyes suddenly glittering with emotion as she looks up into his face. He stares down at her, his gaze unflinching and his jaw clenched but says nothing.

Lilith motions to Mickey, and he silently grabs a control box that lowers Jimmy down so his feet are on the floor and he's eye-to-eye with her. A soft look crosses her features, and I notice Mickey looks away, so I glance at Tony and Matt, who are staring intently at Lilith with curiosity. I turn back to her, and she leans into Jimmy, murmuring words into his ear, and he nods, then murmurs something in response.

She then grabs him by the head, twisting his neck as her mouth latches onto his carotid, and he screams as she sinks her teeth in viciously, shaking her head like a dog. Blood rains down on her, soaking her hair and her shoulder where she's pressed against him, but she doesn't let go. Lils just sinks her teeth in even more, continuing to shake her head like a rabid dog until he stops screaming and goes limp.

Then she steps back, spitting blood onto the floor as she cocks her head at the mess she made. Mickey tosses her a white towel that she uses to wipe the side of her face.

She turns back to us as if nothing at all just happened. "I know who has Antoinette. So, the bad news is the people who have her, and the bad, bad news is they know we each have a connection to her. And since they would like nothing more than to see the two of us brought to our knees, she's in deep shit."

I glance between Tony and Matt, and I'm sure we're all wondering the same thing. One thing you find in these underground organizations is an extremely short list of trustworthy people. Fuck, two-thirds of the people I trust in the world are standing with me.

Tony and Matt both give me a short nod, indicating they're going to follow my lead, so I return my focus to Lilith, whose attention is back on the man hanging lifeless from the ceiling. She looks a little sad, but just as quickly as the sadness appears, it vanishes.

So, I ask, "What's the good news?"

She straightens and turns to me, a smile back on her face as she says, "Oh, this fucker here told me about the tracker."

I frown. "Tracker?"

She shrugs at me. "At some point in time, these bad people managed to put a tracker in your girl."

I grit my teeth as rage burns inside me once again, and the beast rattles in my chest. My hands clench into fists, and I pace a few steps back and forth as I try to rein in my fury.

Then Lilith's voice cuts in, and I look up as she reaches into a bloody pocket of her pants and pulls out a phone. She presses the screen a few times, and then hands it to me, saying, "Do you know they have an app for everything nowadays."

It's not really a question, and I stare at the screen and the little green light that's blinking on it. I run a hand over my face in relief, then hand the phone over to Matt, who exits the room without comment.

"So, am I going in guns blazing, or do I need a specific approach?"

She looks at me thoughtfully. "No guns. Given where they're keeping her, you're better off doing it as quietly and methodically as possible. I highly doubt anyone important is there now. You can try to wait it out and see if they show up. But since it's likely she's been left in the care of some truly disgusting men, I don't suggest you wait at all. Go in there, eliminate all of them. That's the message you want to send."

I nod but can't help but respond. "I don't have a good feeling about any of this. How do I know you're not full of shit, and I'm about to follow a blinking green beacon to my death?"

It's not really a question either, and I don't expect an answer from her, but she answers anyway. Her eyes lock with mine, her face once again cold and deadly as she says, "You don't. But if nothing else, believe me when I say I would never hurt Toni. I don't give a flying fuck about you or your men; you all can fall off a fucking cliff and die for all I care. But not Toni."

I frown at her, then look at Tony, who's also frowning at her in confusion. I turn back to her and ask, "What the fuck do you care about Toni? You don't even know her."

She gives me a puzzled look, then puts her hands on her hips. "Oh, I didn't tell you?"

I snort, about ready to lose it. "Apparently not."

Once again, her winning smile is back, and she responds gleefully, "She's my sister."

What the fuck?

Chapter Eighteen

TONI

I COME BACK TO consciousness in stages.

First, only unintelligible words are being muttered, random laughter, and broken shouts.

Then, it's the smell. Acrid, bitter sickness and smoke incorporated with old blood.

Then light attempts to prick through, and my eyelids flutter as I try to raise my head from the uncomfortable position of my chin against my chest.

I remember the van. I remember making a move to get into the van, but then everything becomes blurry. I have no idea how long I was knocked out, but the jackhammering in my skull and the sticky crusty stuff on my face indicate that it's been a fair amount of time.

I flick my tongue out, licking at the gunk that settled into the corner of my mouth, and I'm relieved when I taste copper. There's no telling if these people have done anything to me while I was out, but upon a quick review of my person, it seems safe to assume I haven't been violated.

I manage to turn my head slightly and pry open an eyelid to see what's around me. I'm facing a wall, and the first thing I notice is the number of people surrounding me. Surely, having this many people standing guard over one woman who is very securely bound to a chair seems a bit overkill.

So, this means either they're worried I have exceptional abilities as an escape artist and assassin, or they're worried about who might be coming to find me.

Obviously, it must be the latter, which makes me snort to myself a bit, considering I have asked myself the same question repeatedly for what feels like ages now.

Who the fuck is that guy?

I snort again, annoyed with myself for failing to clarify this very important question before fucking him, but sometimes, that's just how things turn out.

I give a little start when I realize a dark-haired man is staring at me, and he nudges a bearded man beside him, motioning in my direction as he says something I can't make out. The bearded man turns his head to look at me, and the smile on his face sends shivers down my spine. I attempt to wiggle in the chair to confirm I'm truly stuck, which I most certainly am. No amateur rope skills this time around.

The two men move closer to me until they're standing directly in front of me, and one of them leans over close and says, "No point in pretending to be passed out. We can see you're awake."

Painfully, I lift my head and look at them but don't say anything. The bearded guy looks me up and down and sneers, "We don't usually get the pretty ones."

It takes all of my self-control not to gag at the implication of his words, and I have to force the anxiety and fear back down into my guts. I've always been a big believer in every person having a time to die, and when it's your time, there is nothing you can do to change it. It doesn't matter if you die of old age or illness, by accident or at the hands of another person—your time is your time. And that will have to be my mantra through this ordeal. If it's my time, then it's my time, and if nothing else, I'll be taking a piece of them with me.

A shout on the other side of the room draws my attention, and sure enough, all eyes are on me. I scan the various faces in hopes I'll find one that doesn't have the predatory gleam of someone just waiting their turn, but no such luck. Every last one of them is leering at me, and I may as well be naked in this chair, waiting for them to queue up.

I try to remind myself that I just have to live through it, regardless of what happens here, regardless of how it all ends. If I can make it through to the other side with a heartbeat and brain function; that's a win.

So, scared as fuck, I steal my spine, raise my chin and laugh. I laugh, and I laugh, and I laugh. Because it all really is preposterous. A few weeks ago, I was a bratty accountant who got off on torturing a coworker, and now, here I am, tied to a chair, potentially waiting to be gang raped and murdered for reasons that are beyond me.

Eventually, I run out of breath, and I attempt to get control of myself. I sit there, letting the occasional giggle escape, and now they're all staring at me like I'm certifiably insane, which seems to be pretty accurate, given how life is going.

I'm feeling just a tad unhinged. I'm 100% sure if given the opportunity, I'll chew out the throats of anyone that comes near me. The problem being chewing out throats takes time and strength, and there are far too many of them for me to get very far.

A door creaks open behind me, and I attempt to crane my head around so I can see, but it's too far away.

A voice barks out through the silence, "You all better keep your hands off the goods 'til the order comes down, then she's free game."

I make a face, unable to stop the flinch that goes through my body at his words. Footsteps echo in the bare room, letting me know this asshole is approaching behind me, and when he comes into view, I recognize him as one of the men who took me off the street. Not the one who grabbed me and spoke to me, but the one who opened the van doors, and I'm assuming throttled me when I didn't move fast enough.

He gives me a blank look and says, "You look like shit."

I guffaw, and my lip curls as I parrot in a completely childish tone, "You look like shit."

He scowls at me. "Don't you think it would be in your best interest to keep your fucking mouth shut?"

I level a bland stare at him and retort, "Seems to me I've got fuck all to lose at this point."

"True. And it's not like anything you say will sway us from taking you apart when the time comes."

My eyes widen, then I glare at him before saying, "And why is that? I feel like everyone is in on the joke here but me. Do I even fucking know you?"

He gives me a puzzled, disgusted look, his arms crossing over his chest as he eyes me suspiciously. "You really gonna try to play that one with me? You gonna act like you don't know what this is about?"

I jerk in my chair, my arms pulling on the restraints viciously as I shriek, "I'm not putting on a fucking act. I literally have no fucking idea what you're talking about! I keep asking questions, but everyone keeps putting me off, and now, here I am tied to a fucking chair with everyone around me assuming I know why!" I flail about in the chair a bit more, yanking my arms and legs until the chair starts sliding around beneath me. "I don't fucking know anything!"

He gives me a pitying look, and I can tell he's torn as he contemplates what I've said. Finally, he snaps his fingers, and a few moments later, a chair appears behind him. He sits down, leaning forward so he's resting his elbows on his knees, his eyes on my face. "Well, I'll happily tell you. I don't feel anybody should be tortured, raped, and murdered without knowing the reason why."

I'm panting from my little tantrum, so I gasp, "By all means."

He leans forward a little closer and opens his mouth to speak, but then a booming bang interrupts him, and his gaze shifts behind me to the door.

All hell breaks loose.

It's hard for me to gauge the size of this room from where I'm positioned, but when the screams start, they seem to go on endlessly. And the man who had been on the cusp of giving me all the answers I wanted didn't waste any time. He didn't attempt to defend anyone in the room, nor did he make any attempts to use me as a shield—instead, he just vanished.

I'm not sure if he managed to escape out a window or if there was a trap door or what happened. All I know is one minute, he was there, and the next, he was gone.

But the screaming.

The shrieks and yells get closer, people scurry around me, looking for a way out. Whatever way that one man left must not be an option for anyone else because they're all stuck. As the screeching nears, the leering men from earlier start to move in on me until I'm surrounded, closely packed in. Eventually, they move in too close and knock the chair over completely. People fall onto me, bang into me, and then someone kicks me.

The screaming reaches a crescendo and then starts to die down, and

I lay there on my side, my eyes squeezed tight, still bracing myself for more impact.

Then, just as suddenly as it started, everything is silent.

I'm not sure how long I lay there, eyes still squeezed shut, but eventually, there are footsteps and other commotion behind me. I open my eyes, turning my head in an attempt to see what's happening, but I can't see anything.

There is only muttering, people walking back and forth, and someone barking orders. Then I feel a strange sensation, like warmth sinking into parts of my body that is pressed against the cold concrete floor, and I jerk around, afraid to glance down.

But I can smell it.

The hot coppery metallic taste hangs in the air, and I know.

I gag as bile rises in my throat, and a strangled whimper escapes as I choke back the scream that's churning in my guts.

Then someone is behind me. They place hands on my shoulders and a familiar voice whispers reassurances as something soft settles over my eyes, blocking my sight. I struggle a bit, and then the voice gets close to my ear, and I realize who it is. "It's okay, Toni. We're here. You're safe."

Lilith.

I don't know how, and I don't know why, but she's here. And from the sound of it, she isn't alone.

Another set of hands grip me and Tony's voice also whispers reassurances, and they both work in tandem to remove the ropes from my arms and legs and then they're helping me to stand on my shaky legs.

I take a step, but my boots slip in the wet there, and again, I have to hold back a gag. I reach my hand up to remove the cloth covering my eyes, but Lilith's voice stops me. "No, no. Don't do that. You don't wanna see."

I nod slightly, allowing her and Tony to take my arms, and they lead me through what I can only assume is a maze of dead bodies. I freeze, my hand grabbing onto Tony's forearm as I choke out, "He got away."

Tony stills beside me, then his hand closes over mine, squeezing it as he asks, "Who got away, Toni?"

I shake my head, swallowing the lump in my throat. "I...I don't know who he was. He was talking to me when you guys showed up, and somehow, in the middle of it all, he vanished."

At first, he doesn't say anything, and I'm sure he's probably looking at Lilith and whoever else who might've heard me like I'm a total nut job.

So, I continue, "I mean it, Tony. He was there, and then he wasn't there. I don't know how he got out, but he got out."

Tony squeezes my hand again and says, "I believe you, Nettie. We'll find him."

I take a shaky breath and allow them to continue leading me through the room. After a few moments of slow going, we stop, and Tony leans closer to me and whispers, "I'm going to pick you up. It'll be easier."

He waits for me to nod in response and then picks me up and carries me through the room. I try one more time to raise my hand to remove the blindfold, and once again, I'm cautioned not to. "It's best if you leave it on for now. At least until we get you home."

He doesn't elaborate or try to explain his reasoning, but I have a feeling I know it's because they're both a mess, and they don't want me to see it. They're protecting me from the carnage.

I allow them to lead me out further until, finally, they're helping me settle into the back of the car. Squirming around, I can tell that I'm not sitting on normal leather seats, and I get a small amount of relief from this small detail.

I scoot into the middle seat, and Tony and Lilith get in, sandwiching me between them. I manage to swallow down the sob that remains stuck in my throat, but they both must notice my internal struggle because they each reach for one of my hands.

We sit like that in silence as the car pulls away from the curb.

Dare

To say that our rescue mission was a bloodbath would be a significant understatement.

I'm rather perturbed at the number of bodies that are laid out in that room by the time we're done. While some did attempt to defend themselves, the vast majority of them were just fodder, bodies to stand in the way.

It seems like we caught them off guard, so I can't for the life of me figure out why they would go through the trouble of taking Antoinette and then not take necessary precautions to keep her. She was surrounded by men who were unarmed and mostly inept at general hand-to-hand combat, so I can only assume they were all there for one purpose—to torture her.

After some debate, we finally decide to torch the building. We don't normally use fire as a means to dispose of bodies; however, in this particular case, there are too many to move without someone noticing. Matt is going to call our fire guy so I can get back to the house to tend to Antoinette.

I asked Lilith and Tony to get her out of there for me because I didn't want her to see the mess, not only in the room but also on any one of us. Relief flooded me when I saw she was safe and that she allowed them to cover her eyes and lead her from the massacre.

Lilith planned on getting her home and cleaned up. Then once I got back to the house, she was going to return here to see if any of the bodies are of any importance. She didn't believe they would be, but when Antoinette said someone seemingly important had gotten away, we figured it was best to double-check.

Finally, I walk through the door of my home, the clean-up taking far longer than I thought, and I immediately head down to the basement to dispose of my bloody clothes and take the first layer of blood off me.

I collapse heavily onto the bench in the locker room area, suddenly feeling exhausted. I'm completely overwhelmed by the deep sense of elation from knowing that she's okay. She had obviously been knocked around a bit but, for the most part, seems to be unhurt.

I'm sitting on the bench, my head resting in my hands, when there's a noise in the doorway. I glance up to see Antoinette standing there. Groaning, I shake my head at her as I say, "Go back to the bedroom, Antoinette. I'll be there shortly."

She doesn't say anything, just stares at me, her blue eyes filled with questions. I haven't looked in the mirror, but I can only assume that I look a fright. The blood that dried on my skin and in my hair and the stickiness as it soaked into my clothes and stuck to my skin. I did manage to at least wipe off part of my face and wash my hands, but that isn't really much considering we took out a lot of people using blades, which tends to create quite the mosaic of blood splatter.

She stands taller and pushes her chin out a bit, then walks toward me. I sit up straight but remain seated, and she stops in front of me and raises one hand to my face, her fingertips stroking along my cheek gently. I close my eyes, reveling in her touch, but then her hand is gone, replaced by a sharp sting of her palm as it makes contact with my cheek.

I flinch back, my hands shooting out to grab ahold of her wrists as she screams in my face, "You motherfucker!"

I barely manage to push her back and stand before she goes completely wild. She gets in a few good kicks, and I effectively dodge her knee to my balls as I attempt to restrain her with my body. I end up having to take her feet out from under her, falling to the ground with her in a heap, where we then grapple for domination. I finally pin her beneath me, using my full body weight to ensure she can only move her head.

The sting from where she scratched me, and the lump that formed when she punched me during our tussle radiates pain. I lean forward and scrape my teeth against her brow as I ask, "What the fuck, Antoinette?"

She bares her teeth at me in response as she shouts, "You should've told me!"

I sink further into her, my head leaning in so I can graze my nose along the side of her face, but I quickly pull back as she lashes out at me, managing to nip my ear pretty fiercely.

I'm at a loss for what I should say. There are so many things I want to tell her, so many things I likely need to tell her, but all of it gets stuck in my throat because it's just not the right time.

Obviously, she now has a good idea of the type of man I am, not that I'm ashamed—quite the contrary, actually. Maybe I've been too easy on her so far, and she missed the part where I'm a controlling, self-serving bastard. Maybe it's far past the time I showed her.

She struggles beneath me, and I glare down at her in annoyance. "Cut it out, Antoinette. Surely, we can speak civilly about this."

She barks out a humorless laugh. "There's nothing civil about you, Dare. You're an animal, a bloodthirsty, unrepentant fucking animal!"

I lean in closer to her. "That's right, my little minx. I'm a fucking animal. And you fucking love it, so don't try to pretend that you don't."

She thrashes beneath me in response, managing to break one leg free that she then uses to kick me, though not very effectively. All that move accomplishes is her spreading her legs even wider for me, and I rub the hard length of my cock against her pussy, groaning at the small moan that escapes her.

I rock my hips again, lowering my upper body as I say, "That's right, baby girl. You like that?"

She shakes her head, a contradiction to the quiet sobs that erupt from inside her. She pulls on her hands halfheartedly and whispers, "Let me go."

I laugh. "Never."

She glares at me again, then attempts to throw me off her as she shouts, "Let go of me! I hate you!"

I chuckle again. "You don't hate me." I rub my cock against her a few more times, then continue, "Your pussy tells me that you don't hate me at all."

Now, she's panting, her eyes squeezed shut, and I feel her hips moving as she pushes back against me. I move my upper body up and away from her and adjust my legs so that I'm fully between hers. The champagne-colored sleep set she's wearing is ruined, bloody smears soaked into the fine fabric in all the places that I've been pressed up against her.

For some reason, this pisses me off. I don't know why I had these grand ideas that Antoinette could be involved with me and remain unsullied, but I wanted to believe it.

And here we are, completely fucking sullied.

I let go of one of her arms to test how she'll react, and when she leaves it limply above her head, I release the other one and sit back so I'm kneeling between her spread legs.

I grasp the delicate fabric of her tank top in my hands, yanking it apart violently, and her hands jerk down to cover herself as she exclaims, "What the fuck are you doing?"

Leaning forward, I use both hands to yank on her sleep shorts until they rip apart and toss them aside as I look down at her. "Seems pretty obvious to me, baby girl. I'm going to fuck you."

She glares at me, then spits out, "Over my dead fucking body."

"Keep running your mouth, and that can be arranged." She gasps, but before she can say anything, I wrap my hand around her neck and cut off her air and her words. I move my other hand between her legs and groan in satisfaction at how wet her pussy is for me.

She may rage at me, she may throw a fit, but deep down, she wants me.

And she'll fucking have me.

Toni

I can't fucking breathe.

I'm flat on my back on a cold concrete floor with this beast of a man lording over me, one hand squeezing my neck and the other fucking my pussy.

I'm still beyond pissed off.

I grab onto the forearm of the hand that is choking me and pull against his hold. My nails dig into his skin, but he doesn't let up, just squeezes tighter as he says menacingly, "That's right, baby girl. You're going to take what I give you. You'll take it, and you'll love it."

I get my feet under me and attempt to throw him off, but all my movement does is push his fingers deeper into my cunt.

Then there's that deep chuckle, the one that sends pangs of arousal deep inside me, and I'm grateful he took my words to prevent me from begging him to fuck me.

Instead, I continue to struggle, though I'm not entirely sure if I'm struggling to get away or to get closer. I do fucking hate him. I hate how he keeps things from me, and I hate how he uses the excuse of protecting me to keep me in the dark. All he's accomplished by not giving me information is opening me up to more danger.

I'm practically seeing spots when he suddenly releases his grip on my neck. I suck in air, coughing and choking as I watch him quickly strip out of his shirt, and I gape at the amount of blood on his body. I glance down at myself and grimace at the dried blood streaked all over me, too.

Fury renewed, I yank one leg loose, and before he realizes what I'm doing, I kick out, hitting him in the chest and sending him sprawling. I scramble on the cold floor, unable to get my footing, and he's on me again before I get too far, but this time, I'm face down with my hands pinned underneath me, my naked ass in the air.

His low voice rumbles in my ear as he blankets my body with his. "Is that how you want it, minx? You want me to fuck you from behind like the animal I am?"

I shake my head in denial. "I don't want you at all."

He lets loose another deep chuckle against my ear, sending more shivers down my spine, then he grits out, "That's too fucking bad because you have me. You can't get out of it now. You're mine, and nothing you say or do will ever change that."

I squirm, but I know it's pointless, so I bite out, "I'm not yours. You can't force me to be with you."

He pauses, then remains silent for a moment, his weight still heavy on top of me, and for a moment, I think he may retreat, that he may give up and let me go.

Then he lets out a feral growl that vibrates through my body and says gruffly, "Oh, but I can. You think just because I've given you choices up to this point that I won't hesitate to force my will on you day in and day out for the rest of your life? I've told you before, baby girl. There's an easy way, and there's a hard way, and regardless of which path you choose, I'm at the fucking end of it."

"What are you gonna do? Are you gonna keep me in a collar? Am I going to follow you around like your little lapdog?"

He reaches a hand between us, undoes his pants, and shoves them down out of the way, and then the hard hot front of him presses against me. His rock-solid cock rubs against my throbbing pussy, and I bite my lip in an attempt to not respond, but I can't stop, and my hips press up, and I push my ass against him in invitation.

Then the deep chuckle is back against my ear, pulsing more arousal through me as he continues to slide his hard dick against my wet cunt, and he whispers, "That's right, baby girl. I didn't wait this long to get you to not keep you. I'll tie you to my bed to be used at my leisure. I'll chain you in my basement for safekeeping. I'll put a collar on you and parade you around on a leash. Whatever it takes to get you to understand that you are *mine*. So, it's the easy way or the hard way, and soon you'll have to make that choice."

He doesn't wait for me to reply, just pulls his hips back a bit as he lines himself up with my wet opening and then shoves inside.

My current position doesn't allow for much movement, so my struggling is futile. He reaches around and squeezes my throat again, yanking my torso so my front is pressed into the floor, my spine curved so my ass is pressed more firmly against him.

His other hand moves around the inside of my thigh, and he gives it a jerk, spreading my legs open so that his cock drives into me more fully. I choke around a gasp and squirm as I try to pull my hands out from under me, but the press of his body on top of me makes it impossible.

One of his hands snakes down under my hips, pulling me against him as he leans over me; then I feel the sting of his teeth on the back of my neck, and a sob bursts from within my chest at the deep sense of ownership that envelops me.

I'm torn. Torn between the yearning inside me that searches for fulfillment, for the soul that fits within the darkness of my own, and that same darkness that prevents me from ever truly being fulfilled. The shame, the anger, the infinite struggle of belonging everywhere while also belonging nowhere at all.

I push it out of my mind, shoving the anxiety and paranoia down, down into the darkness and focusing on the sensations enveloping me. There is no thinking, just feeling—his hand squeezes my neck, taking my breath, his arm pulls my hips back against him, his cock driving into my cunt with a punishing speed. His teeth, tongue, and lips devour my neck and my shoulder, the sound of his growls and his grunts, and his hot breath and saliva leaving wet trails on my skin.

I'm still wearing the silk robe that went with the sleep set he destroyed, but now, it's only covering my mid-back, and I feel it sliding around between the press of our bodies. I'm sure it will be soiled by the time he's finished with me, and I shut off my mind and allow myself to revel in the animalistic drive of him inside me.

His grip eases on my throat, and I drag in air. He adjusts his stance behind me, the arm that is curled around my hip shifting around until I feel his fingers on my clit. My sounds of arousal escalate, even as I attempt to suppress them, and then his lips move from my neck, right up to my ear. His voice is almost unrecognizable, a primal vibration that spikes my desire even more. "That's right, Antoinette. Take my cock. Beg for it."

Somehow, I manage to shake my head, even as I feel my body thrumming towards climax, but all that does is make him increase his efforts and his hips piston in a short staccato that matches the press of his fingers against my clit. Then his voice is once again in my ear, commanding, "You'll come on my cock. You'll come on my cock, screaming my fucking name."

I don't want to say it. I grind my teeth and squeeze my eyes shut as I shake my head in refusal. He lets go of my throat, and his hand moves to my hair, yanking my head back as he stops the rut of his cock inside of me and the movement of his fingers against my clit.

He groans against my ear, a long moan of pleasure as he says, "Open your eyes. You open your eyes and look at me as you take my cock."

I give another small shake of my head and squeeze my eyes tighter, but then his fingers pinch my clit and his cock presses into me so sharply I feel him at the very end of me, and my eyes pop open of their own volition.

My mouth gapes open on a moan, and he growls right in my face, his gaze boring into mine. "That's right; you're mine. You look into my eyes and know that you're mine."

Then he slams into me, short, hammering thrusts, and his fingers pinch and rub my clit in time with his cock moving inside my pussy.

His burning, golden gaze consumes me, and then his mouth is on mine, his lips, teeth, and tongue pulling his name from me as my orgasm rolls over me. My neck twists painfully, but I don't care. I'm completely consumed by him, completely undone by his cock in my cunt and his slick fingers still milking my release from my clit. His mouth draws out every begging word he previously commanded from me as his eyes seem to imprint themselves on my very soul.

He curses into my mouth, then grunts his own release, and I feel the corresponding pulse of his length inside me as he spurts his seed deep, and it's like I'm being branded from the inside.

He holds me upright for a few moments, continuing to pant into my mouth, even though his movements have stilled, and I'm a limp rag doll in his embrace. He eases me down onto my front, his lips leaving a hot trail along my cheek to my ear, where he nips at my earlobe and whispers words that I can't make sense of in my delirium.

Eventually, his lips move to my shoulder, and he slowly eases back from me as he pulls his cock from my body. The proof of his release trickles down my leg, and the only physical connection left is his hand on my hip. His harsh, panting breath sounds behind me and the cooling dampness of his saliva spreads all over my neck and shoulder, the side of my face, my lips, and my chin.

I attempt to keep my mind blank, to keep the darkness pushed down to fester in my guts where nothing can touch me, but I still feel its coldness. I hear its call.

I reach one hand back and grasp his hand where he's gripping my hip, but it's not enough. So, I release him and lower both hands in front of me to push myself up onto my hands and knees. I look around my surroundings, and I see his bloody clothes that he discarded when we first began our battle of wills. There's blood on the bench where he was sitting and my bloody clothing he had tossed aside after he ripped them from my body.

I choke down the gag and brace myself against the darkness that crowds me, away from his protective embrace. I crawl forward a bit and remove myself from him fully, then I slowly stand on my shaky legs.

It's as if I'm outside of myself as I turn to face him, where he's still on his knees on the ground before me. He pulls his boxer briefs up over his cock and zips his pants but doesn't fasten them, and he makes no move to stand up. He just kneels there with his hands resting on his thighs.

Those golden eyes bore into mine, and he gives a small shake of his head and barks, "Don't do this."

Now, I'm shaking my head, and I back up one small step and then another. I look him over from his bent knees to the dried blood on his hands, dotting his torso and his neck, the side of his face, in his hair—everywhere. I glance down at the front of myself and take in the bloody streaks all over my body.

I move my gaze back up at him, my eyes unable to avoid his as I choke out, "I can't."

He's still shaking his head, his words full of frustration that echo throughout the room as he barks, "Don't do this, baby girl. Don't do this. Don't run."

But I'm still backing away, still shaking my head, still repeating on a sigh, "I can't. I can't. I can't."

I feel the panic rise up inside me, and I feel the darkness pull me back to keep me hidden within the cool confines of its protection.

But I can't take my eyes off him or stop the echo as he shouts, "What do I have to do? What lengths do I have to go to get you to see me, to hear me, to accept that I'm yours just as you are mine?" He pauses and holds his hands in front of me, his eyes hard on mine as he continues, "I'm on my fucking knees before you, the blood of your enemies still drying on my hands, yet still you refuse to let me in. Tell me what the fuck I have to do."

I hesitate for a moment, and hot tears run down my face as I whisper, "Let me go."

And then I run.

Chapter Nineteen

DARE

I REMAIN KNEELING ON the cold floor for a long moment after she leaves.

My first inclination is to follow, to chase her down, and force her to submit to me. However, the more rational side of me understands that this would be a mistake, so I let her run from me.

I'm still kneeling there when the door opens, and I look up to see Tony walking toward me.

He stops a few feet from me, his hands on his hips as he asks, "Is that it, then?"

I glare at him. "Is what it?"

He glares back at me. "Are you gonna let her go?"

"What the fuck are you talking about?"

He shrugs. "Don't you know the old adage, if you love someone, let them go? Is that what you're gonna do?"

I scoff at him, rising to my feet and stripping the rest of my clothes off of me. "I think you know the answer to that."

He shrugs again. "I think I do, but with her, I'm never entirely sure. By the way you were in here sulking on your knees, it looked to me like you were just going to set her free."

I scowl at him, standing there completely bare-ass naked, covered in dried blood and other bodily fluids. "Not a fucking chance. You know I don't do that whole set-them-free bullshit. She can run if she chooses to, but that's only so I can hunt her down and shackle her to me for eternity."

He raises his brows at me. "Shackle, huh? Do you mean that figuratively or literally?"

I snort as I walk over to the shower, turning the water on and getting under the spray while the water is still cold. "Both."

He doesn't say anything for so long that I finally turn my head to look at him and see he's just standing there staring at me, so I ask, "Is there something else you want, Tony? Or are you going to just stand there and ogle me?"

"Don't flatter yourself. I'm just waiting to find out what's next. I also need to know if we're removing that tracking device from her or not?"

I nod. "Lilith said she's going to handle that. She's got some kind of plan that we'll discuss soon."

Tony's eyes light up at the mention of Lilith, and I can't help but shake my head and chuckle at his obvious interest in our deranged colleague. "You probably should stay away from her, man."

He looks at me like I'm crazy. "I don't know what you're talking about."

I roll my eyes. "Seriously? You get excited every time her name is mentioned. Your interest in her outside the job is blatantly obvious."

"Maybe I do, but it doesn't matter either way until our current situation has been resolved. You know I'll keep my head in the game."

I nod, remaining silent as I finish scrubbing the blood from my skin, washing it out of my hair. I turn the water off and grab a towel out of the cupboard to dry myself off while I walk over to a locker to grab some clothes. I put on sweatpants and a T-shirt, then grab some socks and trainers from the shelf.

When I turn around, Tony has made himself useful by collecting the bloody garments from the floor and putting them in a trash bag. He looks at me and says, "I called the cleanup crew to disinfect this room again."

I like how he says "again." Seems like every time I turn around, I'm having to wash some kind of blood and guts off me, and we're having to call in the cleanup crew to remove all traces of possible evidence. It costs a fucking fortune, but it's entirely worth it, given I can rest assured that I don't have to worry about anyone ever finding traces of anything here.

I nod my head in thanks, then the two of us walk out of the room and head toward the back stairs that lead to the main living area. I pause at the bottom while Tony detours quickly to the incinerator, where he tosses the plastic bag in along with his gloves. He swings the door shut and locks it, then presses the button, waiting for it to kick on before returning, and we continue up the stairs.

Matt is waiting for us in the living room, sitting on the couch with a mineral water in his hand, and I have to laugh at the fact he's not drinking something much stronger. I stop at the bar and grab myself my own bottle, flashing it at Tony, who nods to grab him one as well. I take the two bottles over to the living area, handing Tony his drink, and we all sit there together, sipping our mineral water in silence for a few minutes before Matt breaks the silence. "So, what's the plan, Dare?"

I can feel my muscles finally starting to loosen. I'm kind of tense, and it's time to shake it off. I sink back into the couch as I reply, "Lilith has a few things that she needs to handle and then we'll step in from there."

Matt nods, staring at his bottled beverage quizzically before raising his eyes to mine and asking, "Toni okay?"

I give him a short nod. "She will be."

Tony gives me an incredulous look that does not get past Matt, so he continues, "Are you sure? She went running through here a little while ago and did not seem okay at all."

I can't think of a response for a few moments. I want nothing more than to abandon these assholes and go in search of her, to take care of her and support her as she struggles with her demons. I want to go to her and explain everything, to word vomit every tiny bit of information from the last few months in the hopes she'll understand the deep level of my commitment to her. But I know I can't, and so I sit here, feeling like an asshole, even though I know my hands are tied and my lips sealed.

Matt interrupts my thoughts, "I get that you have to wait for the right time to come clean. But don't you worry that it may already be too late?"

I swallow the lump that is suddenly blocking my words and just give a small nod, my eyes focused on a spot on the wall over Matt's shoulder. Finally, I manage to clear my throat, but my words are gruff and quiet as I respond, "That's a distinct possibility." I gulp down air again, then clear my throat once more before I continue, "I have to accept there's no definitive right path here. Regardless of my choices and when the right time may present itself, the idea that I can force information on her in the hopes of salvaging a future we might have is futile. She has to know first, or at the very least, she has to ask the right questions in the correct order. Otherwise, I can't. I can't be the one to destroy her."

They're both staring at me, a resigned look of sadness on their faces. We all know that there's a distinct possibility that when we reach the end, there may be no happily ever after for us. There may be no us.

And with that thought on all our minds, we sit back and wait to find out what's next.

Toni

I run from the basement as if the hounds of hell themselves are nipping at my heels.

I'm truly panicked, tripping over myself several times and scrambling on my hands and knees on the cold floor as I attempt to flee blindly. I know I'm acting like a mad woman, but my intensely visceral response to Dare's claiming is nonsensical and irrational—unexplainable. And for someone whose first instinct is always to fight back, my deep desire to run is unavoidable.

Eventually, I make it back to my bedroom. Dare's bedroom. I stand in the middle of the room, panting and sobbing, and I feel the tears on my cheeks, snot running down my face as I continue to break down, to crumble in on myself.

I shake my head, attempting to wrench free from the darkness buried there, but its grip doesn't loosen. I scurry to the bathroom, tossing the ruined robe on the floor as I flip on the shower and get in, letting the cold water run over me. I press my hands against the shower wall, resting my forehead against the cool tiles as the warming water runs down my back.

I can't even pinpoint exactly what I'm sobbing over, but it feels like agony, as if the horrific pain that has settled in my bones is attempting to eradicate itself out my esophagus. And then I'm gagging, retching, and dry heaving, watching as the blood from my skin swirls once and then disappears down the drain.

I choke on my own saliva, and then I laugh and cry, my complete madness echoing off the shower walls as I feel the rush of Dare's seed slide out of my pussy onto my inner thigh. I laugh again, grabbing the removable shower head and raising it to my face, washing away the tears and snot. I move it down my body, along my neck and over my breasts and stomach, and then between my legs, like I'm trying to wash Dare from my body.

I put the shower head back in the bracket, then grab a washcloth and soap and proceed to lather my entire body, scrubbing every inch once, twice, three times until I'm satisfied I'm clean. At least, on the outside.

I sit down on the floor of the shower, curling in around myself, leaning against the wall. I'm no longer crying or sobbing, no longer cursing or laughing. I just sit there and silently watch the water circling and circling the drain.

The water has just started to turn cold when there's movement in the room, and at first, I can't move my head to acknowledge that someone is there. A tiny part of me wonders if it's Darius coming to collect me, but I scoff at the thought.

He wouldn't. I rejected him. He'll let me go.

At that thought, a tiny whimper escapes, but I manage to keep the agony down and then I start when I feel a hand on my shoulder, and I look up. I'm surprised to see Lilith looking down at me, her blue eyes soft with understanding as she shuts the water off then reaches for the towel and wraps it around my shoulders.

She takes both my hands in hers and helps me to my feet, then leads me out of the shower, placing me in the chair that I sat in previously when Darius was taking care of me. I have to suppress another whimper at the thought, and I shake my head a bit to center myself back to the present. Lilith is speaking to me, but it takes me a moment to focus on her words before I understand what she's saying. "It'll be okay, Toni."

I shake my head, pulling the towel more firmly around me, as I reply, "But will it?"

She gives me a small smile, nodding her head in response. "Things will be as they should be."

I snort, feeling a tiny bit better at the sentiment, even if I feel she's entirely full of shit. She comes over with a smaller towel and starts to dry my hair with it. Surprisingly, I let her. I don't know that I've ever allowed another woman to care for me. But for some reason, with her, it doesn't make me feel uncomfortable, my normal urge to escape alluding me.

She finishes drying my hair and then takes the length of it and twists it up, clipping it out of the way. She pulls one side of the towel away, unwinding it from my body and placing it in front of me, where I clutch it against me. I hear her putting lotion in her hands, and I shiver again as she applies it to my back, and I can't stop the small laugh that escapes at how strange this entire scenario is.

She laughs behind me. "I bet when you met me you never thought anything like this would be going on."

I giggle again, the tension inside me easing a bit more as I respond, "That's for fucking sure. I'm still not convinced you're not here to slit my throat, but let's just put some lotion on me first."

Lilith laughs outright, and there's something strangely familiar about the sound of her laughter, how melodic it is. I don't think too much of it, though, and lean forward a bit, allowing myself to relax as we sit in comfortable silence for a few moments. When she's done applying lotion to the parts she can reach, she hands the bottle to me, then turns away to clean up the trail I left when I first came into the bathroom.

I massage lotion into the skin on my torso and arms, taking comfort from the familiar smell as I watch her pick up my destroyed robe and stuff it into the trash can. She pulls the bag out, tying a knot in it, and then leaves the room. I can only assume she's throwing it out into the hallway because the door opens and shuts, and then she's back, washing her hands in the sink.

She walks back out into the bedroom, and the sound of drawers opening and closing echoes to where I'm sat, and then she's in front of me, handing me a clean pajama set. Once I'm dressed, I follow her back out into the bedroom, and she motions for me to sit in the chair in front of the vanity, and so I do. I can tell she has something to say, so finally, I blurt out, "Just spit it out, Lilith."

She gives a short nod, then replies, "Somehow, you have a tracker somewhere on your person, and we need to remove it."

My eyes widen, and I stare at her as I ask, "What do you mean a tracker?"

She gives me a serious look, "Someone implanted a chip that tracks your movements. I have no idea how it got there, and I have no idea how long it's been there, but we need to take it out."

I frown, but I don't speak, so she continues, "And we really should replace it with one of our own."

I scoff at her, shaking my head. "Not a fucking chance."

"Antoinette, the only reason we found you this time was because I was fortunate enough to pick up a person who knew you were being tracked and also someone who happened to have the means to locate you. The odds of this happening again are very slim. I don't know who put the tracker in you. I don't know when they did it, but I can fucking tell you right now that I'm incredibly grateful that they did because, without it, you would likely be dead right now."

I sigh, annoyed that she's right, and seeing my change in demeanor, she adds, "The likelihood that these people will try to take you again is one hundred percent. Sure, we can watch you every second of every day, but at some point, they will get you. The only way we'll be able to find you is if we have a tracker on you. It 's for your safety that we do this."

I take a deep breath, resigned to the truth behind her words, and I nod. "Fine."

She nods in return, then goes over to the door and opens it, ushering somebody else inside. I turn to see who it is, and I'm relieved it's Matt who walks in, carrying a case with him and I'm certain I don't want to see its contents. Lilith motions for me to stand, so I do, moving around toward the center of the room where Matt is waiting for me.

She doesn't say anything else, just stands before me, raises her arms out, and moves her legs apart so she's spread eagle, and I do the same. Matt waves the wand thing all over my body until, eventually, it beeps. I continue to stand there uselessly. Finally, Lilith drops her arms, and I huff out a sigh as I follow suit.

Matt scrambles around in his case for something, and then he's standing behind me. "I'm going to need you to remove your shirt, Toni."

I look at Lilith, who nods at me reassuringly, then comes closer to help me out of my shirt. I hold it in front of me while Lilith takes my right arm and pulls it across my body so the skin and muscle of my back is pulled taunt. I feel something wet and cold slide over where my back meets my armpit, and I smell alcohol in the air. I feel a pinch and then a slice of pain that causes me to hiss, and I squeeze my eyes shut as Lilith steps in closer to me.

Matt works quickly to remove the foreign body, and before I know it, he has me stitched and bandaged, and he and Lilith are discussing where to place the new tracking device. Apparently, they need to put it in a spot that will be hidden enough that it won't be noticeable at first glance.

Matt pauses, then says, "Maybe we should put it in the same spot. Seal it up with some super glue and hope no one notices?"

Lilith shrugs and replies, "If they know to look for it at all, they'll just get her to remove it. I don't think it really matters at this point. At least, in this game."

"Well, I guess there's no point in poking a new hole in her, then. Sorry, Toni. I'll be as quick as possible."

I give a brief nod, turning my head away as I feel him snip and remove the stitch that's no longer necessary. There's some pinching and a twinge of pain as he inserts a new tracker, and I can't decide which is a stranger feeling: knowing that someone has been tracking me for an unknown amount of time or the knowledge that I'm agreeing to people I know tracking me for an indefinite period of time. I suppose the sense of violation stems more from the former; however, this doesn't make the latter feel any less vulnerable.

Matt finishes up, and Lilith helps me put my top to rights before reaching her hand out expectantly to Matt. He hands her a little bag which I assume has my old tracker in it, and she looks at it for a moment before looking between the two of us and saying, "It may be time to play a little game."

I frown, unsure of what she means by "little game", but I'm certain that it can't be good.

All I know is I'm tired.

They must sense my unease as they both shift gears simultaneously, and Lilith motions me over toward the bed as Matt says, "I'll let you get some rest, Toni. I'm down the hall if you need me."

I don't say anything as I walk over to the bed and sit down. Lilith is standing in front of me, and she reaches a hand out to caress the side of my head. I give her a weird look and a dry laugh. "Am I your pet now? Got me microchipped and everything?"

She laughs. "It would appear so, though I can assure you, we will only use the tracker in cases of emergency."

I frown, confusion lacing my words as I ask, "How come they didn't follow their tracker here? Or are you all worried they're going to show up at some point?"

Lilith shakes her head. "No, we were able to turn it off from the device we got off one of their men. We've been monitoring it constantly to make sure no one tried to turn it back on to pinpoint your current location. Matt assures me it would take at least three minutes of active status for that to happen. So, so far, we're good."

I tilt my head, grimacing slightly, then lie down, pulling the blankets up over my head. Her footsteps get quieter and further away as she leaves the room, the door clicking behind her, and I lie there in the darkness, contemplating my entire existence up to this point.

Eventually, I fall asleep, and I can't be sure, but I think at some point, Darius joined me, the press of his hard body against my back, the comfort of his breath in my hair.

And my sleep was dreamless.

Dare

When Lilith first came to me with the little game she wanted to play, I was dead set against it. Her idea that we plant the old tracker back on Toni and have her lure the enemy on a merry chase is far from ideal.

Sure, we have a tracker on her at this point, but all it would take is one glance from them to see that their site has been tampered with. The first thing they're going to do is dig that thing out, and if that's the case, she'll be lost.

I figure it would be better to have one of us guys be the decoy, but Lilith is correct in the theory that we're a little too conspicuous to pull that off. I hate that she's right.

So, after agreeing to her tentative plan, I make my way up to my bedroom, quietly opening the door and walking toward the bed. I can make out her body under the blankets, but she pulled the blanket up over her head, so I pull them back on one side so I can get in beside her. She's restless for a moment, and worried I might wake her, I tense up, not knowing how she might react to having me in her space so soon. When she stops her fidgeting, I gently pull her into my body, wrapping myself around her from behind, and she instantly settles, sinking back into me with a sigh.

I rest there with her for a few hours, just until the dawn lights the sky, then I gently extricate myself from the bed so I can shower. With a new pair of slacks and a navy blue button-up on, I exit the bathroom, and she's still sound asleep, so I leave the bedroom and make my way down to the kitchen, finding Matt, Tony, and Lilith already there.

I walk up to Lilith, and she meets my gaze head-on, her blue eyes staring into mine blankly as I snake a hand out and wrap it around her throat. She doesn't flinch or wince, just stares into my face as I squeeze tight enough to take her air away.

"What you did was reckless." She gives a curt nod, and I continue, "Your arrogance, your inability to see the big picture, and your refusal to believe that anyone other than you might know what's best—you almost got my girl killed."

I squeeze my hand even tighter, cutting off her air entirely, yet still, she just stares up at me, unflinching. I lean in close, so close my nose brushes against hers, as I whisper, "I should slit your fucking throat."

I straighten, my hand relaxing enough for her to take in some air, but I don't let go, and she doesn't attempt to fight me. My blood is boiling in my veins, and my hand around her neck twitches with the urge to choke the life out of her, but I'm held back by that tiny little voice in my head, reminding me that we still need her.

Finally, Tony's hand squeezes my wrist, and his voice is in my ear, telling me to stand down, so I release her.

She bends over at the waist, coughing and wheezing as she gets her breath, but then she stands and looks at me as she says, "If anything had happened to her, I would've slit my own throat."

We stare at each other for a few long moments, but finally, I give her a nod and step away. I don't bother dancing around the other elephant in the room and ask, "So, who's going to tell her?"

Lilith raises a hand, saying, "I will. I think she will be more receptive to a plan that comes from me."

I can't really argue with that. I give her a long look, asking, "You know what they want, don't you?"

She nods a little too enthusiastically for my liking. "I have a good idea, but I'm not 100% certain."

All three of them are staring at me, waiting for me to say something, so I ask, "And you think that'll end it?"

She gives a little head bop in response, and I can see the looks of resignation on Matt and Tony's faces.

I smile. "Well, I guess it's time I get myself caught."

Chapter Twenty

DARE

IT TAKES A SIGNIFICANT amount of maneuvering to get these asshats to take the bait.

And this was after giving them so many opportunities to pick me up that I was beginning to get concerned that an unrelated enemy would notice the giant target on my back and take a shot at me. And that's their first mistake—not just eliminating me when they had the opening.

That's what I'll never understand about the so-called bad guys in books and movies. If they just went in quick and efficient, without asking any questions, it would save them a lot of trouble and a lot of blood. Although, I suppose, sometimes blood is the point.

My biggest concern is Toni's reaction when she finds out what we've done. Sure, we told her one story and then went a completely different direction without telling her. I have a feeling she's going to be a bit *disgruntled*. Maybe even outright angry, but even if it turns out badly for me, I won't regret it.

Trading my life for hers is a small sacrifice, given the depth of my affection for her. And honestly, it was all starting to feel a little uncomfortable for me, anyway.

Matt and Tony are also not at all impressed, and they've had no issue vocalizing their malcontent with the "dumbest fucking plan ever put together by two possibly suicidal maniacs." Their words.

It seems the only two people involved in this plan, who have any confidence in it working out with me not being dead, are Lilith and me. Of course, Lilith may feel that way just because she actually doesn't give a fuck if I live or die. Can't say I blame her.

Caring about another person to the point where I don't want them to be hurt by anyone, especially by me, is a foreign concept. Sure, I care about Tony and Matt, but not wanting to hurt their feelings isn't something I've ever had to worry about. I've spent my entire life being content with only ever having to worry about myself, and since romantic attachments were never a priority, it didn't really take a lot of energy to check that I was happy.

Then I met that sassy little bitch.

Honestly, even when I first met her, I wasn't overly concerned with possibly developing an attachment to her. At one point, I even considered attempting to lure her in just to fuck her into silence, but then I accepted that it was far more enjoyable for me to keep my pants zipped and let her continue bothering me. Of course, the more she bothered me, the more I wanted her to bother me.

And then, one thing led to another, and we ended up even more entangled than ever, so deeply entrenched in our own individual stories we almost lost sight of the bigger picture.

Then jackoff happened, and that's when the whole world changed.

When that incident first occurred, I wanted nothing more than to completely overwhelm her with my presence, railroad her into accepting me, regardless of how much she pushed back. If it hadn't been for Tony and Matt talking some sense into me, I probably would've tried it. They were right, though. If I had attempted then what I had done now, it all would've ended terribly.

And not just because she would've run for the hills but also because the target on her back would've been more significant than it is now. That's one thing you learn in the criminal world: having any type of collateral damage against you is detrimental to the possible outcome of the mission. That's one reason none of us has ever really gotten any emotional attachments. That and the fact that we're just not emotional people. It takes a certain kind of person to be able to withstand the constant pressure of having a target on your back.

Even now, knowing that she may be safer without me, I would do it. I'll spend the rest of my life dreaming about her as long as I know she's okay, but now with her connection to Lilith, she's double damned.

There's not a chance in hell Lilith will let it go without the end-of-days bloodbath she's been longing for. She's a fucking blood-thirsty hellcat, and she won't rest until she feels retribution has been met for the great wrongs done to her. Sometimes, it feels like they should be more worried about her than me, but I guess only time will tell on that one.

And here I sit, tied to a chair in another damp, rank warehouse. Definitely not my favorite position to be in, but hopefully, this will be worth it.

They've already said they'll make a deal with me. A deal where Toni can go about her merry way, free and clear, but in order to do so, I have to put on a show where Toni basically thinks that I've been working for the other people the entire time.

In theory, I can pull this off pretty easily. One very tiny, small, itty-bitty part of me, though, worries that she'll see through it. And by she'll see through it, I really mean that I'll do some fucking stupid shit thing and blow my own cover. That's the most likely.

Because I have zero self-control around her.

And, because there's this part of me that's beside myself that I've never confessed how I feel. And I don't know if I can go on keeping that information inside because I know if something goes wrong, it will be lights out for me.

I did explain to these assholes that for this to work, she would have to be allowed to bring Tony and Matt with her. I made the two of them swear up and down on everything they ever held dear to them in their entire life that they would not do anything more than accompany her and worry about her. Regardless of what happened and what position they felt I was in; they needed to take her and turn their back on me.

Neither one of them are fucking happy about it, but I got them to promise that they would focus on the mission, and I was not the mission. Lilith, on the other hand, had made no promises and basically rolled her eyes at me and said she'd see me later.

That bitch is crazy. I think that's my final decision on that matter.

When the crew of assholes finally show back up to tell me it's showtime, I'm more than a little over the situation. They remind me of the plan for the millionth time, and then I sit there while they give me a rundown of all the terrible things that are gonna happen to me if I fuck up.

I give the big talker a bland look and say, "Yeah, I fucking get it already."

He glowers at me and snarls, "I guess we'll fucking see, won't we?"

It's all I can do not to roll my eyes. These fucking yahoos really believe they managed to catch me unaware and take me as their prisoner. It's laughable. They want to own me, for Toni and my people to believe I have given up my life as Darius, and to resume my deep dive into the underground as the beast. Because if I can make it believable to Toni, then she'll turn her back on me, and since my crew has orders to stay with her indefinitely—regardless of my own circumstances—they'll have no choice but to abandon me to whatever fate awaits me.

We move to a different part of the warehouse, one that's almost clean but still smells like shit. We're kind of milling around, and I have to tell them ten times that they may want to at least pretend to be relaxed, or else this isn't going to work. They shuffle around some so they're not crowding me, and I lean against the desk as nonchalantly as possible. It's pretty difficult, considering I'm kind of pissed off.

I'd like nothing more than to slash the throats of every fucking last one of these idiots. Don't get me wrong, they'd have maybe a half dozen bullets in me before I got to the third one, but just the satisfaction of knowing I got a few of them would be pretty good for me.

I hear her before I see her. She's running her mouth spectacularly, just like I figured she would be. At least, this part I'll enjoy.

They step further into the room until she's only a few feet from me, and that's when she notices me hanging out on the side of the bad guys.

Her eyes widen, and she tilts her head at me in confusion as she whispers, "Dare?"

I raise my brows at her and smirk. "Do you ever shut your fucking mouth?"

She looks taken aback, then her eyes narrow as she puts her hands on her hips. "Excuse the fuck out of me, but what the hell is going on here?"

I can practically feel the men that surround me holding their breath, and it takes some serious effort on my part for me not to turn the entire thing into a bloodbath. And I would if I thought for one second the person in charge was in the room, but from the information Lilith gave me, I'm pretty sure that's not true.

I manage to keep my features blank as I give her the once-over, and she's full-on glaring at me when my eyes finally track back up to her face. I give her the most arrogant look I can possibly muster as I ask, "Whatever do you mean?"

She stomps her foot petulantly, her cheeks getting flushed as her anger rises. "Quit fucking around, Darius, and tell me whats going on. What are you doing here?"

I snort, my arms crossing over my chest as I respond, "Just wrapping up some loose ends."

Her eyes narrow even more, and she steps closer to me, so I put up a hand to stop her. "No need to come closer, Toni. You won't be staying long."

She raises her brows at me this time, her arms crossing over her chest defensively. "Oh, really? I'm no longer welcome near you? Am I hearing that correctly?"

"That sums it up nicely, thank you."

She grinds her teeth, then spits out, "I'm going to need a better explanation than that, Clark."

I roll my eyes. "I don't want you anymore. This has been a fun little interlude, but it's over."

"Over?"

"Yes, Toni. It's over. You're no longer useful to me, and I have other responsibilities that require my attention."

I can see the anger in her eyes, but also the pain, and it twists my guts painfully. I manage to hold her gaze without flinching, and eventually, she looks away, then down on the ground. So, I figure this is a good time to turn the asshole switch up and deal a solid death blow, painful and choking as it may be.

I rest my hands on the desk and lean forward, smirking at her as I say, "And a bit of advice for the road. Make sure you act a bit more responsibly than you have previously. I won't be there to save your ass next time you get yourself roofied."

She gasps, flinching as my words settle around her, but she doesn't say anything. She just continues to stare at the floor.

Then she takes a deep breath in and raises her eyes to mine, and all I see is the rage burning in those blue depths.

And here we go.

Toni

I have no idea what the fuck is going on, but all I'm getting from this situation is fucked-up vibes.

Matt got a call and then said we had to report to this warehouse out in the middle of bloody nowhere, and I have to say, I'm entirely fucking sick of warehouses and people getting calls and having to run to do their bidding.

And after all the fuckery that has gone on over the last few weeks, now I'm standing in this shithole listening to Darius fucking Hughes run his mouth like he's the goddamn kingpin.

Like fuck.

I don't say too much as he gives me his official asshole speech, but I can see Matt and Tony are tense beside me, their hands fisting at their sides and their jaws clenched. But, otherwise, I don't see any great surprise on their faces, so I can't help but feel a bit suspicious.

I glance over at Tony, lifting my chin at him as I ask, "You know anything about this?"

He raises a brow at me and shrugs. "Not likely."

I nod, then turn my attention to Matt, who's already shaking his head at me. "You know we're with you, Toni."

I turn my focus back on Dare and see he's still leaning back on the desk like an arrogant fucking jackass. I take a hard look into his eyes, normally full of fire, only to find them dull and cold, and I deflate a bit. "So that's it, then? We're done? You won't be going out of your way to protect me anymore? Is that what you're saying?"

He nods and spits out, "That's exactly what I'm saying. Why am I having to fucking repeat myself?"

"I just want to make sure I'm hearing all of your douchery clearly, you insufferable fucking prick."

He gives me an ugly look, his face twisting as venom pours from his lips, "Get the fuck out of here, and stay away from me or you'll be sorry."

"Believe me, Dare. I'm already sorry," I growl, then I spin around and take a step away from him, but my feet feel like lead, and I'm incapable of a hasty escape. I barely manage to keep the sob in my throat, and I'm sure my shoulders are drooped, so I attempt to square them and take a deep breath.

Then I hear it, words whispered so quietly I almost miss them.

"I love you."

I stop in my tracks, slowly turning around and tilting my head at him, my eyes narrowing as fury builds in my guts and chest. I scan the room, my gaze scanning over the strangers scattered around Dare in a broken horseshoe pattern. At first glance, I assumed they were with Dare, but now, something doesn't feel right. They all look cagey, obviously armed and on guard, like they're waiting for something big to happen.

That motherfucker.

"*No!*" I bellow as I attempt to charge him, but strong arms hold me back. I kick, punch, and fight against them as I shout, "Fuck you, Darius! Fuck you and your lies and fuck all your bullshit declarations and promises! You don't get to give those words to me, and I'll be damned if I give you anything while you're making me leave. Fuck you!"

He gives me a pained look, his lips pressing together as he grinds his teeth in frustration. He gives Tony a pointed glare, then spits out, "Get her the fuck out of here."

Tony tries to tighten his grip on me, but I crack him in the face with my elbow, and he falls back, releasing me. Matt attempts to secure his hold on me next, his hands grappling on my arms as I whirl around, kicking him in the side. His grip on me loosens, and I yank out of his grasp and then I'm sprinting toward Darius, whose pained expression deepens as I leap onto him, wrapping myself around him.

He catches me, pulling me tight against him, and I bask in the strength of his body, the heat and smell of him. I squeeze my arms and legs as tightly as I can, soaking up everything in the few moments I have left with him.

"Don't do this," I'm whispering now, my lips pressed against his ear, my arms locked around his neck, and my pounding heart thumping erratically in my chest. "Please, don't do this. Whatever it is, we can fix it."

His arms tighten around me, and he presses his face into my neck, inhaling deeply as he whispers, "I have no choice, baby girl." He leans his head back to look at me, pressing his forehead against mine so he can stare into my eyes as he whispers, "It will always be you."

This can't be happening. There must be something we can do, or there must be someone who can fix this. There must be some way for this nightmare to be over, to pause it, to change it.

I shake my head, sobbing, "No. No. No. No. No." It's the only word I can get out, and I can't stop the tears from falling freely as I clutch at him, trying to keep him close to me. "No. No. No. No. No."

I feel him gesture behind me, then strong hands are on me, yanking me away as Dare pulls my arms from around his neck and then my legs from around his waist. He makes sure Tony and Matt have a secure hold of me before releasing me and stepping back.

He doesn't look at me, the resigned expression on his face sending chills down my spine as the broken horseshoe closes ranks around him, but I can't look away. Even when I can only catch tiny glimpses of him in the middle of the swarm, I still don't look away.

One of the men pulls his gun out, raising it up and smashing it down across Dare's face, once, twice, knocking him to the ground, and then a gunshot breaks through the chaos, and once again, I'm screaming, kicking, punching, and biting to get back to him.

Tony and Matt hold me tighter, taking my blows as they come without flinching, refusing to turn back, unable to ignore the order to get me out of there. To protect *me*. To save *me*.

They carry me out of the warehouse and down the block to a waiting van. They maneuver me into the back, Matt sitting behind me to keep me in a submission hold.

I vaguely make out his whispering in my ear, and I hear the pain in his voice as he tries to tell me everything will be all right.

But it won't be all right.

And I'm still screaming as darkness surrounds me.

Chapter Twenty-One

TONI

Six months ago...

I'm unsure why I keep agreeing to go out with this jackoff. I know I tend to be a glutton for punishment; however, this form of punishment extends beyond acceptable norms, even for me. I feel like I'm holding it together well enough, laughing in the right places, staring intently in the right places, but a part of me only sees how hollow it is. And another part of me keeps getting this odd twinge of unease, like there's just something about the look in his eye that twists my guts.

I agree to one last drink, but after that, I'm out of here, and he's definitely going on the block list since he seems to be the type who doesn't understand when you're just not interested.

I excuse myself to go to the restroom so I can freshen up a bit and suck down some city water from the tap. I know that's gross, but desperate times call for desperate measures, and I don't have time to circle back to the bar.

When I get back to our table, our drinks are already there, and he looks as pleased with himself as ever. I figure it's time to just get this over with. So, I sit right down and throw that drink back like it's going out of style, then stand up and attempt to excuse myself. Of course, he can't just let me leave, nope. He's got to pretend to be all gentlemanly and walk me out to my car.

I wish I hadn't parked at the rear of the building, so we could go out the front door, but it's too late for that now. I stand and feel a little woozy, so I brace myself against the table and shake my head a bit to clear it. He takes my arm as we head out toward the back entrance, and that twist of unease deepens, so I attempt to stop and turn around, but he's right there, herding me toward the exit. I try to say something, but my tongue is heavy in my mouth, and I frown as I attempt to concentrate on the words that are jumbled up in my throat.

The next thing I know, cold air hits my face, I take a deep breath in, and it works to clear the fog a little. He grabs onto my arms, his fingers digging in a bit painfully, and I straighten my spine, then shove his hands off me. "Don't touch me."

He laughs, and the menacing undertone is not lost on me, so I glance up at him. A shiver runs down my spine as he snarls, "I'll fucking touch you all I want."

My stomach drops as my eyes widen, and I gasp in outrage, furious at myself for not being more careful, while also recognizing that it's a little too fucking late for that now. I step closer to him and open my mouth to tell him to go fuck himself when a squeal of tires turns into the parking lot, and that's when I know I'm fucked.

The black SUV screeches to a stop beside us, and jackoff turns to me and says, "Get in, Toni."

I balk and take a few steps back, but he's right there behind me, shoving me towards the vehicle as the door opens, and then I'm sprawled inside. I attempt to struggle, but my limbs feel heavy. I try to scream, but my mouth is dry, and before I know it, he gets in beside me, slamming the door shut as I feel the vehicle take off.

I've watched a lot of crime shows, and I've read way too many dark romances and suspenseful thrillers. To say this is dire is a significant understatement, and even my blurry mind acknowledges the full extent of the deep shit I'm in.

I go to sit up, and that's when I realize that my wrists have been zip-tied.

Fuck, I didn't even feel him do that.

I try to lift them, but I can only move about an inch before they fall from the heaviness of them. Somebody's talking, but I can't quite make out the words, and it's only the implication of their tone that makes their intent clear.

I'm not sure what drug they gave me, but for the moment, I'm weightless, and it makes me consider what very limited options I have at this point. I'm deeply inclined to fight but given I don't seem to have any control over my body or my words, it doesn't really seem possible.

But, every once in a while, I get this weird zap, almost like the spark plugs of my nervous system are attempting to ignite, like they're attempting to call the light in time to jolt me back to now, but then it's gone. So, all I can think is that at some point, the heavy-weighted feeling is going to dissipate, and the full force of that spark is going to jump through me, reigniting me into being.

It reminds me of those instances where people play dead, waiting for the perfect opportunity to retaliate or escape. It's far easier to separate yourself from the now when things become blurry and disconnected, to save up the rage and malcontent for a moment where it's most useful instead of wasting it on the questions that weave in and out of consciousness.

Have I been in this vehicle for five minutes, five hours, or five days?

Will I ever really know? Are we even moving? Has the world stopped? Have I stopped, or is this just what death feels like? Is this death, my bodily death, or merely the death of the mind which has fragmented in order to let me escape into the void? Will we survive? Do we care?

Even when you allow yourself to squeeze down between the cracks of your psyche into that dark realm where nothing can touch you, there's the odd kaleidoscope of rage and pain cloaked in shame. With nowhere to direct it, this aching shame turns inward, wreaking a scarring path of destruction on your mind until you end up so pushed down into the pitch black that you can no longer see beyond it. It is limitless, endless, depthless.

But there's still that spark, that excruciatingly agonizing spark that insists you move beyond the hurt, agony, and shame you're suffering. The sharp spark that commands you to open your fucking eyes and do literally whatever you have to do to overcome this and walk away from it.

They say the majority of people who are drugged tend to remain complacent and accommodating, but there's a small percentage of people who eventually turn. Where all that complacency finally builds up and twists in the guts to the point where it bubbles and boils over into complete mania, where no amount of drugs will assuage the raging bloodlust that takes over. And then, you burst through the first obstacle of your befuddled and broken mind and manage to acknowledge the effect of man-made weapons.

That's when the blood starts to flow.

I don't know if I 've ever previously considered whether or not I was a murderous person. Does it really matter if it's self-defense or revenge? Murder is murder, right? Even the most docile animals in the wild will lash out viciously if they have to defend their own.

I suppose that's how, in the blink of an eye, I went from being limp and incoherent in the back of an SUV to unleashing all the pent-up rage that had been festering inside me for an unknown amount of time.

At first, it's like a faulty fuse, and I finally understand the words they're using equate to a conversation about them getting rid of me. And not get rid of me as in killing me, no; death would be a blessing considering they're discussing the shipping option—humans for sale.

I've heard rumors about skin trade in the past, but until it's in your face as your possible future, it's hard to even fathom the horror of it all. I have no idea how long I've been here. All I know is that the pain is real and as long as there's pain, that means I'm still alive, and as long as I'm still alive, I can attempt to fight back.

It was the searing pain that truly woke me up. I had been lying like a limp rag on what appears to be a mattress on the floor, listening to unknown voices discuss that their time with me is almost up and it's time to get rid of me. The van is coming. I need to be prepared to be transferred for sale.

I can still feel the drugs coursing through my veins, and even those words don't do much to bring me back to reality, the searing pain between my shoulder blades has all those sparks igniting at once, and it was only due to these men's idiocy that they miss the growl that's brewing inside me. They all pal around for a bit, but eventually, they start to wander off, one by one, until finally, only one person remains.

I open my eyes and look up at him. It's not jackoff; it's some person I've never seen before except for within the inky darkness of my memory. He smiles at me, leering at my naked form as he says, "Did you wake up for one last go?"

If I had any emotion left, I would cringe, but there's no time for that now. I attempt to smile at him, but the pain in my face prevents it, and I can only assume they must've knocked me around at some point. So,

I raise my upper body off the mattress, bring my legs up so I can spread them wide in invitation.

The fact he doesn't find my behavior shocking is a pretty good indication as to how the last bit of time must've gone. I try not to think about it, pushing it back down past the pain and focusing on my present self.

He drops down between my spread legs and unbuckles his belt, opening his pants and pulling out his cock. He strokes himself a few times and spits on his hand to lube himself up before grabbing my hips and jerking me closer to him as he shoves inside of me.

I don't allow myself to recoil; instead, I reach up and pull him down closer to me, wrapping my legs around his hips and locking them to keep him there. He chuckles in my ear, hot breath and spittle coating my skin, and I manage to push back my sense of self and shove back the shame trying to sink me down deep into the darkness.

I tighten my legs around him, then pull my arms tighter, bringing him closer until I'm clinging to him. I turn my face into his neck, my arms tightening further to lock him into place as I latch on, sinking my teeth into the skin over his carotid like the rabid fucking animal I am. He screams in my ear, and my eardrum thrums in pain, but I don't let up.

I hold tight with my grip, my legs banded around him, and my arms holding his head down so I can gnash at his neck with my teeth. I adjust my bite on his skin, sinking in deeper and being rewarded with a gush of blood that washes over me. It's in my mouth and up my nose. I squeeze my eyes shut in order to push back the darkness that dances before me.

I don't know how long I lie there with his limp body on top of me before I finally loosen my grip, spitting blood as I push him away from me. I roll painfully over onto my stomach and retch over the side of the mattress, blood and bile splattering everywhere. Rolling back onto my side, too exhausted to even attempt to wipe the blood and vomit off me, I catch my breath.

A tapping noise in the distance catches my attention, and I slowly push myself up onto my knees and for the first time, take a look at the eerily dark room they've been keeping me in. I don't waste any time taking a tour. I just scour the area for any kind of weapon. All I find is a four-inch utility knife someone left behind when they'd finished cutting up an apple.

Perfect.

Footsteps move down the hall, so I scurry back to the mattress, pushing the dead guy off onto the floor and then lie down so I'm partly on my front with the knife hidden beneath me. I focus on controlling my breathing, keeping my eyes closed, so I can focus on the sound of the person coming into the room.

He curses, his footsteps becoming hurried as he sees the mess I made of myself and the mattress. "What the fuck did you do, Curtis?"

I hold back my snort of disgust, remaining motionless even as I want to jump up and watch the look of surprise on his face as he bleeds out. I know how all of this will pan out if I don't take all the precautions I possibly can, the biggest and most important being the element of surprise.

I wait for him to inch closer, my eyes closed and unflinching as I feel the mattress sink down under his weight, feel the weight of his hands settling on either side of me as he leans closer, likely to see if I'm still breathing or not. He tenses as he catches sight of Curtis, and he curses again as he eases off the mattress to go check on his friend. "What the fuck happened to you, Curt?"

I take a beat after he moves away from me before I open my eyes and see him kneeling down on the floor with his back to me. I quickly and carefully ease myself off the bed, creeping closer to him as he assesses the damage on *Curt's* neck. There is no way this knife is sharp enough to slit his throat in one shot, so I'm stuck with no super-efficient way to get the job done. I try to hold in my huff of indignation.

I sneak up behind him until I'm standing so close I'm surprised he can't feel the heat from my body on his back. I click my tongue to get his attention, and when he starts to turn around, I grab him by the hair and twist his neck around as I stab downward with the knife as hard as I can, sinking it into his neck. He attempts to stand, and I push him forward on his front, crawling onto his back and twisting the knife with as much strength as I can muster. He thrashes beneath me, and I yank the knife out, then stab him again, this time in the throat, and the vibrations from the knife hitting bone reverberates up my arm.

Tightening my grip on the knife, I yank it back and slam it into him repeatedly until he stops moving, and I'm leaning over him, fighting to breathe. I roll off him onto my back, the bloody knife still gripped in my hand as I pant, and I have to coach myself not to vomit again.

More footsteps sound. I sit up, glancing around to see if there's a quick escape. Or clothes. Seeing neither, I decide playing dead again likely won't work, so I hurry across the room to stand against the wall by the open door. I force myself to breathe normally as I wait, the footsteps coming closer, and I try to make out how many people are about to enter this room.

Once I'm outnumbered, things will escalate more quickly, likely with me being disarmed and punished and then either killed or shipped off to the skin trade. I try to push that thought from my brain; instead, I center on my objective of survival at all costs.

There are three of them, and they don't notice me as they walk into the room, having a conversation with each other, but they quickly stop talking and stare at the scene in front of them in horror. Two of them hurry over to the dead men on the floor while the third stands there looking around while I sneak up behind him. I switch the knife to my other hand, wanting to stab him and grab the gun in the waistband of his jeans simultaneously, but he spots me in his peripheral vision and turns toward me.

The knife grazes his arm, but I manage to hold onto it, and step into him, swing up and over, and drive it into his neck where it meets his shoulder. He screams, drawing the attention of the other men with him, and I scramble, yanking him closer by the knife stuck in his body and reaching for the gun.

I pull the gun out of the waistband of his jeans, then kick out with my foot, catching him in the chest and knocking him down. Raising the gun toward the two men rushing at me, I point and shoot, center, repeat.

Boom. Boom.

The noise echoes off the walls of the room, the old windows rattling as both men drop down to their knees, and I quickly turn the gun toward the man on the floor near me. He looks up at me, raising his hands in surrender, but I don't even blink; I shoot him in the face.

Walking over to where the other two men are bleeding on the floor, without hesitation, I aim and shoot them both in the head. I don't see any point in having a conversation with any of them, and we all know that's the best way to get yourself killed.

I'm not even sure how much longer I can keep myself awake now that the adrenaline is starting to wear off. I take another look around the room, and this time, I find a coat hanging on the back of the door, so I slip it on and zip it up over my naked body.

Scanning the area one more time, I spot my purse on the cluttered table on the other side of the door, and I grab it, a rush of relief flooding through me as I find my phone inside. I push the power button, almost sobbing as it starts to power up, and I have to grip it tighter as my hands start to shake.

I'm so focused on my phone that I don't realize someone else is in the room until they're practically on top of me. I'm too slow to bring the gun around to defend myself, and it's knocked out of my hands, skittering across the floor.

Jackoff grabs onto my arms, squeezing painfully as he shakes me, screaming in my face, "What the fuck have you done?"

I smirk at him, then bring my knee up as hard as I can, right into his balls, and he shouts in pain, his hands releasing me to cup himself. I don't wait around for him to recover. I spin around and run out the door, turning right down the long hallway and sprinting to the double doors at the end, only to find it chained.

Fuck, I should've grabbed the gun.

I whirl around, sprinting back the way I came, and turning into a stairwell that leads upward. I take the stairs two at a time, my bare feet slapping on the cold concrete, and when I bust through the doors at the top of the stairs, I come onto a roof with an ominous sky with no stars overhead. It's dark, rainy, and cold, and I almost consider going back inside and finding a better path, but the pounding of feet behind me pushes me further out onto the rooftop as jackoff and some of his men burst out of the door in pursuit of me.

I race across the rough asphalt, hearing them closing in on me until I run out of room, and I have no choice but to climb onto the ledge and contemplate my limited choices. I'm definitely too high up to survive a jump, and even with adequate momentum, there's no way I can make the jump to the next building.

"You have nowhere to go, Toni," jackoff yells behind me, so I whirl around to face him, straightening my spine and lifting my chin in my last bit of defiance. He has a gun in his hand, but it's pointed downward as he walks toward me. He steps up onto the ledge and is now standing a few feet from me.

I raise my brows at him and say, "And I think if you had the option of killing me, you already would have."

He glowers at me, and I know I'm right. For some reason, he needs me alive, so I test this theory by taking a step back. "I won't let you take me."

He laughs humorlessly with a seedy look in his eyes as he takes a step toward me, saying, "You don't have to let me; I'll just take you anyway. Just like we all did."

I glare at him, my hands fisting at my sides as fury ignites inside me again. "I don't see what you have to gain from any of this."

It's not really a question, but he can't stop himself from answering. "Don't worry, sweetheart. When you get to your end, you'll be too fucked up to care. Because that's what hell does to you."

I can't even imagine what the fuck he's talking about, and I'm entirely fucking sick of listening to the sound of his voice. So, I steel my spine again and take a small step closer to him so he'll move to close the distance between us.

Then he's directly in front of me, his arrogant hateful face smirking at me, still. So, I laugh in his face, screaming and spitting laughter that has him staring at me like the lunatic I am.

As quickly as it started, I sober, my face becoming cold as stone as I spit out, "Then you're coming to hell with me."

I grab onto him as tightly as I can as I jump backward, using the leverage of the drop to pull him over the ledge with me.

And then we're falling.

And then everything is darkness.

Chapter Twenty-Two

TONY

TONI HAS BEEN OUT for hours. One moment, she was screaming violent rage, and the next, she was silently calm. A sudden transition I can only assume was brought on by her mind dragging her down into safety. Because what went down in that warehouse is enough to traumatize even the most hardened soul, and hardened she is not.

Matt and I haven't said a word to each other since we got back, but I'm sure we're both thinking the same thing.

Heads are going to roll.

Of every possible scenario we ran of the mission, we never once considered the fact that we may have to turn our backs on our brother. I have no idea if Dare went down with that gunshot, and the unknown leaves a crushing weight on my chest. We've had many near misses over the years, potentially mortal wounds that ended up being survivable. We've survived gunshot wounds and stab wounds, head trauma, and even some near drownings. But this one—this one seems different. It feels final.

I was too focused on trying to keep Toni from running back in there to see all of what was going down, and my glance at Matt only earned me a resigned shake of his head, confirming that he also had no idea what happened.

Dare isn't known for always disclosing his plans to us, but this really takes the cake, and I can't wait until I see him again so I can knock the ever-loving shit out of him.

And now, sitting here, waiting for something to happen, is torture. As soon as I was able to, I put word of the situation out onto the streets, but then all we could do was sit back and wait for the information to come to us.

I called Lilith and let her know what happened, and all I got for my trouble was her hanging up on me. When this is all over with, that little bitch and I are going to go a few rounds, see how long it takes me to get her on her knees.

I shake those thoughts from my head and try to refocus on the mission at hand. Worst case scenario, Dare is dead. If that's the case, then we're going to have no choice but to retaliate. Well, actually, even if he's not dead, we're going to have to retaliate, but if he's alive, we may not have to burn it all to the ground.

I glance at my phone for the millionth time, then give a start as Toni says something from the couch she's been lying on. I get out of my chair and walk over to her, kneeling down beside her and breathing a sigh of relief as I note the blue eyes that meet mine are clear and alive.

She reaches a hand out, gripping my shirt firmly before she yanks on it and says, "It was you."

I frown, shaking my head a bit as I respond, "What was me, Nettie?"

Her features tighten as she whispers, "It was you on the roof."

My heart almost stops in my chest. My words are stuck in my throat, and my mouth drops open in shock.

"I know it was you. It was all of you. I remember."

I finally manage to close my mouth, and I give her a small nod because there really isn't much I can say without blatantly lying to her, which she'll never buy at this point. We've been waiting months for this moment, for the time when she'd clearly be able to face her past demons, a time where all the truth could be spilled without fear it would further traumatize her injured psyche.

We always assumed it would be Dare who'd have to do the explaining, but here we are. Matt went off to meet a possible contact, and Dare could possibly be dead. So, that leaves me. The asshole.

She's still gripping my shirt in her hand, and she gives me a little shake with it, drawing my focus back to her face as she says, "Tell me what happened, Tony. Now."

This is the last thing I want to do. In previous discussions, the mere idea that I would be the narrator of her trauma was laughable, but I suppose there's no way around it now.

So, I get up and pull a chair over beside her and sit down, facing her. And then I let the words fall.

Tony

Six months ago.

When Dare called me about losing Toni to a possible date rapist at the bar, I rolled my eyes, mostly thinking it was an awful lot of hassle to score some pussy.

I know; I'm a huge fucking asshole. But in my defense, Dare has been panting after this woman from a distance for ages, so I wasn't inclined to get my panties in a twist on the possibility that there might be some drama. I attempted to ignore the first set of messages, and I planned on ignoring it indefinitely, but the asshole went and took it a step further, requesting information from some of our contacts.

Matt and Dare are both at the warehouse by the time I get there, and Dare is glaring daggers at me when I nonchalantly stroll into the room. But I mean, really, how up in arms am I supposed to be about some bratty cock tease who he isn't even officially invested in? So, to say I'm a bit surprised by how clearly upset he is by the new turn of events is kind of an understatement.

Apparently, this fucker is more invested in this bitch than I initially realized, which means he's been keeping his cards pretty close to his chest, something that's rather unusual for him when it comes to pussy. And it's a clear indication that his dalliance with her possibly meant more than I thought.

Begrudgingly, I sigh, crossing my arms over my chest as I ask, "What do you need?"

Dare's glare intensifies, and for a moment, I think he's going to take a step toward me, but Matt reaches out and grabs his arm, giving him a very pointed look that I can only assume means for him to take it down a notch.

He doesn't have to take it down a notch for me. If he'd like to go a few rounds, I'm more than happy to oblige. He does stand down, and some of the tension leaves his body, but he still isn't saying anything, so I ask again, "What do you need? Someone needs to tell me what's happening."

Matt moves over to the monitors and starts poking buttons on the open laptop on the desk as he explains, "Dare just happened to run into her while she was out on a date with some guy he's calling jackoff. When she went to the restroom, Dare saw that shitbag dosed her drink, and before he could intervene, she came back and downed it. So, he decided to wait and follow them out to the parking lot, where he was going to teach the guy a lesson. But when he got out there, they were gone."

I frown, considering the very short list of possibilities on what occurred between the time they left their table and when Dare made it out in the parking lot. I turn to Dare, asking, "So, it was a set-up then? How much time went by before you made it outside?"

Dare shrugs, shaking his head with a disgusted look on his face. "It wasn't very long, maybe a minute or two."

I nod, then walk over to the monitors. "Any sign of her on the cams?"

Matt shakes his head. "No. Coincidentally, the ones that would have a direct view of that area were turned off. There are a few vehicle possibilities from some of the outlier cameras, but nothing that stands out."

I scan over the data before me, verifying for myself that it's a dead end. "How about her phone?"

Matt shakes his head again as he replies, "The last ping was near her last known location. They must've turned it off immediately after snatching her."

I glance at Dare, and I see he's wound pretty tight, a look of agony on his features as he leans over the desk, staring out into nothing.

I walk over to him and rest my hand on his shoulder, then lean down closer and say, "You're gonna have to let it go, man."

He turns his head, narrowing his eyes at me as he retorts, "Let what go?"

I raise my brows, then squeeze his shoulder a little harder as I reply, "The regret. The hindsight. The blame. Push all that shit to the side. Focus on the endgame."

He inhales deeply through his nose and gives me a short nod, and I give his shoulder a final squeeze and then walk back over to the monitors and ask, "How many we got working on this?"

Matt responds, "Everyone."

I can't hide my grimace. "How many leads?"

"None. Which is pretty fucking suspicious given how easily some people like to give up information."

I look over at Dare and wait for him to meet my gaze before I say exactly what he doesn't want to hear. "You realize the likelihood that it's too late, right?"

Dare's jaw clenches, and his eyes are practically glowing with anger, but he nods in acknowledgment. I walk over to the lockers and grab myself a duffel bag full of all the fun shit I like to use in times like these. I sling the strap over my back and grab my favorite leather gloves from the shelf, a smile on my face as I slide my hands inside.

I head to the door with Matt behind me, he asks, "Where the fuck are you going, Tony?"

I don't turn around; I just keep walking toward the door as I say, "I'm gonna go fuck around and find out. Keep your phone on."

It has been an interesting state of affairs, to say the least.

Once I left the warehouse, I made my merry rounds across the city. I'm sure I've pissed off quite a few people in the process, but I'm also sure that everyone is aware that I give zero fucks.

The only problem with acquiring information by force is that not everyone is super honest when speaking under extreme duress. Most of the time, I can assure honesty as long as I know I have some type of collateral to hold over their head once they're dead. Most people have at least one loved one who they'd rather not see tortured and murdered so that always works in my favor. But that doesn't prevent the handful of people who literally have no reason to stick to the truth to try to shove it up my ass later on. Unfortunately, we won't know if someone's ass fucked us until it's too late, but in these kinds of circumstances, it's just a chance we have to take.

By the time I find out who jackoff is, quite a bit of time has gone by, and all we can do is hope that Toni is alive and physically in one piece. Even if she has been taken out of the area, there's still a small chance we can locate her, but if she's dead, that is the literal end of being.

When I make it back to the warehouse, I'm a huge fucking mess. I've been feeding Matt and Dare updates as I've acquired them, so when I first walk in, I hold up a hand and then detour to the showers. It doesn't take me very long to scrape all the blood and guts from my body, and when I exit the shower, someone has already picked up and likely destroyed the mess of clothes I had left.

I'm just coming back into the main room, fully dressed and ready to get down to it, when an alarm blares. Matt and Dare both snap to attention, snatching up the nearest device to determine which alarm it is.

Matt exclaims, "It's her phone. Someone turned it on."

The look on Dare's face is a mix of relief and fear. The phone turning on suddenly is not at all proof of good health, and we wait with bated breath as the system works to triangulate her location. The device pings again, and Matt mirrors the screen to the wall-length monitor before us. We see little green dot blinking, and Matt frowns and asks, "Dare, isn't that one of your buildings?"

Dare shakes his head and replies, "No, that's one of the few in that area that I don't own, and offhand, I'm not certain who does own it—"

I interrupt, "Well, we don't have time to find out now. Let's go."

We grab what equipment we're going to need—so basically weapons—and head out. The warehouse where she is being held isn't too far from us, so I instruct Matt to drive over with the SUV while Dare and I go over on foot.

We double time in that direction, and I have to keep bitching at Dare not to overdo it since we don't know what we're walking into. The warehouse comes into sight, and I slow up, taking my phone out to make sure her location hasn't moved. The green dot is still blinking right in front of us, so I hand Dare a COM, and we split up.

We'll both circle the building in different directions and enter in through the first door we see. I have it set up so we can see ourselves on the same screen where Toni's location is being shown, so at least we're not entirely blind to each other's locations.

I circle around the back, and the first door I try is locked, so I move down a ways until I see another one, which, thankfully, is open. It's eerily dark in the building, and I wait a moment to let my eyes adjust and then move further inward. I hurry cautiously, so probably not as cautiously as I should, considering I have no information on who or what is happening here.

This first floor appears to be some kind of chop shop, which is pretty standard for the area. I circle back around in search of a staircase, and that's where I see Dare heading in the same direction.

Matt's voice comes over the COM, yelling he sees movement on the roof, and we immediately throw caution to the wind and run up the stairs at a sprint. We burst through the open doors onto the roof and then stop, glancing around.

Out through the rainy darkness, I can make out a group of people standing facing the ledge. Lightning flashes in the sky, and Dare's curse breaks through the silence as we see Toni standing on the ledge, soaking wet and visibly beaten up, with some asshole creeping out toward her.

Dare and I both take out our knives, not even needing to communicate or plan as we quietly approach the unsuspecting group and each take out two people without anyone noticing.

Lightning ominously flashes again, and Toni's screaming laughter mixes with the thunder claps around me, sending a shiver down my spine. She's laughing and screaming and completely losing her shit over there, and I can sense this is headed nowhere good, fast.

Then Dare is running, shouting for her to stop, to wait, but it's no use. He's barreling through men, stabbing them with one hand, shooting and punching anyone standing in his way, but it's too late.

We watch helplessly as she grabs that asshole in a tight hold, just two dark shadows in the dark landscape, and in the blink of an eye, they both disappear over the ledge.

I stand there, frozen for a moment, but then a slice of pain in my arm wakes me up to realize that the fight isn't over. I quickly and efficiently engage and eliminate the rest of the men on the rooftop to the looped soundtrack of Dare screaming in the background.

I run over to him, where he's leaned over the edge, blindly reaching into the darkness. I hear Matt occasionally over the COM, and it sounds like he's also engaging somewhere in the building.

I pull on Dare and attempt to get him away from the ledge, but he is like stone, cold and immovable. I get on the COM and tell Matt to go down to the backside of the building and assess the situation, and then I bodily tear Dare from the ledge, knocking him back every time he attempts to return.

Never, in all the years that I have known Darius, have I ever seen him so detached, so utterly destroyed that he loses sight of the mission. I grasp his head in both my hands, bring my face directly in front of his and shout, "Wake up!" Then I head-butt him directly in the face.

He barely flinches, but he blinks, shakes his head as if in slow motion, and reaches a hand up to touch his busted nose. But then, his eyes meet mine, and the absolute rage burning in those depths raises the hair on the back of my neck.

I figured this version of Dare was a distinct possibility once I fully grasped his deep affection for this woman. That if things went wrong, if we weren't able to bring her in alive, it would not just mean the end for her; it would also be the end for all of us.

I can see it in his eyes now. That pitch-black fire, the thirst for blood written all over his features.

And I know one way or another, the city will burn.

But I also know that all three of us will burn with it.

Chapter Twenty-Three

TONI

IT'S DIFFICULT TO PUT into words what it's like to lose a memory. To feel it poking in the recesses of your mind, that constant little pin-prick of pain and disappointment that you can't control or even explain. To be aware that something is missing, regardless if it hurts, regardless if it is dark and empty, it's still part of who you are.

Then on the other side of that is the knowledge that maybe you were happier without it. You may feel a sense of homecoming knowing the full landscape of your being, but it's possible that the end was a more comfortable landscape for you. But now you're stuck with this sticky black mass of anger, pain, shame, and regret that you're supposed to stuff back into that empty space; except now, it doesn't fit. It will never fit. It will constantly attempt to crawl out, leak out, and seep out into the better parts of you. And then what do you do?

Tony told me his side of the story, matter-of-fact and detailed, and I'm grateful for it. There are still so many blank spaces that need to be filled in, but I lack the emotional bandwidth to get into those tiny details at this point. I remember what happened in that warehouse with those men. Certain parts of it pass through my brain like flashcards; some other ones are more like the lava lamps from my childhood—like little flashes of color dancing in my psyche.

But I remember the blood. I remember the blood, and I remember the deep, maniacal satisfaction of wrapping myself around that despicable piece of trash and dragging him to his death. I remember falling; I remember peace. I remember hanging in limbo, watching the black of night fall away from me with the cold rain washing me clean again.

Tony's voice breaks me out of my own thoughts as he says, "Do you have any questions? I'll do my best to answer them."

"I have infinite questions. I just don't feel it's the time to dig too deep into it."

He nods. "If there's anything in particular now, just throw it at me."

I stare at him for a few moments and then ask, "How exactly did I survive jumping off a roof?"

That makes him laugh, and I can't help but smile and shake my head. "It's a perfectly reasonable question, Tony. I jumped off a fucking building and lived."

"A miracle? A merciful act of god? I have no idea how you didn't die in that fall. It looked like you managed to turn over in the air, so that fucking asshole absorbed most of the impact."

I swallow the lump in my throat, then ask, "And you're sure he's dead?"

Tony's eyes widen a bit, then he gives a humorless laugh. "He's most definitely dead. His brain was splattered all over the pavement. I scraped him off there myself and then set his body on fire. No way he lived through that."

"Jesus, Tony," I huff out, choking on a small laugh at his description.

He shrugs, straightening in his chair and stretching his legs out in front of him as he continues, almost whispering, "We thought you were dead." He pauses, his eyes glancing downward for a moment before moving back up to my face. "Dare, man. That guy was beside himself before we even got down to the parking lot. Matt had to hold him back, and he ended up with a busted nose for his troubles. When I got to you, fuck. You were a mess."

He stops talking and just stares into space over my shoulder. I reach a foot out and poke his shin. "It's okay, Tony. I want to know. I need to know."

"You were wearing someone's jacket, and that was it. I could see you were covered in a rainbow of cuts and bruises, and then there was the blood. Even with the rain, there was so much blood. It wasn't until we got you inside that we realized most of the blood wasn't yours, but for those first few moments, it was like time stood still. And then, Dare went completely ballistic, which was, you know, super fun. It wasn't until he picked you up to take you out of there that we found out you were, indeed, not dead."

"So, I was saved from certain death by landing on top of jackoff. That's insane."

"You're not fucking kidding," he retorts. "We took you to Dare's house and had one of the docs come in with his staff. They managed to nurse your physical wounds easily enough, but there wasn't anything they could do about your mind."

I frown, sitting back on the couch as I ask, "Did I suffer a head trauma or something?"

Tony shakes his head. "No. Your loss of memory was caused by mental trauma, which meant all we could do was wait for you to remember. All the doctors Dare spoke to, and there were many, were all very clear about not pushing information on you for fear it would push you further over the edge. So, Dare decided it would be best for you to go about your daily life as if nothing had happened, and we would watch you from a distance until the time came when you needed us to fill in the blanks for you."

"And this was no easy feat, given he had to come up with countless cover stories for all the people in your life, from your job to your mysterious family. Luckily, your family was mostly silent, but explaining to your employer that you'd had a debilitating accident while also coming up with a feasible backstory for your own missing memories. I mean, it was exhausting for the first few weeks there. And then there was the stress of accepting that you weren't remembering anything at all, and it was obviously going to go on indefinitely. Dare had an excruciating time accepting all of that."

"But you've all been with me this entire time?"

"Oh, yeah," he says. "We used to argue over who got to follow you in the fun places."

I smile. "And who usually won?"

"No one. We'd all just go because it's better to have more eyes on you in public situations like that."

I laugh quietly, amused as well as appalled that these men have been my shadow for months. A sob gets caught in my throat, and I choke out, "What now, Tony? What do we do now?"

His features shift into coldness as he replies, "Now, we figure out what went down in that warehouse. We find out who's behind all of this bullshit and then get the answers we need."

"And after that?"

His eyes meet mine, and I can see the fire raging there. "We burn the motherfuckers to the ground."

This time I do smile, a full-blown megawatt smile that must be bordering on maniacal.

That's right. *Burn, motherfucker, burn.*

At some point in our discussion, Lilith showed up. At first, I didn't even realize she was there, but then I caught movement in my peripheral vision and there she was, standing just inside the doorway, staring at me.

I realize now our first meeting in the back of the limo was likely not our first meeting at all. When she introduced herself to me and said that she'd been waiting so long to meet me, what she really meant was that she's been waiting so long to meet the new me. I think this new knowledge is what makes me recognize the look in her eyes, that dark affection overshadowed by distant memories.

While I remember what happened all those months ago in that warehouse, there's still a lot of my past that I don't recall. I don't necessarily remember Lilith as anything more than a current acquaintance, but that doesn't shake the feeling of familiarity that envelops me whenever she's in the room with me. The warmth of overall affection, a feeling of recognition, of home.

This is all unbelievably confusing because I have a very clear memory of my family growing up, and for some reason, she doesn't fit into the puzzle.

I stand up from the couch and walk over to her, and the look of surprise on her face melts away into a smile as I wrap my arms around her and pull her in. She returns my embrace, a small shudder going through her body, and it makes me smile because Lilith does not seem to be one who becomes overcome with emotion very often.

I don't say anything, just squeeze her a little tighter before pulling back, and her hands come up on either side of my face as she looks into my eyes and whispers, "Are you in there?"

I give a small shake of my head, tears pricking my eyes as I reply, "Not quite. Sometimes, I feel her in there, looking for a way out, but only bits and pieces sneak out."

She smiles again and drops her hands, then we walk further into the room, where Tony is still sprawled in the chair. He gives her a quick up and down before saying, "Nice of you to show up, Lils."

She glares at him as she stops in front of his chair. "Don't think I won't stab you in front of Toni."

He laughs. "Oh, I'm sure you would. But the thing is, I'd like it."

She doesn't reply, just shakes her head at him as she walks over and sits down on the couch, motioning for me to sit beside her. She looks between us and asks, "So where are we at?"

Tony inclines his head toward me as he replies, "She remembers the warehouse."

I look over at her, frowning as I ask, "Do you know about the warehouse?"

Lilith turns her gaze on me and nods. "Well, I wasn't there, but I know about it. There's always a lot of chatter in the city, and when I investigated further, I found that you were in pretty good hands. So, I consulted the higher-ups on how to manage it, and after a few weeks of surveillance, we decided to leave it be."

My frown deepens as I think over what she said, "So you just abandoned me to the care of these people?"

She raises her brows at me, leaning back on the couch and crossing one of her legs over the other as she replies, "Believe me, Toni. Being in the care of these people was far safer than anything we could've provided for you. On our end, a lot of people just thought you were dead, and frankly, sometimes you're better off being left dead—"

Tony interrupts, "She's right, Nettie. Dare was actively putting up walls and barriers around you to prevent people from getting to you. If Lilith had come for you, that would've sharpened the target on your back."

I hear what he's telling me, even though I don't exactly understand it. Lilith reaches her hand out and squeezes my arm as she says, "I'm not going to bother regaling you with a bunch of information about your past because as far as I'm concerned, the past is irrelevant. I'll answer any questions that you have, though. But just bear in mind that the majority of what you have forgotten is better off left forgotten."

Tony asks, "Do you remember anything other than what went down in that warehouse?"

I don't answer for a few moments, mulling over the question in my mind before answering. "It's not so much memories but feelings. I'm cold. A deep sense of hunger but not necessarily a hunger for food. Thirst, but not wanting to drink. Anger. Sometimes, it's like these black shadows seep in so deep that I can't shake them. And there's no color. It's all different shades of light and dark, but no actual color."

I fall silent and glance over at Lilith, who's giving me a small smile, though the sadness in her eyes gives her away, and her hand is back on my arm, squeezing as she says to me, "And that description is exactly how it should stay. The only thing you need to know at this point is that I'm here. I'm your sister. And I won't leave you again."

I blink at her a few times, taken aback by her confession that she's my sister. I go to respond, but Tony's voice breaks through, "And I'm here, too, and I'm not going anywhere."

Then Matt walks into the room, saying, "Don't forget about me. You know I'm not fucking going anywhere."

That makes me chuckle, but then I fall silent again, my eyes on the floor as a deep sadness sinks into my bones. "And what of Dare?"

Matt perks up, moving to crouch down in front of me, his eyes meeting mine as he says, "I have news."

Tony tenses in his chair, his hands fisting as he asks, "Is he alive?"

"It's not that cut and dry, fuckface." Tony grumbles a bit and leans back in his chair with his hands up. Matt looks at all of us one by one and then continues, "I received information from a so-called reliable source that the Beast was taken to an old warehouse earlier today, and he's being held there."

I frown as I ask, "The Beast?"

Lilith laughs. "Oh yes, that has to be him!"

I look between the three of them in confusion, and finally, Matt explains, "That's what they call Dare in the underground. He's known as the Beast."

I can't help but snort a little as I ask, "What does that even mean? I mean, he's certainly hard to miss, but he's not that big of a guy."

Tony and Matt glance at each other before Tony responds, "When you come out of any gate as a bloodthirsty, raging beast, it doesn't matter how big you are. It doesn't take very long to get yourself a reputation."

My eyes fly wide open, and I gape at him. "So, you're saying that Dare is basically the equivalent of a murdering animal?"

Lilith laughs, clapping her hands in front of herself almost gleefully. "Oh, yes, indeed! It really is delightful."

I shake my head at her as I say, "For fuck's sake, Lilith."

She watches me, still smiling. "Listen, Antoinette. I get that you don't remember most of what has gone on in your life, but one thing I'm going to tell you is if you can't get over the more nefarious parts of all of us, then it's best if you have an exit strategy."

I frown at her. "Exit strategy? What does that even mean?"

She gives me a patient look, but Tony chimes in, "All she means is that if you feel you're not suited to the type of life that we lead, then we'll help set you up far away from it. You have a chance for a completely clean slate here, Nettie. You have the opportunity to remove yourself from all this darkness and keep your hands free of any more blood. And if that's what you want, then that's what we'll provide for you."

I sigh, looking down at my hands as I whisper, "And what of Darius, then?"

No one says anything for a few moments, and I glance up to see the three of them looking at each other, but then, finally, Tony replies, "If Darius makes it out of this alive, and that is a very big if, he'll want you to do whatever is best for you. He won't fight it."

I lick my lips and take a deep breath, blinking against the stinging behind my eyes. "That's not what he said. He said there was a hard way and there was an easy way, and regardless of which path I chose, he'd be at the fucking end of it." I lift my head, meeting Tony's gaze as I continue, "And I'm gonna fucking hold him to it."

Both Tony and Matt give me relieved looks, and Lilith beams at me gleefully as she says, "You don't remember a lot about your past, but I bet you remember more than you think you do, and when push comes to shove, I have a feeling some of those life skills may just come popping right back."

I can't help but give her a pained look as I say, "Please define life skills."

Her smile widens and she stands up from the couch, holding her hand out to me as she says, "I think I'd rather show you."

I give her a skeptical look, then shrug my shoulders and reach my hand up to take hers. "By all means, lead the way."

Lilith was not kidding when she said she would show me some life skills, and Tony and Matt were all too happy to assist.

The first thing they did was take me down into the basement. I'm not entirely sure if it can be called a basement, considering it's more like a maze of very specialized rooms. I had never taken a good look down there before as the only room I had been in was the locker room where Dare marked me like the animal he obviously is.

While Lilith got herself situated with which skill she wanted to show me first, Matt filled us in on some of the conversation he had with his so-called reliable source. Matt figured that the source may be correct, but there's always the possibility that people are being fed misinformation simply to lead us all into a trap. Both guys agree that the problem with the majority of the places where he is likely being held is that there aren't too many ways out once you go in.

It's in the middle of a random conversation about tracking devices and microchipping that I feel a little shock in my brain, and I stand there for a few minutes, trying to puzzle it together. I'm unsure if I'm remembering something that's true or something that's irrelevant, like a movie plot line. Am I recalling a favorite book, or have I suddenly remembered one of my earlier sneaky deeds?

Tony's voice breaks me out of my thoughts. "Nettie, are you okay?"

I glance up, asking, "Does anyone recall what Dare was wearing in that warehouse?"

All three of them are now giving me a puzzled look before Matt eventually replies, "I'm not entirely sure, but what would that have to do with anything?"

I nod, feeling a bit uncomfortable, but I press on. "I think at some point in the past, I may have given Darius a watch. Do you think he was wearing the watch?"

Tony and Matt look at each other, then both return their gaze to me and reply at the same time, "Yes, he never takes that fucking watch off."

My heart skips in my chest, and I bounce a bit with excitement that

I may be onto something. "Do you think they would let him keep it?"

Matt shakes his head slowly as he replies, "I don't fucking know. Probably not. But if they took it from him, then somebody who knows something would have it."

I pull my phone from my back pocket and start scanning all the random folders that I always create for no real reason other than the fact I refuse to have more than two pages of apps. Of course, this just means I have files inside of files instead of files. Finally, I find an unlabeled app that just shows a bullseye, and I click on it, my eyes widening as it opens up to a map. I stare at it, holding my breath as it updates, not daring to move until suddenly, I'm staring at a blinking green dot.

I hold the phone up in the air, practically squealing with delight as I do a little victory dance. I stop and look around, and all three of them are now looking at me like I'm a complete fucking maniac.

"I found it!" I practically scream.

Tony walks over and yanks the phone from my hand, staring down at it in shock. "What the fuck is this, Nettie?"

I grin at him, then look over at Lilith as I say, "Apparently, a while back, I gave Darius a watch. A watch that just happened to have a tracking device in it."

Lilith's mouth drops open, and she gazes at me proudly. "Oh, that's my devious little sister, right there."

Chapter Twenty-Four

TONI

IT FEELS LIKE THE metal barrier in my brain has acquired little pin-prick holes, starting with the initial rush of memory from the warehouse. As time has gone by, I've gotten small bits that fall out of nowhere, and then, occasionally, those bits shift into a feeling that eventually takes on a shape.

The downside of this is that not all the bits that come back to me are ideal. I've spent the last short while believing that beneath my tendency to be a bratty little bitch, I'm a good person, but if these new bits are any indication, then it turns out my earlier belief is entirely false.

Given this new enlightenment of who I was previously, I'm starting to understand what they were talking about when they gave me the option of a clean break. It certainly would've been easier if I had taken them up on it, but since I've also gotten back some good, fond memories, I'm glad I chose not to.

It's as if fleeting clouds envelop me and attempt to carry me away in an array of recollections that seem impossibly real, and in this waking dreamscape, the evolution of my relationship with Dare also begins to lighten and take on a shape. They bring to life those little nuances that come from two people doing the dance between what they should do and what they want to do. While we definitely had a tumultuous relationship, it turns out we also had the occasional toe over the line, the fleeting harmless dalliance that we then turned away from, never to speak of again.

It's these memories that are like warm butterflies in my mind, sparking an intense feeling of warmth only extinguished by the sharp edge of reality. Regardless of how fleeting, I embrace it just as I embrace the belief that everything will be okay.

We've been watching that green dot for days, waiting for it to make a move. We've been surveying the area, tracking the people going in and out in the hopes of being able to confirm who is in charge, but so far, we've managed to find out nothing of consequence.

I find the waiting game to be incredibly annoying because I was under the impression we would just go in there, guns blazing, and take Dare back. All three of them vetoed this idea quickly, all in agreement that taking him back now would only make it worse.

"I still think we should just go get him," I mutter rather petulantly. Again.

Okay, fine; I'm a broken record. I shake my head furiously, my hands clenching in frustration as I grit out, "We don't even know for sure that he's alive. For all we know, he's been bleeding out in that place for days."

The look on Lilith's face isn't very reassuring as she says, "We do have a couple of sources who confirm that he's alive and *mostly* uninjured."

My eyes widen, and my brows shoot up as I place my hands on my hips, raising my chin at her defiantly. "*Mostly* uninjured? What the fuck does that even mean?"

She shrugs. "It doesn't matter. Mostly uninjured means breathing, and that's really the important part."

Tony cuts us off, "Nettie, sit down. Let Lilith explain since she's the only one who understands the inner workings of this so-called mastermind."

I walk over and sit on the couch, and Lilith sits beside me as she says, "Sometimes, I can't decide if this entire thing is my fault or not. All these fucking men run all this shit, and they've spent generations using women as pawns. I just couldn't handle it anymore."

Matt pipes in, sighing as he says, "What did you do, Lilith?"

Lilith looks away, obviously feeling uncomfortable, as she continues, "Growing up, there were always expectations of how us girls would help the organization. We're all trained with certain skills to defend ourselves, defend our family, but at the end of the day, we're still just pawns. For the most part, Antoinette was kept out of it since she was lucky enough to come up with a surrogate family. Our father always knew that you never keep all your ducks in the same basket, so we grew up more as distant cousins than sisters, and very few people knew the real connection there."

She pauses for a moment, closing her eyes and taking a slow breath in and out, obviously needing a moment before carrying on, "It was maybe four or five years ago that I overheard those fuckers talking about bringing her in. There were a bunch of fucking yahoos from some European organization there for a meeting, and they asked what the options were in terms of joining forces. One thing I've always excelled at is going unseen. Probably not a difficult skill to learn in the household I grew up in, but I feel that it served me well for my entire life. So, I had to sit there, silently fuming, when he brought up your name.

"Don't get me wrong, there have been many arranged marriages that turned out just fine, but I'd done my research on these fuckers, and they would've happily destroyed you. Even if you could learn to toe the line and keep your mouth shut, you would have been brutalized—physically, emotionally, and mentally. I couldn't let that happen."

I frown, completely stunned by what I'm hearing. "So, our father would have yanked me from the only life I had known and handed me over to some man who would treat me poorly?"

Lilith snorts. "'Poorly' is a serious understatement. Part of my job within the organization is to know everything about everyone. One of the reasons I was staying so close to these meetings was because I was concerned about any kind of deals they might be trying to make. If I had been the one offered up on the block, maybe I wouldn't have done anything, but I know that I'm a whole different breed of woman at this point. There's nothing left to destroy. But you—"

She breaks off, her eyes meeting mine intently as she reaches her hand out and rests it on my arm. "Seeing you destroyed would've rendered my entire life pointless. Every shady deal I've ever made, every quid pro quo that never worked out, it would have all been for nothing. And that fucking pissed me off—"

Matt interrupts, "I take it you did something to put this idea to bed for good?"

She nods, then explains, "Well, I thought it was put to bed for good, but apparently, I didn't go deep enough."

Tony chimes in, and I can't help but notice his excited tone as he prods, "Come on, tell us what happened."

I roll my eyes and tsk at him. "Fuck's sake, Tony. You can at least pretend not to be excited about the impending story of bloodshed."

He laughs as he says, "No point in pretending I'm someone I'm not. Please, Lilith, carry on."

I spot her smirking as she shakes her head at him, but then she continues, "I did try to talk our father out of it, in a subtle way, of course. I even outright offered to take her place, but that only made him laugh because he, at least, knew me better than that. He told me that these men would want someone unsullied and easy to control, neither of which could ever be used to describe me. And he knows this because that's how he raised me. And our brothers didn't give a shit and wouldn't be of any help, so I did the only thing a single person who had an army to eliminate could do."

She pauses, glancing around the room until Tony raises both hands, waving them impatiently at her to continue. She gives him a stern look, then turns her gaze back on me as she says, "I waited for them to fall asleep, and then I snuck in and slit all of their throats in their beds."

Tony barks out a laugh and claps, "Brilliant! I do enjoy your clandestine tactics."

Lilith gives him a bland look. "I don't know about clandestine, but all's fair, as you already know. This was also a tactic I took from somebody else in the hopes that it would get blamed on them. Which it did, for the most part; however, our father and brothers knew better. That's when shit really got ugly. I wondered if they would kill me outright, but then I remembered that killing someone is actually a merciful end. And as it turns out, the men I killed didn't eliminate the real problem because in this business, just as soon as you take care of one problem, ten more show up."

I sigh loudly, my head swimming with this new influx of information. "How many brothers do we have?"

She glances over at me as she replies, "Well, four. I thought we had none left, but apparently, one survived."

Matt interjects, "So you thought you had killed all four of them?"

She nods. "That sums it up. And I'm pretty fucking mad that I didn't know that the fourth one was still alive. You can blame fucking Jimmy for that."

I squint in confusion and ask, "Who is Jimmy?"

Tony laughs again as he answers for her, "Jimmy is the guy she had strung up in the warehouse who told her about the tracker inside you."

I shake my head. "And what happened to Jimmy?"

Tony cackles even louder, obviously getting a kick out of being able to tell the story. "Oh, Nettie. Jimmy's dead. She chewed that fucker's throat right out. It was epic."

I shudder a bit, knowing how gross that is. "But who was Jimmy? Was he a lowlife pawn or something?"

Lilith has a sad look on her face, and her eyes seem far away as she replies, "No, Jimmy was my husband."

Tony gives her a strange look and asks, "Wait, you're married?"

She levels him with a scathing look and replies angrily, "Well, technically, I'm a fucking widow."

Tony glares at her. "You killed your own husband? I mean, you didn't just kill him; you literally ripped his throat out with your teeth."

"And your point?"

He put his hands up in surrender, saying, "I guess I don't have one. Carry on."

Lilith looks over at me and explains, "Jimmy and I go back a long way. He's been around the organization since he could walk, and our families have always crossed paths pretty regularly, and they decided we should solidify the bonds between the families. Honestly, that was one punishment I didn't find too unbearable. Jimmy wasn't horrible. I mean, it could be kind of boring sometimes, but occasionally, I could pretend he loved me.

"Of course, I see now it was all part of a bigger ruse. I thought the majority of people who knew about you were dead, but I never took into account that Jimmy also spent his life in the shadows, so he knew a thing or two about staying out of sight in order to acquire information without anyone knowing. Turns out he was the one who helped them find you initially. Seems Jimmy and that asshole crossed paths at some point, and the ridiculous plan to steal you away and deliver you into the hands of the enemy took root. It wasn't until they took you this last time that I started to put the pieces together. Like, who in my inner circle would've known what I was up to? When I first got the call from Matt asking about your whereabouts, Jimmy was there, and all I mentioned to him was that there seems to be a rat about. The look on his face..."

She drifts off for a moment, lost in thought, and it's Tony clearing his throat that snaps her back to the now. "Of course, he tried to point the finger at other people, even going as far as to implicate Mickey, if you can fucking believe it. Goddamn, he was so fucking stupid. That guy, Mickey, he practically raised me. He would literally lay down and die at my feet before ever betraying me. But not Jimmy, nope. What I find the most amusing is that I genuinely believe he thought he was going to get away with it. I mean, you can say whatever you want about me, the worse it is, the more likely it's true, but the absolute worst thing you can do to me is insinuate that I'm stupid. That someone could pull the rug out from under my feet, and I would be none the wiser. Now, that just pisses me off."

She stares off at the wall on the other side of the room, then chuckles softly as she continues, "And when I set up the scene like we were going to interrogate Mickey, that arrogant fuck actually thought it was working. I'll never forget the look on his face when he realized he was the one who was truly fucked. You know what they say about a woman scorned—back us into a corner, and we're going to show you our fucking teeth."

She falls silent again, and remains quiet for a few moments, her hands falling onto her lap as she stares down at the floor with a lost look on her face. Then just as quickly as it arrives, she blinks, and it's gone. She looks up at me and meets my eyes as she says, "I'll tell you right now, Toni. If you find any person in this world who would lay down and die for you, you either find a way to be with them or you go to the grave with them. Because that shit doesn't happen twice."

Matt interjects again, "Well, you look like you have a plan."

She gives him a look of complete uncertainty, shrugging her shoulders. "Well, not exactly. But I think under these circumstances, we're just going to have to go back to that dumb saying I keep hearing you all use."

Tony cocks his head at her in question. "And that would be?"

She turns her head to look at him, the smile growing on her face as she replies, "We're gonna fuck around and find out."

Chapter Twenty-Five

Dare

I have on an occasion or two, heard the last words of dying men. People always assume that they're going to be poetic, or at least in some way revolutionary, but I have found, in most cases, they're either angry or bitter or just out of fucks. That's why when I finally managed to peel my eyes open into the darkness and said to myself, *what the actual fuck*? I figured it was unlikely that I was dead.

The last thing I remember was someone bashing me in the head with a weapon and the sound of a gunshot. Not entirely sure which one came first, but regardless of that, it was complete nothingness after.

I attempt to sit up and squeeze my eyes shut against the pain in my head before giving up and lying back down. My tongue feels thick in my mouth: I try to swallow, but my mouth is so dry it proves impossible. I clear my throat a few times, stretching my jaw out and rolling my tongue around in my mouth in an attempt to get things moving again.

From the stiffness of my body, I feel like I've likely been here for a while, and I lay still for a few moments to get my bearings on what type of room I might be in. Everything remains motionless, and I release my breath in relief to find it is very unlikely that I'm on a boat because being on a boat would fucking suck.

I stretch myself out, slowly taking inventory of my injuries, grateful that I don't seem too worse for wear, considering they likely knocked the shit out of me while I was down. Other than what is likely a concussion and a few rather large contusions, I seem to be mostly in one piece. I'm also relieved to find most of my clothing is still on, especially since no one wants to be in a cold, dark room with their ass hanging out.

I reach my left hand over to my right wrist and smile when I feel my watch is still there. Antoinette gave me this watch a while back, and I basically never take it off. Over the last few months, she has asked me about it a few times, unaware that it was a gift from her. She always teased me, asking if it was a gift from my secret lover, and I had no choice but to tell her, "Only in my dreams."

Not that I would take any of it back with Antoinette's life hanging over my head. I snort to myself. I never thought I'd see the day that someone could have collateral over me, but here I fucking am. Knocked on my ass, likely being prepared for shipment to the vilest location on Earth.

I'm still not entirely certain at what point my fascination with Antoinette turned into complete infatuation. I'm even less sure at what point my infatuation turned into a complete obsession. Adoration, really.

For the first few months that we worked together, I mostly ignored her. Of course, the more I ignored her, the more she sought me out, so I guess that plan worked in my favor. For the most part, I would just sit on the outskirts and watch her and how much she enjoyed her life, imperfect as it was.

She didn't seem to have any friends, and she wasn't overly close to her family for reasons I only had ideas about. She came off as abrasive, but I always knew once I managed to break through that bitchy exterior, there would be nothing but molten heat inside. And I was fucking right.

I remember the first time I broke through. I know the only reason things went as far as they did was because my behavior shocked her so much. I had her pinned against a wall with my thigh pressed against her pussy, my hard dick pressing into her stomach, and my hand pinning hers behind her back. I used my other hand to dig into her hair at the back of her head, pulling just short of the point of agony as I squeezed the back of her skull until her mouth fell open, and I dove in like a fucking animal.

She certainly stopped talking then, and when I finally backed off and let her go, she stared at me, panting for breath. I could see the look on her face, the confusion, the uncertainty, and just as quickly as the flare of need sparked in her eyes, I shut it down, turned on my heels, and left. Just left her standing there. I'm sure that pissed her off even more.

Then, just to add insult to injury, I ignored her for a week. I worked from home, took a short business trip, and by the time I came back into the office, I was able to pretend it didn't happen at all. I did get some satisfaction from the glares she shot at me the first few times she came into my office, her hands on her hips, waiting for me to engage. I never even looked up, and she would eventually stomp off, but I found I couldn't maintain that level of distance for very long, and eventually, we shifted right back into our old patterns.

The same scenario happened a few times over the span of a couple months. She'd go out of her way to rile me up, poking at me until I'd fucking snap and maul her in a closet or in the hallway, and once, right on top of my fucking desk, but then I'd leave her there and never speak of it again. After the first few times, she stopped attempting to speak about it, but I was always relieved her attitude toward me didn't change—that would've been a real shame.

Now, here I am in this pitch-black room, waiting to find out what's next. I guess that's what happens when you attempt to make deals with snakes. I'm startled out of my thoughts when a metal door creaks open. I don't bother sitting up or even acknowledge that they've entered the room; it's not like I can see who's coming in. There's some muttering across the room and what sounds like someone slapping the wall.

Suddenly, bright light fills the space, and I sit up, covering my eyes with my hands. I lean over with my elbows braced against my knees, fighting the urge to throw up as the pain in my head jackhammers.

I slowly manage to crack my eyes open, staring at the floor while my vision adjusts to the light. A pair of shiny black shoes appear in my line of sight, and I painfully manage to remain upright, squinting up at my new visitor, and I immediately frown, shaking my head, and then regretting it as I say, "Fuckwad."

He smirks at me, putting his arms over his chest as he replies, "Really, Darius? I don't think it's time for names."

I give half a shrug because that's all I can manage, then lower myself back down to a prone position in the hopes my head will stop swimming. His steps move around me before chair legs scrape against the concrete. I crack an eye open to see him sitting in front of me, one of his legs crossed over the other, and his palms resting on his thighs as he leans back and eyes me. "It seems we have a problem."

I snort, unable to control any response at this point, and then give a little chuckle. "I can't imagine what that could be."

He glares at me. "And now we joke? It doesn't appear that you're in a position to be joking."

I give another nonchalant shrug, but I don't say anything this time. I'm not in the position to do much of anything, and I lack the strength to even pretend to give a fuck about that, but I'm unable to control my chuckles. I lift one arm up, motioning weakly for him to continue before letting it fall back to the bed limply.

He shifts in his chair, and both his feet hit the floor before he continues, "You didn't exactly uphold your end of the deal since it's apparent our initial story wasn't believed at all. I'm not entirely sure what went down to make Antoinette lose her shit like that, but I have my suspicions."

I give another shrug, as it seems that's all I have the energy for, something as indelicate as shrugging. "Antoinette is not a stupid woman. She probably picked up more from us saying nothing than she did from the words that came out of my mouth. But I don't see why it matters, either way, since I'm here."

He nods. "I wish I could say that she wasn't going to be a problem, but I have a feeling that's not the case. And don't even get me started on that crazy bitch that keeps lurking around, Lilith Ferro. She's like a disease that will fester until it is eliminated."

I attempt to sit again, but only manage to bring my elbows up under me as I try to stare him down, but I mostly just mumble, "You better not lay a fucking hand on either of them."

He laughs. "And what are you gonna do about it, Darius?"

I squint back at him, then lay down as I mutter, "You know the motto, fuckwad. You fuck around, you find out."

He raises his eyebrows at me, shakes his head. "You boys and your stupid fucking motto."

I laugh again, rolling over all the way onto my back and pressing my hands against my face, likely jumbling my words even more as I reply, "Well, it has served us pretty well so far, and I imagine it will continue to do so until the bitter end."

He shifts in the chair, and then he says, "Well, it seems your bitter end will be coming sooner than some. I've decided I'm still going to ship you out, and then you'll be somebody else's problem. I'm sure I'll be able to get a good price for you on the old retribution market. Turns out there are a lot of fucking people out there who aren't very fond of you."

I attempt to roll my eyes behind my hands, but all the movement does is make my stomach lurch. I have to say, I'm feeling pretty juvenile, which is kind of ridiculous given my circumstances. I know there's nothing I can say at this point that will change the outcome or his current decision, and it isn't like I can do anything since I can't even sit up without feeling like I'm going to vomit. If I have to fight my way out of anything right now, I'm definitely a dead man.

Fuckwad doesn't say anything else; he just stands up and exits the room. The slide and click of the deadbolt sounds as he locks me in. I wouldn't say I have a death wish, but I also won't go into my death with any sadness or regret. He's correct about Antoinette not buying our attempted ruse in the first place, which is why I felt the need to whisper my true feelings for her, and I'm relieved that she knows.

I would feel far worse about my imminent demise if I hadn't told her, and since I was mostly certain my end would be coming regardless of how the events in the warehouse panned out, I figured it was best this way. She'll forgive me eventually and move on with her life, and I'll be a distant memory that she can frown over on the odd occasion I come to mind. At least I know that Matt, Tony, and Lilith will look out for her. They'll lead her into a good life, and everything we've done in these last months won't have been in vain.

I'm not sure how long I lay there half-dozing and ruminating on my life's work thus far, but the next thing I know, the locks on the doors click and the door creaks open and then a bunch of footsteps move toward me. I'm not feeling quite as shit as I was before, but I'm still not great, so all I do is crack an eye open and peek up at the group of people standing over me.

I don't recognize any of them at first glance, but none of them look too happy to see me. They continue to just stand there, looming over me, so finally, I open both eyes and squint up at them, asking, "Can I fucking help you?"

The tall blond guy standing closest to me smirks. "About to meet your end and still running your fucking mouth. How fitting."

He has a fair point. I've never been one to push the envelope in unknown situations, but part of me acknowledges that it might be easier on myself if I push one of these yahoos into putting me down now rather than going up on the auction block to be handed over to some deviant who I'm sure has a huge grudge against me. But then, there's the other part of me, that stubborn cunt part of me, who knows that the likelihood of me coming out of this in one piece increases significantly if I'm not barred into these four walls.

If there's one thing I've learned throughout my years in this life, it's that, generally speaking, people are inherently stupid. Regardless of your reputation and regardless of how well you've presented yourself as a badass who is not to be fucked with, there's always gonna be that one yahoo out there who thinks it's all bullshit. That one yahoo who believes it's all a myth and takes it as a challenge to prove it to the world. And I'm sure as fuck hoping it's that yahoo who bids on me and takes me on.

So, I close my mouth and lay back, and close my eyes as I reply, "Fair point. Carry on."

I feel hands on my arms, so I open my eyes and realize they're trying to get me to sit. I haul myself upright and sit on the side, leaning heavily on my thighs as I attempt to get my bearings.

The tall, blond guy says, "Time to go. Got a whole bunch of people waiting on you. If you live to see tomorrow, you're gonna fucking regret it."

The whole group of men laugh at this, and I have to roll my eyes in response because I'd rather be dead than listen to another word out of their stupid fucking mouths.

Once I appear to be steady on my feet, they release me. I slowly take a few steps without the room swimming around me. They lead me out of the room and down the hallway. It turns out I'm in some kind of warehouse, which, of course, I'm not at all surprised about. Seems all of us disreputable assholes do our business in warehouses, and there are a lot of fucking warehouses in the world.

We turn the corner and enter another room with a chair set in the middle of a small stage. Three bare walls, then the far wall is a mirror. I assume that the mirror is just the one-way window where whoever may be wanting to purchase me is sitting.

Now, I'm torn between theatrics and just being tired. Do I want to go on stage as a beaten man? Or do I want to put on a little show of bravado just to tease the crowd? I attempt to walk up the stairs and stumble a bit, and by the time I fall into the chair, I have to accept there's no bravado left in me, false or otherwise.

This doesn't mean I'm a beaten man; this just means I'm fucking tired, but none of these assholes will know that. They're all out there, congregated, patting themselves on the back, getting their little fucking high-fives that they finally managed to bring in the Beast.

I can't help the little smile that forms on my lips as I stare out at the mirror, a chuckle falling from my lips as I ponder who is the most likely to pay top dollar for me.

And that's how I remain as I wait to find out.

Chapter Twenty-Six

DARE

I FEEL LIKE I'VE been sitting in this room on the damn stage for days, though I'm sure it's only been hours. Surely, it didn't take this much time to get someone to pay a lot of cash for me as I have an extensive list of enemies, who I'm sure would be frothing at the mouth to take me home with them. So, them having me sitting up here on a pedestal awaiting someone's retribution is hilarious.

It seems rather fitting, given how I've basically led my adult life with both middle fingers, and very few people have ever attempted to step up and knock me down. It's been so long since I've been properly put on my ass that I'm probably due for it anyway.

I've been playing a little game here, trying to decide who's gonna come through that door. The problem is there's such a long list of possibilities that I get confused about who would be the most pissed at me that they'd pay the most money for me. There are a few people who would like nothing more than to stab me in the throat, but they're far too proud to pay for me. They'd continue to bide their time until they could take me out properly, but that still leaves a whole slew of people who have more money than sense.

I'm just considering lying down on the stage to get a nap when I hear someone at the door. All the deadbolts slide open, and the door squeaks, and there's fuckwad with a bunch of his shit-ass men behind him. They all walk into the room, and fuckwad stops in front of me and says, "It's done. You'll be moved to your new home soon."

I can't help but snort, leaning back and crossing my arms over my chest as I reply, "And who is the happy bidder, do tell?"

He gives me a stern look. "I think you should be a little more serious about the murky situation you're in."

I shrug and shake my head in dismissal. "I don't think it fucking matters either way. So, where am I going?"

Fuckwad turns away, motioning for me to follow him, and out the door we go, back down the same hallway I came down. He doesn't say anything, which probably should make me nervous, but I honestly can't find any fucks to give about it. He leads me out of the building to a waiting car, and he opens the door, motioning for me to get in as he says, "They're taking you to the airfield that your buyer designated for transport. If you give anyone any trouble, I'll make sure your girl pays."

I give him a nod and then get in the car. I'm not going to give anyone a hard time before I know what I'm up against.

It's a short drive to the airfield, and I'm surprised to find a spiffy little private jet rather than the cargo plane I anticipated. The idea that I'll be riding in luxury to parts unknown kind of creeps me out. I'd much rather be getting into the back of a cargo plane because, at least then, I know what to expect.

The door opens, and I get out of the car and follow the man toward the plane. He motions for me to go up the stairs and then stops me and says, "I need your watch."

I start, giving him an incredulous look. "I'm not giving you my fucking watch."

The man sighs, standing his ground as he says, "I have orders to take your watch, and that's what I'm gonna do. You already heard the boss, so let's not cause any trouble for anyone else over a piece of jewelry."

He's right. I don't want to tell him he's right, but it's difficult to argue when someone is making good sense. That doesn't change the fact I really don't want to give him my fucking watch.

He must sense my indecision on the matter because he leans a little closer to me and whispers, "Solid 80% chance you'll get it back someday."

I tilt my head, my surprise obvious by my expression, and frown, but instead of saying anything else, I remove the watch from my wrist and hand it over. I make my way up the steps and enter the jet cautiously.

One good thing about being transported in such luxury is it's highly unlikely I'm going to be brutally murdered when the cleaning bill would be so high. While a lot of these people have more money than sense, the idea of blood splatter all over their pride and joy doesn't really appeal to them. They might shoot me on the tarmac as soon as I land, but at least I'll get one good ride before I go.

Surprisingly, there's no one waiting for me inside. I make my way through the cabin and sit in one of the big chairs, then lean back and close my eyes, willing myself to relax for a few minutes. At this point, I may as well get a nap in and at least attempt to prepare myself for whatever will be waiting for me on the other end of this flight.

Toni

I've now been staring at that little green dot for what feels like weeks. I know it's only been days, but the time that has gone by since we found out we had a lead on Dare has all jumbled together.

I have to actively push down the painful anxiety that's building up in my chest, and I feel twitchy to get out there and do something. I'm still fucking mad that Dare made such a nonchalant declaration of his affections at such an inopportune time. It certainly wasn't at a moment where I could tell him how I felt in return.

Do I love him? Probably. Am I capable of letting those words spill from my lips just because someone else confirmed they feel the same way? Probably not.

Other memories are still slowly trickling in since the warehouse revelation, but it's difficult to determine how accurate any of them are. The one thing that I don't question is the feeling I get when I think about him.

My most recent memories of my relationship with Dare have been contrary, and I'm starting to realize now that he would've had to push down his own true feelings for me in order to fit into the relationship that I decided we were having. Whereas in the past, we were likely building the beginnings of a romantic relationship, this new Toni had wiped that clean, so all we had left was conflict.

Don't get me wrong, intertwined in that conflict, there were a few instances where Dare ripped off that controlled mask and took me for a little ride, only to then immediately snap back to the ever-cool and controlled Darius Hughes. I still have to ask him how he ended up working at the same place that I did, as it seems unlikely that he was there to keep track of the business accounts of a very rich man, considering he seems to be one of those very rich men. And from what I've gathered from the sporadic conversations I've had with Matt and

Tony; he didn't become a very rich man by staying on the right side of the law.

I'm so wrapped up in my own thoughts that, at first, I don't notice the green dot moving. I stand up so quickly that I knock the chair over behind me, and I shout, "He's on the move!" Everyone jumps to attention, and we all run for the door and head out to the SUV. The green dot is moving faster now, and I give Tony directions and tell him to hurry the fuck up. Luckily, it's not rush hour, so we're not hindered by much traffic, and Tony weaves around the cars with ease as he continues to push the accelerator.

My heart is pounding in my chest to the point I'm having a hard time keeping my breath in check, and I lean back against the seat and attempt to center myself. Lilith is sitting beside me. She reaches out and rests her hand on my arm. I shiver, and she says, "We got him. We got him."

I curse as the green dot stops, and I tell them the location, which Matt confirms is an airfield. My blood goes cold. We're still a couple of minutes away, and that's a lot of time for someone to slip away by air.

I reach into the pocket on the seat in front of me and pull out the handgun that's stored there, checking to make sure it's loaded and the safety is in place before I sit back, my leg bouncing nervously. The whole car is tense, and I can practically smell the tension oozing off everyone as Tony barrels ahead, the tires squealing as he turns into the airfield, driving right through the metal gate and racing out onto the tarmac.

I look down, and see the green dot is still there, not moving, but I can make out the tail of a jet at the end of the runway, going at full speed, and I know we're too late even before the jet's wheels leave the ground.

I look down and the green dot is still blinking at me, mocking me, and I scream in frustration as the SUV comes to a halt, and we all exit onto the pavement. This means one of two things: either they brought him here to execute him before making their escape, or I have a little surprise here waiting for me, and he's in the wind.

I glance around, seeing that the green dot is still unmoving, so I wander around a bit until I come across what looks like a square in the distance. I run over and see that it's a gift box, a black one with a nifty silver bow, and I suddenly have flashbacks of *Brad Pitt* in a field, and my urge to vomit intensifies.

The others have caught up to me, and they're all looking at the box with concern. I vaguely hear them muttering to each other over the roaring in my ears, questioning the likelihood that it's a body part. I don't think it looks big enough to be a head, so I guess I should be reassured by that, but if I open that box and there's a hand in there, I'm probably going to freak out.

Tony nudges me then asks me if I want him to do it. I give him a shake of my head and then step forward, crouching down and closing my eyes as I take a deep breath and lift the lid off the box. I peek one eye open, exhaling loudly in relief as I note Dare's watch at the bottom of the box. I reach in, pulling it out to find there's a note underneath. I pick it up and open it. Tony speaks behind me, "What does it say, Nettie?"

I swallow the lump in my throat and read it to them. "Let it go, or he'll die a 17th-century death. And then you all will be next."

I clutch the watch in my hand, then hold the note out to Matt as I mull over the words for a moment. I can see everyone is trying to figure out who the heck may have left this note for us, and it seems like everyone's coming up blank.

I finally look up and see they're all looking at me expectantly, and I'm not entirely sure what they think they're waiting for. All I know is some fucking idiot took it upon themselves to take something that's mine. They've taken something that's mine without my permission and then acted like they have the power to control my next move. And not just mine; they took something that is Tony's and Matt's, and even Lilith's if you want to get down to the dirty details of it all.

Some fucking idiot took something that didn't belong to them, and then tried to put conditions on their thievery.

My blood boils in my veins, my hands fisting at my sides, and it's almost as if that rush of fury clicks some of those missing pieces back into place, and I meet Lilith's gaze. Excitement brims in her eyes, and she whispers, "There she is."

I look at Matt, and then at Tony. I stand up taller, straightening my spine, my jaw clenched so tightly my teeth hurt, and I feel my own beast rattling in my chest as I respond.

"Burn it all."

Dare

Somehow, I manage to sleep the entire flight, which is a relief, but also hugely inconvenient, considering I have no idea how long I've been in the air. So, when I'm jarred awake by the wheels thumping down on the runway, I'm more than a little disoriented.

I sit up and attempt to stretch out while ignoring the pounding in my head. There's a bottle of water beside me that I normally would ignore, considering it could easily be poison, but I'm so thirsty that I have no choice but to open it up and guzzle it down. My stomach lurches from the sudden influx of fluid, and I take some deep breaths as I fight the urge to throw it back up.

The jet comes to a stop, and thumping sounds outside. The door opens, and a man appears. He doesn't say anything, he just motions me to follow him, and so I do. I can't make any moves until I have a full scope of what I'm up against, so in the meantime, I just have to fall in line and figure it out.

I follow him down the steps and across the pavement into the hangar. Inside is a group of people hanging out, apparently in deep conversation since they don't look over when I first enter the building. Given the situation, I would think these people would be more excited to see me, but I guess maybe I haven't gotten to the big show yet.

We get closer, and slowly the group of men disperses, moving to the side, and I do a doubletake at the woman standing in the middle of them. I blink a few times; certain my eyes must be deceiving me or that my concussed brain is playing a huge fucking joke on me because there's no way this is really happening. In all my years of criminal activity and duplicitous dealings, if this is true, this may be the biggest mindfuck that has ever been pulled on me.

I hesitate for a second, then pick up my pace a bit as I watch the expression on the woman's face when she finally looks up at me. The man leading me into the building stops and puts his arm out to stop me while I'm still a good ten feet from the group of people. But I can't stop looking at her face. That fucking face. Those blue eyes bore into mine, and I feel the beast rattling in my chest as I'm all over the idea that the tricky little bitch has pulled one over on me. No one says anything, so finally, I say the only thing I can think, "What the fuck, Antoinette?"

She frowns, then gives me a puzzled look, and the man beside her leans in and whispers something into her ear, and she nods before walking over to me. She stops in front of me, looking up into my face, and my breath catches to have her so close. I can't help but lean forward a bit, and she doesn't flinch away or anything; she just continues to peer up at me.

I inhale deeply, attempting to breathe in her scent in the hopes it will calm me, and that's when I realize something's wrong. She doesn't smell right. I take a closer look, and it's her face, but it's not her face. The body is wrong, too, and the hair is different.

Finally, I focus back on those blue eyes that are so familiar but at the same time are so wrong, and I say, "You're not Antoinette."

One corner of her mouth turns up a little as she says, "How very astute of you, Darius Hughes."

The voice is different. It's not quite as husky, with just a hint of an accent that I can't quite place. I look her over some more and note that she's around the same height as Antoinette but also a bit slimmer. She's more angular, stiffer and more formal in her mannerisms.

Whoever this person is, she's obviously well-versed in the game, as her face gives away nothing. I look into her eyes again as I ask, "But who the fuck are you?"

This time, she smiles, and for a moment there, I see Lilith, and it causes a shiver to run down my spine. She steps back from me a bit as she answers, "My name is Agatha. I'm the third fucking sister."

My eyes widen in horror and I sigh heavily, suddenly overwhelmed by the need to sit down.

What the actual fuck?
TO BE CONTINUED...

Acknowledgements

Well, I finally did it. I wrote a book.

I've been writing stories in my head for most of my life. They've been my constant companion since as far back as I can remember, and its mostly sheer laziness that kept them inside for this long.

You see, writing a book is the equivalent of bleeding on paper. If you're a pantser, like me, you spend countless hours letting this group of strangers do the talking, oftentimes having no freaking idea what's going to happen, and then screaming some variation of "WHY WOULD YOU DO THAT" once they inevitably do something stupid that you had not planned on. For example: jumping off a building. You love them, and you hate them, and you have zero power over them. All you can do is hope they don't screw you over in the end. Or force you into expanding your standalone into a duet. Haha.

Basically, it took hundreds (feels like more) of people to make this book a reality. I know I won't remember everyone, so don't get your underpants in a twist if you're not listed. Small brain, remember. Like super tiny.

To you, the readers: thank you for taking the time to read this book, and for taking the chance on a new author. Without readers, writers would flounder in their sea of creativity with no one to share it with. We appreciate you.

My family: For putting up with my constant book drama. The ranting. The crying. The banging my head on my desk. The regret. OMG the regret.

My Non-Book friends: (But mostly Jess) Sorry, I vanished. I'm still here. I still love you.

Layla Towers: you were the first to see potential in my vision and the first to get a glimpse into my Ends world. Love you forever. Hope you're ready to listen to me piss and moan for as long as my brain will continue to pantser through storylines.

Jay: my delightfully unhinged friend. You commented on my posts probably not thinking I would try to drag you off into my fictional world, but you came willingly and then stayed. I love you. Hope you'll stick around for the twisted fuckery of Tony.

TL Swan and my Cygnets/Spicy Book Nook family: Where the journey caught fire. Extra shoutouts to those who listened to me cry the most—LA Ferro, Margaux Porter, Martina Dale, and LM Fox.

Censored: Carolina Jax and VR Tennent—To making *someday* our *everyday*. First coffee is on me.

Matt and my KGQ family: Amanda, Dani, Heather and Sammy. You were the first to hear me say, "Ima write book" and you told me to go for it. So, I did. So, basically this is all your fault. Love you, my OG bitches.

My Bookish Sisters: Issa Marie (**111**), April, Britt, Stef, Grace – red flag crew for life.

The Bookish Girls Services: thank you for the alpha reads, arc team oversight, and social media push. Appreciate you all so much.

Kayla: you get your own line because I'm the biggest PITA and I know it. Thank you for all your handholding and ass-kicking. You're the best. Please don't leave me.

vo.EROS and my Egirls: Tamora, Lilith, Goldie (twinner), Katarina, Jane Apatova, Amy, Denise, Abby, Elle, Constance, Monroe, LadyT, Erin, Candy. STFUATTBFFDIYPPPLTLWYA. CHFM.

My CABFD crEw: Ashley, Manda, Mags, Aimee, Krystin, Madi and Tara – if ever there was a group of women put on this Earth to drive me to not fail, it is you. I would walk in the dark with you forever, and never miss the light. ILYSM.

Huge shoutout to BookToker/Author Ashley Mack for offering to give my book baby a read before it was even ready. Truly appreciate your giving spirit and willingness to help out the new girl. Your insight and feedback was instrumental in me hitting *upload* on my completed manuscript. You're the best.

Big thanks to the BookTok/Bookstagram worlds for allowing me to start a whole new TBR shelf for you, "Books That Have Not Come Out Yet" and being enthusiastic about it. I apologize for edging you for almost a year. I hope it was worth it.

Also, shoutout to Cyra Wilde for the taking time to read and respond amidst your own busy writing schedule.

To the creators of some of my all-time favorite book boyfriends, in no specific order: Selena, Sam Mariano, LJ Shen, Nashoda Rose, K. Webster, Sophie Lark, Shantel Tessier, Tijan, Bella Di Corte, Rina Kent, HD Carlton, Meagan Brandy and many, more...

Kirsty McQuarrie with **Let's Get Proofed** for putting up with my "But what about" bullshit for months. And months. And months. Cheers to the future "but what abouts."

And to my brother, Jason.
Any ability I possess to articulate emotion
effectively will always be fueled by the
loss of you. You're still an asshole. I love you.

Made in the USA
Coppell, TX
02 August 2023

19870730R00181